ROSES AND REVENGE

An Isle of Man Ghostly Cozy

DIANA XARISSA

❦ Created with Vellum

AUTHOR'S NOTE

When I first started this series, I imagined that Fenella would be making trips back and forth to Buffalo on a fairly regular basis. Things didn't quite work out that way. Finally, now that I've arrived at book number eighteen, Fenella is flying back to the city that had been her home for her entire adult life, right up until she inherited Mona's fortune.

I think my series books work best when they're read in order (alphabetically), but each story should be enjoyable in its own if you prefer not to read them all. If this is the first title in the series that you're reading and the paragraph above didn't make any sense, don't worry. All will be explained in the story.

As Fenella spent most of her life in the US, I use American English and American spelling for these books. The characters who are British or Manx use British terms when they speak, however. I try to keep this consistent, but I know I make occasional mistakes. If you spot one, send me an email and I'll try to correct it.

These stories typically take place on the Isle of Man, a British Crown Dependency in the Irish Sea, but this book is primarily set in the US.

This is a work of fiction and all of the characters have been created by the author. Any resemblance that any character may bear to any real person, living or dead, is entirely coincidental. All of the businesses in the story have been invented for the story and have no relation to any real businesses on the Isle of Man or in Buffalo, New York. Fenella and Daniel do visit a number of real places that actually do exist in Buffalo and the surrounding area (the Buffalo Zoo and Niagara Falls, among others), but all of the events that take place within those locations in the story are entirely fictional.

I always enjoy hearing from readers and invite you to contact me in whatever way you prefer. My contact details are available on the About the Author page at the back of the book. I hope you enjoy the story.

"I can't believe you're going back to Buffalo tomorrow," Shelly Quirk said to her friend, Fenella Woods, as they walked along the promenade on a sunny Friday morning in August.

"I can't either," Fenella replied. "I'm excited, but I'm also nervous."

"What are you looking forward to the most?"

Fenella grinned and blushed. "Spending some time with Daniel."

Daniel Robinson was a handsome police inspector with the Isle of Man Constabulary. Fenella had first met him over a dead body right after she'd moved to the Isle of Man after inheriting her aunt, Mona Kelly's, fortune. A year and a half later, after numerous stops and starts, she and Daniel were settling into a comfortable relationship together. He'd recently purchased an apartment not far from Fenella's and they were both enjoying being able to spend more time together now that he lived within easy walking distance of Fenella's luxury apartment.

Tomorrow they were flying to Buffalo, New York, together for a two week vacation that would include attending the wedding of Fenella's former boyfriend, Jack Dawson. Fenella and Jack had been together for ten years, but she hadn't hesitated to end the relationship when she'd decided to move to the Isle of Man. Jack had struggled with the breakup, but after a visit to the island, he'd returned to New York a changed man. Not long after, the university where he worked had hired a new adjunct faculty member, Linda Hawkins. Fenella had been pleased when Jack had begun dating Linda.

Jack had proposed only a few months later and Fenella was still slightly surprised that the pair were getting married so soon after they'd met. That Jack had invited her to the wedding also felt odd to Fenella, but after giving the matter some thought, she'd realized that she really wanted to be there to help the man, about whom she still cared deeply, celebrate his special day. That she'd also get to spend two weeks in the US with the man with whom she was currently madly in love was a huge bonus.

"That will be nice for you," Shelly said. "Are you staying somewhere fabulous?"

Fenella shook her head. "I didn't want to, well, flaunt my wealth in front of my old friends. Besides, Daniel still isn't comfortable with my money. We'll be staying at a fairly standard chain hotel near the university where I used to work. It's central enough for the places that we want to go."

When Fenella had first arrived on the island, she hadn't been certain of exactly what she'd inherited from Mona. Over time, she'd come to discover that she now owned properties that were scattered across the island, as well as a fortune in cash, stocks, and shares. Each month, what still seemed to be a huge amount of money was deposited into Fenella's bank account, the income from the rents from all of her properties. With fairly low living expenses, the money just seemed to keep mounting up, but Fenella wasn't in any hurry to start spending it frivolously.

Daniel was still struggling to come to terms with just how wealthy Fenella actually was, but he was starting to accept that it was simply a part of her. He'd allowed her to help him purchase his new apartment, but only with a complicated legal agreement in place to protect both of them. He was also permitting her to pay for the trip to Buffalo, as they were going for her friend's wedding, and because she'd promised not to spend more than necessary.

"If I were you, I'd be staying at the fanciest hotel in Buffalo," Shelly told her.

Fenella laughed. "Says the woman who is still refusing to let me help pay for her wedding."

Shelly flushed. "That's different."

"I can waste my money on myself, but I can't treat my dearest friend to the wedding of her dreams?"

"I just don't feel comfortable having you pay for things," Shelly said softly.

"But I really want you to have the most wonderful day of your life."

Shelly's first husband had passed away unexpectedly some years earlier. In the early days of her grief, Shelly had quit her job as a primary school teacher, sold the house she and her husband had shared, and bought the apartment next door to Mona Kelly. Mona had helped Shelly through the worst of her mourning, encouraging the widow to embrace everything that life had to offer.

Shelly and Fenella had met within days of Fenella's arrival on the island and the pair had become the closest of friends in the months since. Fenella had been delighted when Shelly had started dating again and she'd quickly grown fond of Tim, Shelly's first serious relationship since her husband's death. Fenella had even helped Tim pick out the engagement ring that was sparkling on Shelly's finger in the morning sunshine as they walked.

The pair was planning for a January wedding and Fenella was still hoping that they would allow her to use some of her money to make their day extra special. Regardless, she'd already spoken to Tim about giving them a dream honeymoon trip and he was less reluctant than Shelly to accept Fenella's generosity. At some point, he'd have to discuss the plans with Shelly, but for now, Fenella and Tim were mapping out a fabulous trip that would take the pair around the world in luxurious style.

"Are you doing anything different to what you would have done if you hadn't inherited a fortune?" Shelly asked as they reached the end of the promenade and turned around.

"You're just changing the subject," Fenella complained. "But yes, I am doing one thing that's a bit extravagant. We're flying first class, not from the island, of course, but from Manchester to Toronto. From there we're taking a limousine to Buffalo. I'll be renting a car once I'm in Buffalo, but it's easier to rent it once we arrive than to drive ourselves from Toronto. It costs extra and is a lot of hassle to take a rental car across the border."

"How far is Toronto from Buffalo? I know next to nothing about US geography."

"It's about a two-hour drive, although that depends a lot on traffic, of course. That's another reason why I'm happy to rent the car once we get to Buffalo. I'd rather not drive through Toronto traffic if I don't have to."

"I'd much rather ride in a limousine everywhere," Shelly said. "You should just keep it for the whole fortnight."

"Daniel would hate that, and I'd feel odd arriving everywhere in a limo. I'm more than happy to drive around Buffalo anyway, especially since there's no chance of snow in August."

"What time do you leave tomorrow?"

"We're on the earliest flight to Manchester. It leaves the island at five in the morning, so we'll arrive in Manchester around six. Our flight to Toronto leaves at nine."

"And what time do you arrive in Toronto?"

"Because of the time difference, we'll arrive in Canada just after noon, even though the flight takes around eight hours. I imagine we'll both be jetlagged and grumpy by the time we get there."

Shelly laughed. "That will be an interesting test for your relationship."

"Maybe we'll be able to get some sleep in the car on the way to Buffalo," Fenella said. "We're going to need it, because we're supposed to go to a party tomorrow night."

"A party? How exciting."

"If we can stay awake, it might be fun."

"What sort of party? Is someone celebrating your return?"

Fenella laughed. "Not at all. It's an engagement party for the happy couple. It will be my first chance to meet the bride, as well as some of her closest friends. Some of Jack's friends will be there too, and most of them were my friends before I moved over here."

"Were your friends? Past tense?"

She shrugged. "I haven't really kept in touch with any of them since

I moved. I haven't missed any of them, either. It's odd, but if I moved somewhere else now, I know I'd miss you terribly. Most of my friends in the US were work colleagues, but that was all we had in common."

Shelly nodded. "I've been surprised by how little effort I've made to keep in touch with my former work colleagues. I would have said we were all close friends before I retired, but in truth, I barely miss any of them."

"Anyway, assuming we have enough energy, we're supposed to go to the engagement party. It's being held on the university campus, not far from where we're staying. I suspect we'll get a taxi so we can both have a few drinks and relax. After that, Daniel and I will have three or four days to see the sights and enjoy some time together before the actual wedding events begin."

"Wedding events? Are weddings multi-day affairs in the US, then?"

"Not necessarily, but Jack and Linda are celebrating over three days. There's a rehearsal dinner on the night before the wedding. They've invited the bridal party and also all of the guests who are coming from out of town to attend the wedding. I believe Jack said there were going to be about twenty people at the rehearsal dinner."

"Is there a rehearsal, as well? And if so, for what?" Shelly asked.

"There's a rehearsal for the wedding ceremony before the dinner," Fenella explained. "Only the bridal party will actually go to that, though. The rest of us just go to the dinner afterwards."

"That's on Friday night?"

"Yes, a week from tonight. The wedding is a week from tomorrow, on Saturday afternoon. They're getting married on the lawn in front of the history department building on campus."

"What happens if it rains?"

"They'll use one of the lecture halls. It will be less romantic, but the guest list isn't that large. We'll all fit in a lecture hall."

"Then there will be a reception, I assume."

"There will. It's actually being held at the hotel where Daniel and I are staying. The rehearsal dinner is there, too. Jack and Linda are getting a discount for having everything there, and I got a special rate for our room for the days around the wedding as well. It's a bonus that we don't have to drive anywhere after the reception."

"And then there's another day of celebrating?"

"There's a big Sunday brunch for anyone who wants to attend. It will probably be mostly the out-of-town guests and the wedding party again, but apparently they've invited everyone who's been invited to the wedding. It's at the same hotel, yet again."

"So the hotel will be making a fortune off of Jack and Linda."

"No doubt, but, as I said, they've given them a discount on some things to encourage them to have all of the events there. I'm not going to complain as it couldn't be more convenient for me."

Shelly laughed. "It will be lovely for you and Daniel. You won't have to drive anywhere."

"I just hope the food is good. We're going to be eating there a great deal."

They'd reached their building and Shelly stopped. "Did you want to walk further?" she asked.

Fenella glanced at her watch and sighed. "I wish I could, but I still have quite a lot of packing to do. I need an early night, as well. Tomorrow is going to be a very long day."

"And I need to go and make certain that my flat is ready for our special guest who is arriving later today," Shelly said. "Smokey is looking forward to having a friend around for a whole fortnight."

"I can't thank you enough for agreeing to have her," Fenella replied. Katie had walked into Fenella's apartment almost before she'd unpacked her suitcases. Acquiring a pet hadn't been in Fenella's plans, but now she couldn't imagine her life without the small, playful kitten.

"You know Mrs. Jacobson would have looked after Katie if I hadn't been willing to keep her."

"Yes, but she'll have more fun staying with you than she would with Mrs. Jacobson."

Mrs. Jacobson was another neighbor, an older woman who lived with her daughter. The daughter was allergic to cats, so Mrs. Jacobson enjoyed spending time with Katie and Smokey whenever she had the opportunity. As she was retired and had mobility issues, she was nearly always at home, and both Shelly and Fenella had come to rely on the woman to give their cats meals and attention whenever they were away from home.

"I hope she'll enjoy her visit with us. We may spend some time in your flat too, just for a change of scenery."

"You know you're more than welcome any time," Fenella assured her.

They crossed the lobby of the building and rode the elevator to the sixth floor.

"I'll be over around seven with Katie and her things," Fenella said in her doorway.

"I'll be there, ready to welcome her with open arms."

Fenella laughed and then let herself into her apartment. Just a few steps inside, she stopped and stared out the windows at her wonderful view. Huge floor-to-ceiling windows showcased the promenade and the beach and sea beyond it. Waves were rolling slowly towards the sand and then splashing gently onto the shore. The sun was shining, and for a moment Fenella wondered why she was leaving, even if it was only for a short vacation.

"I've nothing from which to take a vacation, of course," she said to Katie, who was fast asleep in a sunny spot near the windows.

The animal opened one eye and then squeezed it shut again.

"It will be nice to be there for Jack, though," she continued. "It's going to be a very special day for him."

"And you're dying to meet Linda," a voice behind her suggested.

Fenella jumped and then spun around. "You said you were going to start appearing in front of me," she reminded her aunt.

"I forgot," Mona replied with a shrug. "I'll try to do better next time."

Sighing, Fenella swallowed a snappish reply. It was bad enough she was sharing her apartment with a ghost. Mona seemed to take great delight in startling her with her sudden appearances and disappearances, and that somehow made the unusual circumstance worse.

"Anyway, I'm not dying to meet Linda, but I will admit to a certain amount of curiosity about the woman," Fenella said a moment later.

"Yes, having met Jack, I'm rather curious about her, too," Mona admitted. "I may have to come along on your holiday."

Fenella frowned. "You can't do that, can you?"

"It won't be easy, but I should be able to make an appearance or two during the fortnight. I've been working on traveling, actually. I'm pretty sure I can go where you go, at least. I was thinking that I should attend the wedding, although the engagement party is tempting, as well. That's where you'll be meeting everyone for the first time. I'd hate to arrive at the wedding not knowing anyone."

"I thought you could only go to places that were significant in your life."

"There are some grey areas," Mona replied with a wave of her hand.

While she wanted to demand more information, Fenella knew better than to bother. Mona rarely shared much about the afterlife, and when she did share, Fenella could never be certain of what to believe.

"I'm glad you're here, anyway," Fenella said. "I need your help."

"You don't know what to wear," Mona guessed.

"Exactly, and I know you'll be able to help me find the perfect outfit for every occasion."

Mona nodded. "Let's go and see what we can find, then," she said, walking toward the master bedroom.

Along with the money, the fancy red sports car, and the fabulous apartment, Mona had left Fenella a wardrobe full of gorgeous clothes. Nearly everything in the wardrobe had been custom made for Mona by a man named Timothy, who had been a local designer. Whatever magic Timothy had sewn into his garments, everything in the wardrobe seemed to fit Fenella perfectly, even though she and Mona had very different figures.

Fenella's suitcase was on the bed. She'd already partially filled it with necessities and the casual clothes that she'd need for lazy days of sightseeing with Daniel. All that she needed to finish packing were the special outfits for the engagement party and the three days of wedding celebration.

"Where do you want to start?" Mona asked as Fenella opened the wardrobe.

"Tomorrow night's engagement party. I'll be meeting Linda for the first time and meeting some of her closest friends, as well. I've no idea what Jack's told her about me."

Mona frowned. "That is a worry. Jack has probably said all sorts of inappropriate things about you, in his charmingly clueless way."

"Exactly. I've no idea what Linda is expecting."

"So you must be beautifully dressed, but not in a way that appears to want to attract any attention," Mona said thoughtfully. "I nearly always dressed to attract attention, of course. This could be more difficult than I'd expected."

"I don't have time to go shopping now," Fenella said anxiously.

"There will be something appropriate here," Mona told her. "Just let me think."

Katie wandered into the room and shouted a greeting at them. Fenella gave her a pat and then watched as Katie jumped onto the bed.

"Blue dress, third from the left," Mona said behind her.

When Fenella turned back around, everything in the wardrobe looked different than it had a moment earlier. While she felt as if she should rub her eyes and look again, she knew she'd only make Mona laugh. Instead, she stepped forward and found the dress in question.

"It's gorgeous, but it looks as if it cost a fortune," Fenella said as she ran her hands over the simple lines of the dark turquoise blue dress.

"Try it on," Mona urged her. "It will look perfect on you."

It took Fenella only a moment to change into the dress. As Mona had said, it was perfect for her. "It still looks as if it was expensive," Fenella said as she twirled slowly in front of her mirror.

"It *was* expensive. I could tell you all about the fabric, but knowing would just make you nervous. It's the right dress for tomorrow night, though, and Daniel is going to love it."

"I can believe that," Fenella replied as she slipped it off. "How do I pack it, though?"

"With tissue paper, of course. There's some in the bottom drawer. I didn't travel much, but when I did, I always took excellent care of the clothes I took with me."

Under Mona's careful tutelage, Fenella carefully folded the dress, layered in tissue paper, and put it into her suitcase. There was, of course, both a matching handbag and a pair of shoes to go with the dress. Fenella added them to the suitcase and then looked at her aunt.

9

"Rehearsal dinner?" she asked.

"Such an American tradition," Mona replied. "I understand such things are increasingly common over here, though. Again, you'll have to do your best to blend into the crowd. One mustn't upstage the bride at her own wedding, or even at her pre-wedding meal."

"I definitely don't want to upstage the bride."

"Is the third dress from the right too pink?" Mona asked.

Fenella pulled out the summery sundress and studied it. The bodice was pink, but the color deepened from the waistline to the hem, ending in a rich, almost burgundy, red. "I hope not, because I love it," Fenella replied.

She loved it even more once she'd tried it on. "It's stunning. So simple, but so beautiful. I want to wear this every day for every occasion, all summer long."

Mona laughed. "It is a lovely dress," she agreed.

It took Fenella only a few minutes to carefully pack the dress, the shoes, and the handbag into her suitcase.

"What's next?" Mona asked when Fenella was finished.

"Something for the wedding itself. They're getting married outside, weather permitting, and then having a sit-down dinner with drinks and dancing."

"What time is the wedding?"

"The ceremony is at two in the afternoon, but the reception doesn't start until five."

"Will you have time to change between the ceremony and the reception?"

"Technically yes, but people would find that odd."

Mona laughed. "Why do you care what people think? I never did."

"I can't draw attention to myself on their wedding day."

"Yes, you've already said that," Mona sighed. "And I was going to suggest the red dress on the left."

Fenella pulled out the dress and raised an eyebrow. It was a slinky, sexy beaded cocktail dress and not at all appropriate for her ex-boyfriend's wedding.

"It will look fabulous on you. Make certain Daniel takes you somewhere where you can wear it once you've returned from Buffalo."

"I will," Fenella replied. "But what do I wear for the wedding?"

"If you will insist on being boring, try the purple dress under your left hand."

Fenella looked at her left hand and blinked. When she blinked a second time, she noticed the purple dress. "This wasn't there a minute ago," she muttered as pulled the dress out of the wardrobe.

"I can't imagine what you mean."

"It's pretty, but boring," Fenella said as she held the dress up to the mirror.

"Try it on," Mona urged her.

"It's less boring when I have it on," Fenella admitted as she rotated in front of the mirror a moment later. Her curves changed the straight lines of the dress into something else altogether.

"It's perfect. Grab the shoes and the bag and get it packed," Mona told her.

"I just need an outfit for the Sunday brunch now," Fenella said when her wedding outfit was safely packed.

"What about a skirt and a light jumper?" Mona asked.

"Maybe I could wear trousers," Fenella replied.

Mona shook her head. "Most of the women will be in dresses or skirts. You said yourself that you want to blend into the crowd."

"As much as I hate to admit it, you're right," Fenella sighed. "Jumper, meaning sweater, I assume?"

"Yes, but a very light one, as it is August. I believe it gets a good deal warmer in Buffalo in August than it does here."

"You're right about that."

The sweater that Mona suggested felt so light as to almost not be there when Fenella put it on. It paired perfectly with the skirt that Mona recommended.

"And I can wear the same shoes with them as I'm wearing for the wedding," Fenella suggested.

Mona nodded. "They'll work and be less for you to pack. I would carry the handbag from the engagement party with it, rather than the one from the wedding, just to mix things up a bit."

"Perfect," Fenella replied, making careful notes about which shoes and handbags went with which outfits. She tucked her notes into the suitcase and pulled it shut.

"Do you think you have everything?" Mona asked.

"Everything except the things I'll need in the morning. I can't pack my makeup and hairbrush until I've used them."

Mona stared at the suitcase for a moment and then shook her head. "You haven't packed anything black."

"Black? I'm going to a wedding, not a funeral," Fenella replied before she felt the color draining from her face. "You aren't suggesting that someone is going to die at this wedding, are you?"

"Of course not, but it's always a good idea to travel with one black outfit, just in case."

"Just in case? Just in case I suddenly have to go to a funeral?"

"Didn't you say that Jack's mother was going to be there? She must be nearly ninety."

"She's in her eighties, certainly, but the last I knew she was in better health than I am. She eats little more than fruits and vegetables, and she walks for miles every day. I expect her to outlive me."

"Do yourself a favor and pack something black. If you don't need it, it's only taken up a bit of suitcase space. If something does happen, though, you aren't going to be in the mood to go shopping."

"Buffalo has a number of malls."

"And they're probably full of trendy clothes for today's teenagers. Do you think you'd actually be able to find something appropriate for a funeral at one of them?"

Fenella really wanted to argue further. She hated the idea of taking funeral clothes on her vacation with her. The thing that made her bite her tongue and start searching for an appropriate black dress was remembering that she'd completely unexpectedly needed funeral clothes on her last vacation with Daniel. As Mona had said, they didn't take up much suitcase space, and it was probably better to be safe than sorry.

With her suitcase as packed as it could be, Fenella made herself a light lunch and then gave her apartment a quick clean. Shelly would be letting herself in to give the cats a change of scenery and to get food for Katie. The last thing Fenella wanted Shelly to find was dust bunnies under the beds.

"She isn't going to be looking under the beds," she muttered to herself as she ran the vacuum.

"But Katie could chase Smokey under one of them. You don't want them both coming out covered in dust," she replied, shaking her head as she realized she was talking out loud.

The afternoon seemed to stretch out endlessly in front of her. A nap would have been a wise way to spend some of it, but Fenella knew she was too excited to sleep. After pacing around her living room for several minutes, Fenella went out for another walk. She found herself wandering around the Douglas shops, looking into windows at the displays. *It will be very different, going around an American shopping mall again*, she thought. "And I can do that tomorrow," she exclaimed out loud, startling the woman who'd been admiring jewelry in the window next to Fenella.

"Sorry," Fenella said, blushing.

"I talk to myself all the time," the woman replied. "Most of the time, I answer myself, too. It isn't as if my husband is ever listening."

Fenella laughed and then headed for home. Between walking and window-shopping, she'd built up an appetite, so she stopped at her favorite Chinese restaurant and got dinner before she went back to her apartment. She and Daniel had agreed that it would be best if they didn't see one another that evening, as they both needed as much sleep as possible, so Fenella planned to eat her dinner and head straight to bed. When she got off the elevator, she realized she was going to have to change her plans.

"Hello," she said to Daniel as he approached her. "Please don't tell me that you're here because you have to cancel our trip for some reason."

He shook his head. "I'm here because I missed you all day and I wanted one quick kiss before I try to go to bed early, that's all."

"You're welcome to come in and eat half of my dinner. I got about three times more than I can probably eat. I was going to give Shelly the leftovers, but she'll never know what she missed out on if we eat it all."

Daniel laughed. His light brown hair had been recently cut and it framed his handsome face and highlighted his gorgeous hazel eyes. Fenella felt herself fall even more in love with him as he dropped a quick kiss onto the top of her head and then followed her into the her apartment.

An hour later the food was gone, and they'd shared more than one kiss. Daniel looked at the clock and sighed.

"I should be in bed, trying to get ready for tomorrow. It's going to be a very long day."

"It is, indeed. I have to take Katie to Shelly's in half an hour and then I'm going to bed."

"Katie is staying with Shelly tonight?"

"She is. I didn't want to have to wake Shelly tomorrow morning at silly o'clock when we have to be away."

"Aren't you worried about being lonely tonight?" he asked, pulling her into his arms.

"I'll miss Katie, but I think it's in everyone's best interest if we all sleep alone tonight," Fenella said when the kiss ended. "We'll be sleeping together for the next two weeks, after all."

"My favorite part of the plans," he whispered in her ear.

She walked him to the door and then let herself get lost in just one more kiss. Snuggling up with him every night was one of her favorite parts of their plans, too.

When her alarm went off the next morning, it took Fenella several minutes to work out where she was and why her radio was blaring out an eighties pop tune that she hadn't cared for when it had actually been the eighties. As her brain slowly began to engage, she found the button to silence the radio and then made sure the alarm was switched off entirely so that it wouldn't be playing to an empty apartment for the next two weeks.

"This is a ridiculous time to be awake," she muttered as she stumbled toward the shower.

By the time she was dressed and had finished packing, there wasn't time to make coffee. Regretting that she hadn't started a pot brewing before she'd gone into the shower, she mixed up some instant coffee with water that she'd heated in the microwave. It wasn't the best, but it got some much-needed caffeine into her system.

She was standing in her doorway when Daniel got off the elevator a short while later.

"Do you have coffee?" he asked.

"Just instant and I drank all of it," she replied, her tone apologetic.

"I'll get coffee at the airport, then," he said before he pulled her into a kiss.

"That's woken me up, anyway," Fenella muttered when he released her.

"Me too," he chuckled.

She grabbed her suitcases and her handbag and then locked her door behind them. After checking that it was securely shut, she followed Daniel down the corridor.

"Did you sleep well?" she asked him as they boarded the elevator car.

"I had trouble falling asleep, as it was much earlier than I normally go to bed, but once I was asleep, I slept well. You?"

"Much the same," Fenella replied, not mentioning the nightmares that had plagued a portion of her evening. No doubt Mona's insistence that she pack something black had played a part in the series of dreams that had featured a seemingly endless parade of funerals. Mercifully, Fenella hadn't known the deceased at any of the funerals, but they'd still been distressing to attend. Now she was determined to put the nightmares out of her head and focus on the vacation ahead.

The roads were nearly empty as they made their way south. At the airport, it took just a few minutes to check in for their flight and get through security. Unfortunately, it was too early for the café to be open, so Daniel didn't get his coffee.

The flight itself was less than an hour. To Fenella, it seemed as if they'd only just taken off before they were landing. Maybe that was because she'd drifted off, her head on Daniel's shoulder, during the flight.

"Did you get some coffee?" Fenella asked as they taxied to the gate.

"I was afraid to try to drink it over your head," he told her. "We can get some after we get through security here," he replied.

Fenella blinked at the bright lights of the airport. "'Welcome to Manchester,'" she read off the sign.

"And now we have to get to the other side of the airport," Daniel told her.

"Maybe the walk will wake me up," Fenella muttered.

"Maybe there will be coffee somewhere," Daniel replied.

When they arrived at the correct airline desk, there was a huge line of people waiting to check in.

Daniel sighed. "I hope we'll be able to get through the queue and security in time," he told her.

"We'll be fine," she assured him, leading him to the special section for first class passengers. They were checked in and then escorted directly through security and into a first class lounge near the gate.

"Someone will come and collect you when it's time for you to board," they were told. "In the meantime, enjoy complimentary drinks and breakfast."

"We're flying first class," Daniel said flatly as the woman walked away.

"And it was worth every penny, just to get through check in and security that easily," Fenella replied.

"Coffee?" a passing waiter asked.

Fenella nodded and, after a moment, Daniel did, too. The waiter was back only seconds later with two huge cups of coffee.

"Sugar and milk are on the table," he told them, nodding to the table next to Fenella.

Daniel took a sip and then sighed. "I can't even be angry that you spent so much on first class tickets. This is wonderful coffee and I really needed it."

"It was the only extravagant thing I did for the trip, but I thought we deserved it. Flying long distances is exhausting. This way we can stretch out and relax. We'll appreciate it even more on the way home."

He nodded and then looked around the room. "I've always wondered about these lounges. I thought they'd be nicer, actually."

Fenella laughed. "I know what you mean. This isn't that different to what's out there. It's just quieter."

"Which makes it worth a lot."

"That's very true."

An hour or so later, a man approached. "Mr. Robinson? Ms. Woods? Your flight to Toronto is ready to board. If you'd care to follow me?"

Fenella felt herself blushing as she and Daniel were escorted past the crowd of people who were waiting to board their flight. They were led onto the plane and shown to seats near the front. Of the dozen or so seats in first class, only two other seats were occupied. The other couple was sitting in seats together, but they seemed to be ignoring one another.

"We'll be on our way shortly," the flight attendant told them. "Have a look over the menus. We'll be serving lunch shortly after takeoff and dinner about five hours after that. Of course, it will only be midday when we arrive in Toronto, so we'll be serving a small snack just before we land, as well, sort of an extra lunch to help you acclimate to the new time zone."

"That's a lot of food," Daniel whispered to Fenella as the man walked away.

"And look at the menus," Fenella gasped. Everything sounded more like fancy restaurant food than airline food. She read through the menus twice and then sighed. "Why am I already expecting to be disappointed by the food?"

Daniel laughed. "You've flown economy too many times. This all sounds delicious. I'm certain it will be better than what the poor folks in the back of the plane are getting."

The pair enjoyed the lunch and then settled it to watch a movie together on the large screens that folded out from the walls next to them. Then they stretched out on seats that went completely flat and napped for a short while. After a delicious dinner, they chatted about nothing and everything as they were served a snack that was almost another meal and before buckling back up for landing.

"They never said one word to each other the entire flight," Fenella whispered as she and Daniel followed the other couple off the plane.

"I noticed that. It was, well, worrying," he replied.

"Maybe they don't even know each other," Fenella suggested.

As they walked into the international arrivals area, she noticed that the woman had opened her large handbag. She pulled out two passports and handed one to the man.

"It looks as if they know each other," Daniel said.

"You want to follow them, don't you?"

"I'm a bit concerned, that's all. It was a long flight and, as you say, they didn't speak to each other for the entire journey."

"Maybe they talked quietly while we were napping."

"Except I didn't sleep," Daniel countered.

He casually but deliberately, walked behind the couple as they approached the immigration desks. The woman headed for one desk while the man stayed behind.

"You can go up together," Fenella said helpfully as she and Daniel got in line behind the man.

"We aren't together," he replied flatly.

Daniel squeezed her hand before she could reply. A moment later, the man was waved forward to another desk. When Daniel and Fenella were called up after another minute, Daniel told the immigration officer what they'd seen.

"They were together on the plane and she was carrying his passport," Daniel explained.

The officer picked up the phone at his elbow and said something to someone. A moment later, another officer approached the desk where the woman was just getting her passport back. She looked surprised when the second officer asked to see it. Fenella deliberately turned her head as the woman began to scan the room. The last thing she wanted was for either of the pair to recognize her and Daniel.

"What brings you to Toronto?" the immigration officer asked as both the man and the woman were led away.

"We're just passing through on our way to a wedding in Buffalo," Fenella explained.

"Who's getting married?"

"My ex-boyfriend."

The man raised an eyebrow. "Interesting," was all that he said as he stamped their passports.

"We'll never know if that was anything serious or not, will we?" Fenella asked as she and Daniel headed for baggage claim.

"I left my card with the man. He may get in touch if he's allowed to tell us anything, but it may simply have been a nasty quarrel that meant neither wanted to be anywhere near the other. It was odd behavior, but it may not have been criminal behavior."

Fenella sighed. "I'm going to be imagining all sorts of reasons why they weren't speaking, and they're all going to be criminal."

Daniel laughed. "You may imagine whatever you like."

Their bags had been pulled to one side where an airline employee was standing guard.

"Ms. Woods, Mr. Robinson, thank you so much for choosing to fly with us," they were told as they collected the bags and headed through customs.

"Why do I always feel as if I'm trying to get away with something I shouldn't when I walk through 'Nothing to Declare?'" Fenella asked. "I have nothing to declare."

"Then stop looking as if you feel guilty," Daniel suggested.

She sighed. "I do feel guilty, even though I'm not guilty of anything."

A moment later they were through the doors and into the chaos that was the arrivals hall.

"There's supposed to be someone here with a sign with my name on it," Fenella told Daniel. "Ah, there he is."

"Dr. Margaret Woods?" Daniel asked.

"I use the title when I travel," she explained. "People seem to treat me better when I use it, at least until they find out that I have a doctorate in history and I'm not a medical doctor."

Daniel laughed. "And you're planning to use Margaret while we're here?"

"It's just easier in this part of the world. No one has ever heard the name Fenella over here, but Margaret is fairly common."

Fenella showed her identification to the limo driver. He took their bags and led them through the airport to the car that was waiting outside.

"Help yourself to drinks and snacks. We should be at your hotel in Buffalo in about two and a half hours," he told them. "If you want to stop anywhere along the way, just let me know over the intercom."

They settled into the back of the car.

Fenella sighed. "I could get used to living this way."

"You could live this way every day."

"Actually, I don't think I want to get used to living this way. I'm really enjoying it right now because it all feels like a real treat. If I had a driver to take me wherever I wanted to go all the time, it wouldn't be special any longer. I might hire someone to clean my apartment, though. I do hate dusting and vacuuming."

Daniel shrugged. "My flat is still so new to me that I don't mind cleaning it. Besides, it's so much smaller than the house I had previously, that it doesn't seem to take any time at all to clean the entire place."

They sat back and watched the scenery go by for a while. It consisted mostly of bumper-to-bumper traffic for the first hour or so. Fenella started to feel excited as they reached the Canada/US border.

"I've never been to the US before," Daniel remarked as their driver joined one of the queues for inspection.

"Never? Have you been to Canada before?"

"Yes, actually, to Toronto and Quebec. I went on a six-week training session in Toronto that included a weekend trip to Quebec. That was my only trip to North America before today."

"I've been to Quebec only one time, although we used to visit Toronto occasionally when I lived in Buffalo. Quebec is beautiful, but as I don't speak French, it was a little bit overwhelming."

He nodded. "I speak a tiny bit of French, but not enough."

Once they went over the bridge into the US, Fenella felt as if they were nearly in Buffalo.

"We're going to visit Niagara Falls, aren't we?" Daniel asked as they passed signs for the natural wonder.

"I'm planning on a day there. I thought we could do all of the touristy things, like take the boat into the falls and walk through the caves behind them."

"Perfect," he grinned at her.

Fenella felt a rush of a dozen different emotions as they got closer to the hotel. They were only a short distance from the university where she'd studied and then worked for many years. The streets were at once familiar and strange. New restaurants and businesses had popped up since she'd been gone and the pizza place that had been on one corner was now an Indian restaurant. She felt a tear slide down her cheek as the driver turned into the hotel's parking lot.

"Are you okay?" Daniel asked.

"Yes and no. I don't know why I'm so surprised that things have changed, but I really wasn't expecting anything to be any different. I know that's silly, but, well, I don't know. I guess I was expecting everything to be exactly the same as I remember it, but, of course, it isn't."

"And you aren't the same person who used to live here," he reminded her.

She nodded. "I'm much happier now."

The driver took their bags out of the car and offered to help them get them inside.

"We'll be fine," Daniel assured him with many thanks.

Inside the hotel, they were welcomed warmly and given the keycards for their room.

"This is nice," Daniel said a short while later.

They were on the top floor of seven, which gave them decent views of the surrounding area.

"There's the university," Fenella told him, pointing to the campus that sprawled across many acres starting just across the road from them.

"Where did you used to work?" he asked.

She pointed out the building and then felt tears forming again.

"What's wrong?" he asked as he pulled her into a hug.

"It's just a lot, that's all. I, well, I haven't really thought about any of this since I've been on the island and now I'm completely overwhelmed."

"And jetlagged," he suggested. "Maybe we should take a nap before the party."

"We need to have some dinner, too. There's going to be food at the party, but only finger foods, or so Jack said."

"Let's try to sleep for an hour or two. Then we can find dinner somewhere. One thing at a time."

"Maybe we could just get room service. There's something about room service that feels like the height of luxury."

Daniel laughed. "Room service it is," he agreed.

"How do I look?" Fenella asked nervously as she powdered her nose for the tenth time.

"Stunningly beautiful," he replied. "Will I do?"

"You look incredibly handsome in that suit. It simply isn't fair that men can wear the same suit everywhere and be appropriately dressed for anything while women have millions of outfits to choose from and usually end up being either overdressed or underdressed wherever they go."

"I think you look perfect, and it won't be you who is overdressed or underdressed, even if everyone else is."

Fenella laughed. "No wonder I, lll, er, love you," she said, stumbling only slightly over the word that was slowly becoming easier for her say.

"I love you, too. That nap did me a world of good and dinner was surprisingly tasty. I'm ready to enjoy the engagement party."

"I'm not sure I'm going to enjoy this," Fenella muttered as she checked that she had the right bag and shoes. "I'm nervous about meeting everyone. I suspect Linda's friends will all think I'm crazy for coming to Jack's wedding."

"You and Jack were together for ten years. I think it's lovely that you can still be friends even after the relationship ended."

"Are you still friends with any of your ex-girlfriends?"

Daniel frowned. "No, but the only one I was with for any length of time was my ex-wife. You know that didn't end well."

"I hope our taxi is here," Fenella said brightly.

"When do we collect our rental car?"

"They're supposed to drop it off for us tomorrow morning. I did all of the paperwork online, so they're supposed to be simply leaving the keys with the front desk for me to pick up at my leisure."

"And you've added me as a driver?"

"I have, but I'm more than happy to do all of the driving if you'd rather not have to deal with being on the wrong side of the car on the wrong side of the road. I appreciate what a challenge that is."

He shrugged. "We'll see."

They rode the elevator down to the lobby and then walked outside. A taxi was idling near the door.

"Mr. Robinson?" the driver asked through the open window.

"Yes, thanks," Daniel replied.

It took just a few minutes to get to the venue on campus. Fenella blinked back tears as she looked around at the place that had been her home for so many years.

"Are you okay?" Daniel asked as the taxi rolled to a stop in front of the building where the party was being held.

"Mostly," she replied.

They got out of the car and he took her hand, squeezing it tightly. "If you want to leave early, I can fake a migraine," he whispered in her ear as they walked toward the entrance.

She laughed. "Have you ever had a migraine?"

"No, but I was with you when you had one. They look pretty awful."

"They are, and if anyone needs to fake one, it should be me. I'll be more convincing."

"Hopefully, we're both going to have fun."

"I'm not sure about that," Fenella muttered. The front door opened into a long corridor. There were classrooms on either side, but they were heading for the large community space at the far end of the building. It had been used for everything from large lectures to faculty luncheons, and Fenella hadn't been surprised to hear that Jack and Linda had chosen to have their engagement party there.

The university's hotel and restaurant management program's students had probably welcomed the opportunity to help with the planning and the menus. The food would be excellent because the students would be getting graded on the finished products.

No doubt the students had had a hand in decorating as well, Fenella thought, as she and Daniel entered what was usually a very boring large rectangle of a room. Tonight, the walls had been draped in huge sheets of white fabric, the tables were covered in immaculate white cloths, and the chairs all had large pink bows around their backs. Short columns were dotted everywhere around the room, each holding vases of white and pink roses. A large bar ran along one wall, and on the opposite side of the room there were several tables seemingly ready for the food that would be coming later.

"This is lovely," Daniel said in a low voice.

"It's really beautiful," Fenella agreed. "There's Jack," she added, nodding toward the man who was standing next to the bar.

"And that must be Linda," Daniel whispered as they headed toward Jack.

Fenella studied the woman on Jack's arm as they approached. She appeared to be around fifty-five, with brown hair that was pulled back into a bun. While Jack looked flustered and a bit bewildered about everything, Linda looked calm. They both looked incredibly happy.

"Jack?" Fenella said when she reached the man's side.

He turned away from Linda and smiled broadly. "Maggie, I knew you'd come," he nearly shouted. After a quick hug, he shook Daniel's hand. "Thank you for coming, as well. But you have to meet Linda. Linda, this is Maggie and her, um, Daniel Robinson."

Linda smiled and held out a hand. "It's very nice to meet you both. Obviously, I've heard a great deal about you."

Fenella felt herself blushing as she shook hands with the woman. "Congratulations to you both," she said.

"Oh, thank you so much," Linda replied.

"Of course, Jack never did want to marry you, Margaret," a sour voice said loudly.

Fenella nearly laughed out loud as she turned to greet Jack's mother, Rosalie Dawson. "Mrs. Dawson, how lovely to see you again," she said.

"Is it?" the woman replied, looking down her nose at Fenella as best she could, being that she was several inches shorter.

"It truly is," Fenella replied. *Because I don't have to be nice to you and I don't care in the slightest what you think of me any longer*, she added silently.

"I was shocked when Jack told me that he'd invited you," Mrs. Dawson said.

"I was surprised and delighted to be invited to be a part of Jack and Linda's celebrations," Fenella replied. "This is Daniel Robinson, by the way."

"Yes, a police inspector, I believe," she said, making the job title sound like something embarrassing.

"I am, yes," Daniel replied. "It's a pleasure to meet you."

"Sorry," Fenella told Daniel. "This is Mrs. Rosalie Dawson. She's Jack's mother."

Daniel nodded. "I thought there was a resemblance. You must be very pleased for your son."

Mrs. Dawson inhaled sharply. "That isn't how I would put it."

"Mrs. Dawson, let me get you a drink," Linda interjected. "What would you like?"

"My son knows what I like," was the snapped reply.

Linda flushed and looked at Jack.

"A gin and tonic for mother and I'll have another glass of wine, please," Jack told Linda.

"Ah, there's a familiar face," a voice said.

"I didn't think you'd ever come back here," another added.

Fenella turned and smiled at Hazel and Sue, two of the women with whom she'd formerly worked. Neither of them had ever been particularly friendly with Fenella, and both women had chased after Jack when Fenella had moved to the island. She imagined they were both disappointed when he'd asked Linda to marry him.

"Sue, Hazel, how lovely to see you both again," she said. She took a few steps away from Jack and his mother before introducing Daniel to the two women.

"It's lovely to meet you," Hazel said, holding Daniel's hand for a moment or two longer than necessary.

"How long have you known Margaret?" Sue asked.

"Since she first moved to the island," Daniel replied.

"He was one of the first people I met after I arrived," Fenella told them.

"Was that before or after you found the dead man that Jack told us about?" Hazel wondered.

"After. Daniel was the police inspector who was put in charge of the investigation," Fenella explained.

"Oh, a policeman?" Sue exclaimed, giggling.

Fenella swallowed a sigh.

"Let me get everyone drinks," Daniel suggested.

"He's much more attractive than Jack," Hazel said as Daniel walked over to the bar after they'd all told him what they wanted.

"I think so, anyway," Fenella replied.

"He's younger, too. You definitely traded up. I'm sure Jack's mother is furious," Sue said.

Fenella laughed. "I no longer care what that woman thinks."

"It's good to see you, though," Sue told her. "Tell us all about your life on the Isle of Man."

She told the pair a little bit about life on the island until Daniel came back with the drinks. Before the conversation could resume, another couple walked into the room. The woman was blonde, with blue eyes. She was frowning at the man who had dark hair and eyes. Linda waved and then rushed over to greet them.

"Everyone, this is my best friend since forever," she said loudly. "This is Melanie Jensen and this is her long-suffering husband, Karl."

A few people chuckled as Melanie smiled tightly and Karl made a face. Linda didn't seem to notice the slightly awkward moment as she dragged the pair over to the bar.

Daniel was telling Sue and Hazel about his work when Linda crossed to them, still pulling Melanie along with her.

"Everyone, I want you to meet Melanie. She's the one who encouraged me to start dating again after my husband left me. She's been my rock through all of this and I want to make sure everyone knows that we wouldn't be here tonight if it weren't for her," Linda said.

"It's nice to meet you," Fenella replied. "There's nothing better than good friends to help you through hard times."

Melanie nodded. "George treated poor Linda quite badly. I was glad I was able to be there for her. She may have to return the favor soon."

Linda gasped. "You and Karl are having trouble?" she asked in a loud whisper.

Fenella glanced over at the bar. When her eyes met Karl's he shrugged and picked up his glass. He'd clearly heard Linda's words.

"It's probably just a rough patch. All couples have them. I don't know," Melanie replied. "I'm determined not to worry about it until after the wedding, though. That's the most important thing happening in the world right now."

"I'm not sure it's that important," Linda laughed.

"Oh, it is," Melanie replied. "But look at your handbag," she said to Fenella. "It's nearly identical to mine. Mine was a gift from, well, from a dear friend."

They compared their bags, which were strikingly similar and then talked about handbags and shoes for several minutes. A short while later, as they were all talking about nothing much, another couple came into the room. They were carrying a huge present wrapped in shiny paper with a massive bow on top. Both had brown hair and eyes and both looked tired and bit unsure of where they were or why.

"Now, I said no presents," Linda said, laughing as she crossed to greet the new arrivals.

Fenella was on her second drink, still chatting with Hazel and Sue, before she finally met the couple who'd brought the gift.

"You haven't met Howard and Gloria," Linda said to them. "This is Howard and Gloria Keller. They're another couple from the crowd I used to hang around with when I was married to George."

Everyone exchanged greetings and then an awkward silence descended.

"You said they were another couple from your married days," Sue said after a moment. "Who else was in the group?"

"Oh, Melanie and Karl," Linda replied. "I haven't explained any of this at all well, have I? When George and I first got married, we lived in an apartment downtown. I'd known Melanie since middle school and I was thrilled when she and Karl bought an apartment in the same building. Howard and Gloria moved into the building a few months later. There was another couple, as well, that we often included in our parties and outings, Donald and Jennifer Harrison, but they moved to Colorado after a year or two. I don't think any of us stayed in touch?" She made the statement a question as she looked at Gloria.

The other woman shrugged. "I didn't stay in touch with them. I didn't really care for Jennifer, and Donald was as dumb as a bag of rocks."

Linda laughed. "Yes, well, anyway, the six of us who were left used to get together at least once a week, even after Howard and Gloria moved out to the suburbs."

"We were ready to have children," Gloria said. "But, of course, it became a lot more difficult to spend time with our friends once the little darlings began to arrive."

Melanie laughed as she joined the group. "That will be why Karl and I decided not to have any little darlings."

A shadow passed over Linda's face. It was gone almost as soon as Fenella had noticed it.

"We wanted children, but we were never blessed with any," Linda said. "Anyway, we all moved out of that building eventually. Melanie and Karl bought a little house just down the road from me and George and we've all been friends ever since. Well, except George left, of course."

Melanie laughed. "And good riddance," she said loudly. "Linda is much better off with Jack. He adores her and he'd never treat her the way that George treated her."

"He had a midlife crisis. It happens," Linda said with a shrug. "In the end, it was for the best. I'm happier now than I've ever been."

"I'll drink to that," Melanie said, holding up her glass.

Half an hour later, Fenella was tired of the small crowd. Melanie had continued drinking steadily, and she'd begun loudly sharing stories from when she and Linda had been in college together with the bartender. It was clear that Linda wasn't enjoying the walk down memory lane anywhere near as much as Melanie was.

Karl was deep in conversation with Sue and Hazel, both of whom seemed to be fascinated by whatever he was discussing with them. Howard and Gloria were talking with Jack's mother, who was frowning and going through gin and tonics at an alarming rate.

Jack mostly seemed to be following Linda around the room as Linda attempted to speak to everyone and ignore Melanie. There were a dozen other people scattered around the room, none of whom Fenella knew and none of whom had been introduced to her and Daniel.

"I think I've had enough of these people for tonight," Daniel whispered in her ear as he and Fenella finally managed to get away from Linda's cousin, who sold used cars for a living.

"Do you think anyone would notice if we slipped away?" she asked. "That migraine we were discussing earlier is becoming a reality."

"Are you okay?"

"Yes, but I'm definitely not having fun."

"Do you want to say anything to Jack and Linda before we leave?"

"I should, shouldn't I?"

He sighed. "Yes, you should."

Jack and Linda were near the door, so Fenella and Daniel headed that way. They were nearly there when the door swung open.

"Ah, good evening," the handsome man in the doorway said. "I hope no one minds me crashing the party, as it were, but I really need to talk to my wife."

"I'm your ex-wife," Linda said flatly.

$\mathscr{H}$ 3 $\mathscr{H}$

There was a long and very awkward pause before Jack stepped forward. "Maybe you should introduce me," he said to Linda.

"Jack, this is George, my *former* husband," she replied, putting emphasis on the word "former" before she continued. "George, this is Jack, the man with whom I will be spending the rest of my life."

George winced. "It's nice to meet you," he said to Jack, holding out a hand.

Jack took it, seemingly reluctantly. "I'm not certain who invited you to the party," he said.

"Ah, yes, well, I wasn't invited, of course, and as I said earlier, I apologize for crashing, but I simply had to see Linda and I couldn't think of another way to manage that. I didn't want to turn up on her doorstep."

"I've moved," Linda said coolly.

He nodded. "Yes, I know."

"So you already tried turning up on my doorstep?" she demanded.

"I drove past the old house, the one that had been our home for so many years. The place where so many of my happiest memories are tucked away in nooks and crannies, on shelves and inside cupboards." He stopped and took a deep breath. "I didn't recognize the cars on the driveway, so I parked across the road for a few minutes. It was obvious, even in those few minutes, that you weren't still living there."

"I wanted to get away from all of those memories," she replied.

He nodded. "I don't blame you. I treated you very badly. You've every right to be angry."

"How did you find out about the party tonight?" Daniel asked.

Fenella glanced at him and smiled. He was always a policeman, even when on vacation and at a party.

George shrugged. "I called a few of my old friends, told them that I was back in town and that I really wanted to see Linda. One of them offered to tell her that I was in the area. When I asked when he expected to see her again, he mentioned tonight's little gathering."

"Which friend?" Linda demanded.

George glanced around the room and then looked back at her. "I'd rather not say. I don't want you angry with him unnecessarily. He told me not to come tonight. This was all my idea."

"As Jack's old girlfriend is here, I can't see why Linda's former husband isn't welcome," Mrs. Dawson interjected, putting unnecessary emphasis on the word "old." "Come and have a drink," she told George.

"I don't want to stay where I'm not welcome. I truly just want five minutes of Linda's time," George replied.

"You can have a drink first," Mrs. Dawson told him. "I'd love to hear all about your marriage and why it fell apart."

George looked uncertain.

Mrs. Dawson walked over to him and took his arm. "Come and buy me a drink," she told him, leading him toward the bar.

"Do you want me to escort him out?" Daniel asked Linda and Jack in a low voice.

"I don't know what I want," Linda said, clearly close to tears.

"I don't want him here, but now Mother will fuss if we throw him out," Jack said.

"What could he possibly want?" Fenella asked Linda.

"I've no idea. He made it clear when he left that he hadn't been happy with me for years. He claimed that he'd stayed only out of a sense of obligation. Maybe he needs money. That wouldn't surprise me, actually."

"You aren't going to give him any, are you?" Jack asked.

Linda shook her head and then sighed. "If he doesn't need much, I might be tempted, if it makes him go away."

"I think maybe we should go and talk to him," Fenella said, looking at Daniel. "Maybe we can persuade him to leave without making a scene."

"It's rather too late for that," Linda muttered.

"We're among friends," Jack told her. "Everyone here is on your side."

"Except for the person who told George about tonight's party," Linda replied. "He might have warned me that George was back in town, at the very least."

"I'm afraid you're going to be very angry with me, then," Karl said as he joined them. "George called me a few days ago. He said he missed everyone and he was thinking of coming to Buffalo for a visit. We spent a few minutes getting caught up on each other's lives and then he asked about you," he told Linda.

"Of course he did," she muttered.

"I said I wouldn't talk about you, not at all, but he was very persistent. He said he just wanted to make sure that you were okay, and I told him that you were thriving. I said you had a good job and that you were busy planning your wedding. I never imagined that he'd turn up here, though," Karl told her.

"You should have told me you'd spoken to him," she replied.

"Yes, clearly," he said ruefully. "I didn't realize he was already in Buffalo. I was more concerned that he might try to crash the wedding than I was about tonight's gathering. I didn't want to spoil tonight by mentioning him, and I certainly didn't tell him about the party. I was going to call you tomorrow and tell you everything."

She nodded. "Next time, call me immediately."

"There won't be a next time. I don't intend to speak to the man again," Karl said firmly.

Fenella glanced over at the bar. Mrs. Dawson seemed to be having a lovely chat with George. Sue and Hazel had joined them and they were all laughing and talking together.

"We'll see if we can get him to leave," Daniel said. He offered Fenella his arm and they walked across to the bar. Melanie followed, staying just behind Fenella as they went.

"Ah, George, this is Margaret," Mrs. Dawson said. "She and Jack were together for a while. It wasn't a significant relationship or anything. Jack never once considered marrying her, but for some reason he insisted on inviting her to his wedding."

"It's nice to meet you," Fenella said to George. "This is my friend, Daniel Robinson."

"Nice to meet you both," George said, shaking hands with both of them.

"How long are you planning to stay in the area?" Daniel asked.

He shrugged. "That depends on Linda, really."

"Why?" Daniel shot back.

George shrugged. "I don't mind telling you that I'm hoping she might take me back. I've learned a lot over the last couple of years. I had a really good thing and I threw it all away. I'm hoping I'll be able to get it back."

"She's marrying Jack in a few days," Fenella said.

"She's supposed to be marrying Jack in a few days," he corrected her. "I have time to change her mind."

"But she's happy with Jack," Fenella argued.

"She was happy with me. I can make her happy again. We were married for almost thirty years. No one knows her the way I know her."

Fenella opened her mouth to argue, but Daniel caught her eye and slowly shook his head.

"It might be best if you simply have your conversation with Linda and get it over with," he suggested. "Let me see if she's willing to talk to you now."

"Now? I mean, I don't want to talk to her in front of a room full of people," George replied.

"There are quiet corners," Daniel told him. "If you're sincere about what you want, you should be willing to take whatever you can get."

George looked as if he wanted to argue, but after a second, he nodded. "We can talk in a quiet corner," he conceded.

"We'll go and see if Linda will agree," Daniel said. He and Fenella crossed back to where Linda was standing with Jack. Again, Melanie followed quietly.

"He'd like five minutes of your time in a quiet corner," Daniel told Linda.

"Don't talk to him," Melanie said quickly. "After the way he treated you, he doesn't deserve five minutes of your time."

Linda nodded. "I'd rather not speak to him."

Daniel sighed. "Of course you don't have to speak to him, but in this case, I think it might be a wise idea. I'm hoping if you let him say what he wants to say now, he may leave you alone after that."

"What could he possibly want?" she asked.

"He told us that he wants you back," Fenella told her.

Linda and Melanie both went pale.

"That's out of the question," Linda said.

"It's a crazy idea," Melanie added. "What could he possibly be thinking?"

"He's thinking I'll go back to looking after him," Linda told her. "He's probably just lost his job or something. Maybe his most recent girlfriend dumped him and bruised his ego. Maybe he simply wants to prove to himself that he can get me back if he wants to."

"Don't talk to him," Melanie said angrily.

Linda took a deep breath. "I need to speak to him," she told Jack. "I need to tell him that I'll never take him back, not in a million years."

"I'll come with you," Jack offered.

"No, you wait here," she replied. "I don't know what he's going to say or do."

"Do you want me to come with you?" Daniel offered.

"I'll come," Melanie suggested. "I'd love to tell him exactly what I think of him."

"I'll be fine. I'll give him exactly five minutes and then he'll go away and I'll never have to see him again."

Linda took a deep breath and squared her shoulders. "Here goes nothing," she said in a low voice.

Fenella and the others watched as she walked over to the bar. After a brief exchange with George and Mrs. Dawson, George got to his feet and followed Linda to one of the corners at the back of the room. For several minutes, George talked and Linda listened. She started crying about halfway through the five minutes. When George was done talking, he held up a hand to stop her from replying.

Jack gasped and muttered something under his breath as George pulled Linda into a kiss. When he finally lifted his head, Linda said something and then pulled away from him. Jack met her before she was halfway back across the room. George leaned against the wall, a satisfied smile on his face while Jack and Linda had a whispered conversation.

"Now what?" Daniel whispered in Fenella's ear.

"I wish we'd left an hour ago," she whispered back.

"We'd have missed all of the excitement."

"Exactly."

"I'm sorry, everyone, but the party is over for tonight," Jack announced a moment later. "Things haven't exactly gone as we'd expected. I appreciate you all for coming. Thank you."

"Is the wedding still going to happen?" Howard asked loudly.

Jack flushed and looked at Linda. "Is the wedding still going to happen?" he asked.

"I can't make that decision right now," she replied with tears streaming down her face. "We'll let you all know what's happening in the next day or two," she said.

"Thank you again for coming," Jack said.

"I wouldn't have missed it for anything," Jack's mother said, cackling with laughter.

Fenella frowned. "Poor Jack," she whispered to Daniel.

"He and Linda seemed really happy together before George arrived," Daniel replied.

"I can't imagine why Linda is thinking of taking George back."

"We don't know that she is. Maybe she's simply feeling a bit overwhelmed."

"George seems really happy, anyway," Fenella replied, nodding at the man who was watching the scene unfold with undisguised glee.

"This is crazy," Melanie said loudly. "Linda, you can't possibly be considering taking that man back. He treated you badly for years and then broke your heart."

"Thanks for the support," George said, laughing.

"Don't you dare even speak to me," Melanie snapped back. "I have nothing to say to you."

"Really? Give me five minutes," George told her.

"Oh, I'll happily give you five minutes," Melanie shouted. She stormed across the room to the man's side.

It seemed as if almost everyone in the room watched the conversation. Whatever was said, Melanie spun on her heel almost exactly five minutes later and stormed across the room.

"We're leaving," she said to Karl who was at the bar, seemingly ordering another drink.

"Everyone is leaving," Daniel said in his senior policeman's voice. "Jack said the party is over. Let's not make this any more difficult than it already is."

Around the room, people finished drinks and began to head for the door. Gloria rushed over to give Linda a hug before she followed Howard out of the room.

Melanie dragged Karl away, waving to Linda as she went. "I'll call you tomorrow," she shouted to her friend.

Linda nodded, but didn't reply.

Sue and Hazel were still talking to Mrs. Dawson. Fenella stared at them until they finally gathered up their handbags and headed for the exit.

"Mother, let's get you a taxi," Jack said, crossing to where his mother was standing at the bar.

"I think you should stay with me tonight," she replied. "After everything that's happened, you need your mother."

Jack's back stiffened. "Thank you for the very kind offer, but I'll be fine at home."

Mrs. Dawson was still fussing as Jack led her out of the room. Fenella crossed to Linda, who was still standing in the middle of the room.

"Are you okay?" she asked gently.

Linda looked at her and then looked away. "Not really, but, well, I don't know what I am. I need to think and I can't do that here, not while he's standing there, smirking at me."

Fenella nodded. "Do you need a ride somewhere?"

"Jack and I came in a taxi so that we could have a few drinks. We were going to have a champagne toast. Now everything is ruined."

"Let me get you a taxi," Fenella offered.

"I can take her home," George said as he crossed to them. "Let me take you home," he told Linda.

"No," she said flatly.

He sighed. "I know I hurt you, and I'm genuinely sorry. I want to make it up to you. We need to talk."

"We can have lunch tomorrow," she told him. She named a local restaurant that wasn't far from the university's campus. "I'll be there at noon," she said. "You can say whatever you need to say over lunch."

He nodded. "Thank you for the opportunity," he replied.

She shrugged. "You didn't give me much choice."

Jack walked back in and frowned. "Ready to go home?" he asked Linda.

"I think I should go home alone," she told him. "I have a lot of thinking to do."

Jack tried to argue, but Linda was adamant. In the end, they all walked out of the building together. Fenella rang a taxi service and requested multiple cars. They all stood together and watched as George rode away.

"Linda, darling, we need to talk," Jack said as the car disappeared around a corner.

"Jack, my dearest, I know that we do, but I need time to think first. I didn't expect to ever see that man again and, well, him being here has thrown me badly. I need to go home and think about some things."

"What things?" Jack demanded.

She shook her head. "We'll talk tomorrow. I'll come to your office after my lunch with George. I'll have answers for you then, I promise."

Jack looked as if he wanted to argue, but after a moment, he shrugged. "I won't push you. If you need time to think, take it, but remember that I love you desperately and I'll do anything to make you happy, even if that means walking away graciously so that you can get back together with your ex-husband."

Linda blinked back tears and she pulled Jack into a hug. "Thank you for being kind and understanding. I'll see you tomorrow. I do love you, so very much." She climbed into a taxi before Jack could reply.

"Anyone want to buy me a drink?" Jack muttered as Linda's car disappeared from view.

"I'll buy you a drink, or ten," Fenella offered. "That was horrible."

Jack sighed. "It wasn't the best night of my life."

There was only one taxi left, so they all climbed into it and took it back to the hotel where Daniel and Fenella were staying. There was a small bar just off the lobby.

"Scotch, neat," Jack told the waiter.

Jetlag and too many drinks at the party were starting to catch up to Fenella. She asked for a soda and Daniel did the same.

"I assume you've never met George before," she said to Jack after the drinks had been delivered to their small table in the corner.

"Never. I'd never even seen pictures of the man. Linda got rid of everything that reminded her of him, including all of the pictures of their wedding and of their life together."

"So she threw away thirty years of pictures?" Fenella asked, unable to imagine doing anything similar.

"She did. She said the historian in her hated to do it, but she needed to purge everything to keep her sanity."

"He must have hurt her very badly," Fenella said.

Jack nodded. "He broke her heart in ways I can't even imagine. I was devastated when you ended things with me, but from what Linda has said, she was very nearly destroyed when her marriage fell apart."

"And now he's here and he wants her back," Daniel said.

"Or so he claims," Jack said darkly. "I wouldn't be surprised if he dumped her again in a month or a year, however long it took to satisfy his ego that he'd truly won her back again."

"You think this is all about his ego?" Fenella asked.

"I don't know what to think. They've been divorced for a few years now. He hasn't been back to Buffalo in all that time. It can't be a coincidence that he turned up right before Linda was due to get remarried."

"Are you okay?" Fenella asked him.

He shook his head. "I love Linda in a way that I've never experienced before. I'm sorry, Maggie, but I never loved you as much as I love Linda. You and I were more like close friends. Linda truly is my soul mate, or so I believed. Now I don't know what to think."

"She's just overwhelmed right now," Fenella said.

"After all the things she's told me about the man, I can't believe she's giving even a single thought to the idea of taking him back."

Fenella patted his arm. "You told me that he left her while she was writing her dissertation."

"Yes, and that was the kindest thing he ever did for her. If he'd have stayed, she'd still be writing it and never quite getting it done," Jack replied. "She was working full-time while she was writing and he still expected her to spend all of her time at home looking after him. She did all of the laundry, shopping, cooking, cleaning, whatever, and held down a job and studied on the side. After he left, she suddenly had a lot more hours every day to concentrate on her dissertation."

"Once she'd recovered from the emotional upset," Fenella suggested.

"Yes, well, she told me that she buried herself in her research to help her forget about what was happening in her life. Maybe she didn't give herself enough time to properly recover from the end of her marriage, though."

"I assume you still want to marry her," Fenella said.

"Of course I still want to marry her. If she gets back with George and then he dumps her again, I'll take her back and marry her then. I'd do anything for her. She completes me."

Fenella looked at Daniel, unsure of what to say next.

"Tell me everything you know about George," Daniel said.

"I don't know much, really. Linda doesn't talk about her marriage with him."

"What does he do for a living?" Daniel asked.

"He works in human resources," Jack replied. "He was working for some company in the Southtowns, but he quit when he decided to leave Linda and leave Buffalo."

"Where did he go?" was Daniel's next question.

"He told Linda that he was going somewhere warm where he didn't have to shovel snow again. She never said anything more specific than that."

"How did they meet?" Fenella asked.

Jack shrugged. "They met in college." He named a small liberal arts college elsewhere in the state. "She got a teaching degree and he was studying economics. I'm a little fuzzy on the details, but I think he was a year behind her and I'm not sure he ever actually graduated."

"And then they moved to Buffalo together?" Daniel wondered.

"She was offered a job here, teaching at one of the high schools in the Northtowns. It was only meant to be a temporary thing. She was covering for someone's maternity leave, but the other teacher decided not to come back, so Linda simply stayed. She was still there when she finally earned her doctorate and left to teach at the university instead."

"Melanie said that George treated her badly. Did she simply mean because he'd left her or were there other issues?" Fenella asked.

"As I said earlier, he was very demanding, getting her to do every-thing around the house even though she worked as hard as he did, maybe even harder. Beyond that, I don't know much, except for the not having children thing."

Fenella thought for a minute. "Did you tell me that he'd had a vasectomy and never told her?"

Jack nodded. "He told her, when he left her, that he'd decided when he was young that he didn't want children, so he'd had himself fixed so that it would never happen. That broke her heart in a different way."

"What a horrible thing to do to someone," Fenella said softly. An unexpected pregnancy many years earlier had resulted in a miscarriage that had left Fenella unable to have children of her own. It was a sorrow she'd never fully recover from and she couldn't imagine spending years trying to get pregnant to find out only after it was too late that her partner had deliberately prevented her from getting pregnant.

"That's one of the reasons why I don't think she'll take him back," Jack said. "At least, I really hope she won't take him back."

"I think you need to get some sleep," Daniel said. "Tomorrow is another day."

Jack nodded. "I think I may just get a room here for tonight. That seems easier than going home. Linda's been staying with me for the last few weeks. Home will feel, well, empty without her, anyway."

"Let me help," Daniel suggested. He stood up and held out a hand to Jack. Jack let him pull him to his feet.

"I'll wait here," Fenella said, feeling as if a few minutes on her own were just what she needed.

"I'll be right back," Daniel promised, dropping a kiss on the top of her head.

She watched the men leave the room and then sat back and took a sip of her drink. Closing her eyes, she counted down from twenty to one, letting her mind clear.

"This is a surprise," a voice said near her ear.

She jumped, nearly spilling what was left of her drink. "Mr. Hawkins," she said in surprise.

"Call me George," he said with a chuckle. "May I join you?"

"Of course," she replied automatically.

"So you're Jack's ex, is that right?" he asked as he settled into the chair next to hers.

"Yes, that's right. And you're Linda's ex."

He shrugged. "For the time being."

"I don't understand why you'd turn up after all this time and try to get her back."

He sighed. "I know I'm coming across as the bad guy here, but I'm really not. Okay, maybe I am. I never set out to be the bad guy, that I know for sure."

"As I understand it, you left Linda."

"I did. I woke up one morning and realized that life was short and I was stuck in a rut." He shrugged and then laughed ruefully. "It was a classic midlife crisis and I'm deeply embarrassed about my behavior now, but at the time I became somewhat obsessed with the idea that I was missing out on something. Linda and I met in college. She was my first, well, my first lover and I suddenly realized that I was nearly fifty and I wanted more, not just in bed, but out of life. I'd been working a boring, dead-end job for years, paying the bills and plodding through my days. I wanted a complete change. Maybe you can't understand how that feels."

"I understand completely," Fenella countered. "I quit my job, sold my house, and moved over three thousand miles away less than two years ago."

"And no one has cast you as the bad guy?"

"Jack has forgiven me for breaking his heart. Our relationship wasn't that serious, though. We'd been together for ten years, but we'd never even lived together, let alone talked about marriage."

George laughed. "I'm going to guess that it was you who never wanted to marry Jack. He seems like a nice enough guy, but way out of your league. You're a lot younger and far too attractive for a man like him."

Fenella wasn't certain how to reply to that. She glanced at the door, wondering what was keeping Daniel. "It's all water under the bridge now," she said after a moment.

"It was nice of you to come all the way back here for the wedding. It can't have been cheap."

"I can afford it."

He raised an eyebrow. "What did you say you do for a living?"

"I didn't say."

"No, you didn't. Are you deliberately trying to intrigue me?" he asked, leaning closer to her.

"Not at all," she snapped, sliding as far back in her seat as she could.

"What did Linda say after I left? Is she going to give me another chance?"

"I've no idea. I met her for the first time today and we barely spoke."

"I feel bad for Jack. I truly do. If there was a way to do this without him getting hurt, I'd do it."

"Why don't you just go back where you came from and leave Linda alone?" Fenella suggested.

"Linda and I have unfinished business."

"What does that mean?"

"You know why I really feel sorry for Jack? His mother is horrible. She was unbelievably pleased that I'd crashed the party. She told me that she's hoping that Jack will be so brokenhearted that he'll move back in with her so she can look after him."

Fenella thought about her reply, biting her tongue as she considered her options. "She never cared for me," was what she finally decided to say.

"No, I got that," he laughed. "She doesn't like Linda, though, either. She's hoping the wedding gets canceled at least as much as I am."

"I hope you're both disappointed."

"Really? Why? What possible difference will it make to you?"

"Jack and I were together for ten years. I'll always love him and I want him to be happy. Linda seems to make him happy."

"She's good at seeming to be something. He'll learn the truth once they're married, if she goes through with it."

"What does that mean?"

"I'm more than willing to admit that I walked out on our marriage and broke her heart, but she wasn't totally blameless in everything that happened over the thirty years we were together."

"All relationships have their ups and downs."

"Yeah, and those are easier to negotiate if both people stay rooted in reality."

Fenella raised an eyebrow. "I'm not sure what you're suggesting."

He shrugged. "It doesn't matter. What matters is that I still love Linda, in spite of her faults, and I want us to have another go at being together. Tell Jack not to despair, though. It may well not work out."

"She told Jack that you had a vasectomy and never told her," Fenella blurted out, blushing over the words.

George stared at her for a moment and then slowly shook his head. "That's exactly the sort of thing I mean. She lives in her own world where she rewrites history to suit her purposes."

"It isn't true?"

He sighed. "I can't see why it matters, but it isn't true. There were other reasons why we never had children. Linda knows the truth, but I suppose Jack preferred to hear that it was all my fault. No doubt Linda enjoyed telling him that, as well."

"Sorry that took so long," Daniel said as he dropped into the chair opposite George. "I wasn't expecting to see you here," he said to the man.

"It's a nice hotel and it's convenient for everything," George replied.

"You're staying here?" Daniel asked, frowning.

"Is that a problem?" George shot back.

"Of course not," Daniel replied. "Ready for bed?" he asked Fenella.

"Yes, I am," she replied firmly.

"Good night," George said.

"Good night," Fenella muttered as she and Daniel got up from the table.

4

When Fenella woke up the next morning, she was determined to put Jack, Linda, and especially George out of her head. Today was her first opportunity to show Daniel everything that made Buffalo so special and wonderful and she couldn't wait to share it with him.

"I can't believe I stayed away this long," she said over breakfast in the hotel's restaurant. "I love Buffalo."

"I'm looking forward to seeing more of it," Daniel replied as he tucked into pancakes and bacon.

"I thought maybe we could go to the Buffalo Zoo this morning," she suggested. "It's a really nice zoo. It's larger than the island's Wildlife Park, but smaller than Chester Zoo."

"Will it take all day?"

"I imagine we'll be able to see everything in a few hours. Then we can get lunch somewhere. I'm not sure what we should do this afternoon."

"You'll think of something."

She laughed. "I'll probably think of a dozen things. I want to go everywhere and see everything."

"I hope Niagara Falls is still on the list."

"Yes, of course. I thought it would be sensible to stay closer to home today, though, while I'm getting used to the rental car. I'm only a little bit worried about being back on the other side of the road."

After breakfast, they picked up the keys to the rented car from the hotel's front desk and headed outside.

"It's very, um, sensible," Fenella said when she saw the small blue SUV. "I thought about renting a sports car, but I have one at home."

Daniel laughed. "This is probably smarter for getting around town, anyway."

"I hope I remember how to get to the zoo," she muttered as she adjusted the seat and the mirrors.

Twenty minutes later, she pulled into the zoo's parking lot.

"I was expecting to see more cars," Daniel said.

"I don't think they're open yet."

She parked and then they walked to the entrance.

"We're two minutes early," she said. "We didn't hit as many red lights as I thought we would."

A minute later, as a small crowd of women and children grew behind them, the ticket windows opened. Fenella paid for their admission and for a parking token that would let them out of the parking lot when they left.

As they walked away from the window, she handed Daniel the map. "Have a quick look and see if there's anything you definitely don't want to miss," she suggested. "I'm planning to try to see it all, but there's always a chance we might miss something."

"I don't care what we see or don't see," he told her. "I'm just happy to be spending the day with you."

She blushed and then took his hand and pulled him eagerly toward the otters.

"I didn't think, after all those pancakes this morning, that I was ever going to be hungry again," Daniel said just after noon. "But I'm starting to get hungry."

"Just the rainforest to go," Fenella replied. "It's really interesting, and it won't take long to go through it."

Half an hour later, they walked through the gift shop on their way back to the car. Fenella stopped in front of a large display of stuffed red pandas.

"Does Chester need a friend?" Daniel asked.

Fenella blushed and then nodded. "You remembered his name."

"Will you call this one Buffalo?" he asked as she picked up and put down several different animals.

"I'm not sure I want to call a red panda 'Buffalo,'" she mused. "Which one is cuter?" she asked as she held up two different toys.

"I prefer the one that's lying down. He looks as if he'd be good company."

Fenella laughed. "I think you're right about that. I have to have him. Chester will love having a little brother."

Daniel insisted on paying for the toy in the same way he'd bought her Chester at the zoo in Chester. As they walked back outside, she clutched the bag tightly.

"What can I call him?" she asked as she put the bag into the car's trunk.

"It's definitely a boy panda?"

"Yes."

"You could call him Douglas, after the island's capital."

"Oh, that's very good. I like that a lot."

"Should I keep thinking, or is he definitely Douglas?"

"He's definitely Douglas."

"Excellent. Lunch?"

"I used to go to a little pizza place that's tucked up in one of the strip plazas not far from here. The food was amazing and the place was nearly always empty. It's probably some chain restaurant now, but if it's still there, it would be my first choice for lunch."

"Let's go and see if it's still there."

"Not only is the food good, but it was always a fun place to people watch," Fenella said as she drove. "Because it's sort of out of the way, I always felt as if most of the other customers were meeting blind dates or secret lovers there."

Daniel laughed. "Did you used to go alone?"

"I usually went with one or two of the other professors. Whoever was around, really, when I started craving their food."

"So maybe everyone else in the place thought you were on a blind date, too."

She laughed. "I never thought about that. You could be right."

A few minutes later, she turned into the large parking lot. "It's still there," she said happily.

"I don't see anything that looks like an Italian restaurant."

"It's that one," she said, pointing to a small storefront in the corner of the strip plaza.

"If you say so."

"The food used to be amazing," she told him.

"I can't wait to try it."

They walked across the parking lot. Daniel held the door for her.

"I can't see a thing," Fenella laughed as they stood in the dimly lit entryway.

"It's very bright outside today," Daniel replied.

"Table for two?" a voice said.

Fenella nodded toward the speaker, squinting as her eyes slowly adjusted to the sudden change in light.

"Right this way," the man told them, heading through the door behind him.

Fenella and Daniel followed. The large dining room wasn't any more brightly lit than the entrance had been. Fenella felt as is she was still struggling to see as the man stopped at a table in the corner. As her eyes adjusted, she was surprised to see that nearly every table was full. She was even more surprised when she recognized the man at the table next to theirs. She exchanged glances with Daniel as they were handed menus.

"Go ahead and say hello," he whispered from behind his menu.

"That isn't Melanie," she whispered back.

"Maybe it's a work colleague."

Fenella looked over at the couple that were holding hands and staring into one another's eyes. They'd clearly just finished eating. They may have been work colleagues, but they seemed to be something more, as well.

"Hello," Fenella said brightly as she put her menu down on the table. "I didn't recognize you at first, because I could barely see. It's not very well lit in here, is it?"

The man at the next table looked at her. For a moment, he looked annoyed before the expression was replaced with something like resignation. "Hello," he muttered.

"Friends of yours?" the pretty blonde across from him asked.

He sighed. "Cindy, this is Margaret Woods and Daniel Robinson. This is Cindy Paxton."

Fenella smiled. "It's nice to meet you."

"Likewise," Cindy replied. "How do you all know one another?"

Karl frowned. "I don't see that it matters. We have mutual friends."

Cindy looked at Fenella. "Are you one of his wife's friends?" she demanded.

"Not exactly," Fenella replied, glancing at Daniel. He raised an eyebrow.

"But you know her?" was Cindy's next question.

"We've met her," Fenella said cautiously.

"Drinks?" the waiter asked.

"Yes, please," Fenella said, grateful for the interruption.

"You were telling me how you know Melanie," Cindy said a short while later as the waiter walked away.

"Cindy, leave it," Karl said.

"What are you hiding?" she asked him.

"I'm not hiding anything," he snapped. "Melanie and I are separated. What else do you need to know?"

"Are they separated?" Cindy asked Fenella.

"I just met them both last night," Fenella told her. "It was a party. I barely spoke to either of them."

"Last night?" Cindy echoed.

"I told you I had a thing," Karl said.

"You told me you had to work late," Cindy countered.

"I did have to work late," he told her. "And then I had to go to a thing with Melanie. I told you her best friend is getting married this weekend. Last night was the engagement party. I was there only because I had to be."

"I don't understand why you had to be there," Cindy replied.

"I told you, it's Melanie's best friend who's getting married. She doesn't want to tell her friend that her marriage is falling apart right before the wedding," he explained.

"I thought it had already fallen apart," Cindy said coolly.

"Yes, of course. It's over. We're separated. Linda, Melanie's friend, is the only one who doesn't know that," he said quickly.

"And these people," Cindy said, gesturing toward Daniel and Fenella. "They didn't know that you and Melanie were separated."

"I just met them last night. I barely spoke to them. Besides, Melanie doesn't want Linda to know. We did our best not to talk about our relationship last night," he defended himself.

Cindy sat back in her seat and took a sip of her drink. "I don't trust you," she said eventually.

"Ready to order?" the waiter asked Fenella and Daniel.

Fenella nearly waved him away, but Daniel asked a question about one of the pasta dishes. It didn't matter, in the end, as no one at the other table spoke until the waiter left again with Daniel and Fenella's order.

"I told you that this is going to take time," Karl said to Cindy. "Melanie and I have been married for thirty years. Undoing everything that ties our lives together isn't going to be quick."

"I've been waiting for six months already," Cindy said flatly.

"I know and I love you for being so patient. This is the last hurdle, I promise. Once the wedding weekend is over, Melanie and I will be separating properly, and you and I will be able to be together. I just need this one more week," Karl said in a pleading voice.

"When we met, he told me he was divorced," Cindy said to Fenella. "We met on a dating app and I wasn't sure what to believe. I've met so many married men on those apps that I'd very nearly given up, you know?"

Fenella nodded. "It's hard to find single men over the age of forty."

"At least ones who aren't looking for women in their twenties," Cindy said. "I went out with ten different men last year and nine of them were married and just looking to cheat. The tenth was a narcissistic moron who truly was divorced. He was trying to sleep with as many women as he could to make himself feel better about his wife leaving him for another woman."

Fenella laughed. "I can't imagine."

Cindy looked at Daniel. "He's probably not single and he's definitely gorgeous."

Daniel blushed as Fenella laughed again. "He's single, or rather, he's not married, but he's taken."

Cindy nodded. "The good ones always are. The thing is, I thought my luck was finally changing this year. I met Karl," she nodded toward the man. "He told me he was divorced and he seemed so sincere and trustworthy that I gave him a chance. That was a mistake, of course."

"No it wasn't," Karl said forcefully. "I'm separated and I'll be divorced by the end of the year. You just need to give me time."

"That's what he always says," Cindy told Fenella. "That he just needs more time. And I keep giving him more time, and more time, and more time."

"I'm doing my best," Karl muttered.

"Things keep coming up," Cindy said. "Melanie got sick and nearly died back in April. It was horrible. There simply wasn't anyone else to take care of her."

"I didn't have a choice," Karl said tightly. "I couldn't leave her to die alone. I owed her that much after all these years."

Cindy shrugged. "It took her months to recover, but she was finally well again, right before her birthday."

"She'd been planning a big party for months," Karl said. "She hadn't been certain she was going to make it to her birthday, so once she started feeling well again, she started planning for the party. I couldn't very well leave her right before one hundred of her family members and friends all came together to celebrate, could I?"

Cindy shrugged. "That takes us to June. But then Karl had to go to Hawaii for work and Melanie had to go along for some reason."

"I told you, the trip was a reward for my work performance, and it included spouses. The company believes in happy families, so we had to go along and pretend to be a happy family for a little while," Karl replied.

Cindy rolled her eyes. "Whatever. He's been back from Hawaii for a month, but now he won't leave Melanie until after this wedding. He doesn't want to upset the bride, but he's happy to upset me. Having said that, I'm not even sure I believe there is a wedding this weekend."

"There is a wedding this weekend," Fenella assured her. "And Melanie is the bride's best friend."

"Here we are," the waiter said, putting plates full of delicious smelling food in front of Daniel and Fenella. "Is there anything else I can get you for now?"

"This looks great," Fenella said. "Thank you."

"So he's telling the truth about that one thing, anyway," Cindy said as the waiter walked away. "What about the rest of it?"

"I've no idea," Fenella told her.

"So what would you do, if you were me?" Cindy asked her.

Fenella took a bite of spaghetti while she tried to work out how best to reply. She looked at Daniel who shook his head slightly. *What did that mean?* she wondered.

"I can't imagine getting into your situation," Fenella said after she'd swallowed. "How did you find out he was still married?"

Cindy laughed. "We were sitting here, actually, having dinner one night. Someone from Karl's office came in to get something to go and he spotted Karl. After a very awkward conversation where Karl tried to convince the man that we were cousins, he finally told both me and his work colleague that he and his wife were in the process of separating."

"I think I would have walked out then," Fenella said.

Daniel turned a chuckle into a cough as Karl frowned at her.

"I should have," Cindy said with a sigh. "It was only our third or fourth date. I didn't have all that much invested, really. Now, after six months, it's a lot harder to end things."

"I love you," Karl told her.

"Just not enough to actually end your marriage," she shot back.

"The marriage is over in everything but name," he replied.

"You could just tell him to call you when the ink is dry on the divorce papers," Fenella suggested.

Cindy laughed. "That's a wonderful idea!" she exclaimed. She turned to Karl. "I'm a nice person. I've always been really careful not to knowingly get involved with married men. You managed to persuade me to give you a chance and then another and another and now I've had enough. I'm done until you're actually, truly, legally divorced. Send me a photo of the signed papers and I'll let you buy me dinner."

"Please, just give me..." Karl began.

Cindy stood up. "I've given you everything I'm going to give you. I've waited for six months for you to leave your wife. I won't feel sorry for you if you have to wait a few months for the lawyers to work out your divorce. Who knows, maybe I'll find someone else before you get it all done."

Before Karl could reply, she'd spun on her heel and walked out of the room.

"Thanks," Karl said angrily to Fenella. "She only had to wait one more week."

"Did she?" Fenella replied. "When I spoke to Melanie last night, I didn't get the impression that she thought a divorce was imminent."

"She's putting on a good show for Linda's sake. Our marriage is over and Cindy makes me a million times happier than Melanie ever did. If you've ruined everything between us, I'll never forgive you," Karl snarled before he jumped up and stomped out of the room.

"He isn't very happy with you," Daniel said.

Fenella sighed. "I shouldn't have told her to wait for him to be divorced, but she did ask what I would do under the circumstances."

"You'd have walked out the minute you found out he was still married."

"Relationships are built on trust. He lied to her from the beginning."

Daniel nodded. "I doubt anything he's told her has been true."

"It would be interesting to compare his version of events with Melanie's," Fenella said thoughtfully.

"At least you'll have something to talk with her about at the wedding," Daniel teased.

"If there is a wedding," she sighed. They'd both been avoiding the entire subject all morning, but now Fenella felt as if they needed to address it.

"George and Linda were supposed to have lunch together," she said.

"I thought you'd suggest that we have lunch at that same restaurant."

Fenella sighed. "I thought about it, but I really don't want to get involved. I thought about meeting Jack for lunch too, just to try to keep his mind off Linda and George being together."

"Have you heard from anyone today?" Daniel asked.

She shook her head. "I sent Jack a text this morning, telling him to let me know if he needed anything. He still hasn't replied."

"The food is good," Daniel said after a short silence.

"I'm thinking too much to taste it," Fenella sighed. She took a deep breath and tried to push everything out of her head except the delicious meal. By the time the waiter returned, she'd managed to enjoy her last few bites of lunch.

"Would you like to see the dessert menu?" he asked.

"I wish I had room, but I don't," Fenella told him.

"We can package anything up to go," he suggested.

"Thank you, but we're staying in a hotel. We wouldn't have anywhere to keep it," she replied.

They were walking back to the car when Fenella's phone buzzed.

"It's Jack," she said when she'd found the device in the bottom of her bag.

George never showed up for lunch. Linda is upset.

Fenella read the message twice and then read it out to Daniel. "I don't know how to reply to that," she said.

He frowned. "Ask him if there's anything we can do," he suggested.

She nodded. *Can we do anything to help?* she texted back.

Can you meet us at the hotel where you're staying? I'm still here and Linda is on her way.

Fenella read the message to Daniel and then let him reply in the affirmative while she drove. They were back at the hotel a short while later.

Jack was pacing in the lobby when they walked through the front door.

"Linda was only a few blocks away, but she isn't here yet," he said anxiously.

Fenella looked at Daniel. "Maybe George turned up late," she suggested.

The Wedding March began to play somewhere. Fenella frowned and looked around.

"It's my phone," Jack said, blushing. "It's my ringtone for Linda."

He took a few steps away and answered. Fenella heard nothing but a few monosyllabic replies, but when Jack turned back around, he was clearly upset.

"What's wrong?" she asked.

"Linda took a wrong turn and ended up on the thruway. She was crying so hard that she ended up on Grand Island. She's now sitting in a parking lot at a fast food place, sobbing her eyes out."

"She shouldn't be driving," Daniel said.

"No, she shouldn't," Jack agreed. "I told her to stay there and that I'd come to her."

"Are you okay to drive?" Fenella asked, studying the clearly shaken man's face.

He shrugged. "I don't know."

"Why don't we drive you to Grand Island," Daniel offered. "Then you can drive Linda's car for her so she doesn't have to drive."

"I suppose we could do that. I'd have to leave my car here, though," Jack said, seemingly feeling overwhelmed by the situation.

"It will be fine here," Fenella assured him. "Let's go."

"I'm sorry about this," Jack said as they all climbed into the rental car. "I'm so worried about Linda that I can't even think straight."

"It's going to be okay," Fenella told him.

"I hope so," he replied. "I don't even care if she wants to go back to George. I just want her to be okay."

"You do care if she goes back to George."

"Yes, but if that's what it takes to make her okay, I can live with it."

"You love her a lot."

"It scares me."

"Is Grand Island actually an island?" Daniel asked from the backseat.

"Yes. We'll have to go over a bridge to get there," Fenella told him.

"I hate the Grand Island bridges," Jack muttered.

"It's a good thing I'm driving," Fenella replied.

Jack sighed. "I can't believe Linda drove over the bridge while she was crying. She could have...I can't.... I could have lost her."

"She should have stayed where she was," Fenella said. "You could have met her there."

"I should have suggested that," Jack said miserably. "When she called me, she was upset. She'd sat in the restaurant for ages, waiting for George. Eventually, when she realized he wasn't going to show up, she just wanted to get away. When we spoke then, she sounded more angry than anything else."

Fenella paid the toll and then drove carefully over the bridge.

"It's higher than I was expecting it to be," Daniel remarked.

"It's not high at all," Fenella said, patting Jack's arm. "We're practically at ground level. And it's really, really short. We're nearly to the other side already."

"My eyes are shut," Jack replied. "Tell me when we're back on solid ground."

"We're back on solid ground," Fenella said a moment later. "Where am I going?"

Jack named a local coffee shop chain. "They're at the next exit," he told her.

Fenella pulled off the highway and followed the signs to the coffee shop.

"That's her car," Jack said, pointing to a small car that was parked at an odd angle near the door.

There weren't any empty spaces near it, so Fenella pulled into a spot nearby and then the trio crossed the parking lot together. The car was empty.

"Maybe she went inside for coffee," Jack said hesitantly.

"There you are," a voice said loudly.

Fenella looked up and smiled at Linda, who was standing in the doorway to the building. It wasn't immediately obvious that she'd been crying.

"I didn't mean to drag you all to Grand Island," Linda said apologetically.

"Jack said you were upset," Fenella replied. "We thought it might be best if Jack were able to drive you home, so we brought him to you."

Linda nodded. "That does make sense, but for now, I'm having lunch. Come and join me."

Fenella exchanged glances with Daniel as they followed the woman into the building. Linda led them to a table in the corner where she'd left a cup of coffee and her half-eaten sandwich.

"Do you want anything?" Daniel asked Fenella as Jack sat down next to Linda.

"I'd love a cup of coffee," Fenella replied.

"Jack, can I get you anything?" Daniel asked.

Jack blinked several times and then shook his head. "I'm fine," he said.

As Daniel walked to the counter, Fenella took a seat at the table. "Are you okay?" she asked Linda.

"I'm more than okay," she replied. "Crying on the highway clarified some things in my mind." She looked at Jack and sighed. "I love you, Jack Dawson. I can't wait to marry you on Saturday and start our new life together."

Jack looked as if he might burst. "Really? You're sure?"

"I'm positive," Linda said, pulling him into a kiss.

"But what about George?" Jack asked when the kiss finally ended.

"He had his chance to explain, to apologize, to beg, whatever he wanted. He didn't bother to show up, but even if he had, I wouldn't have taken him back. He hurt me terribly in the past, but he can't hurt me any longer. I'm done with him, with his lies, with his empty promises, with, well, everything. I'm all yours now, if you're willing to have me."

Jack grinned from ear to ear. "I love you," he said.

"Coffee," Daniel said, handing Fenella a paper cup.

"Thanks," she replied.

He sat down next to her and looked over at Linda and Jack. "I feel as if I missed something," he said.

"The wedding is back on," Jack told him happily.

"It was never actually off," Linda protested. "I was just, well, upset and confused for a short while. But I'm not confused any longer."

"That's good news," Daniel replied. He took a sip of his drink and then frowned.

"What's wrong?" Fenella asked.

"I asked for lemonade. I was expecting something different."

Fenella laughed. "In the UK, lemonade is carbonated lemon-lime soda," she explained to the others. "Over here, it's water and sugar and lemon juice," she told Daniel. "And I love it, so if you don't want to drink it, we can trade."

Daniel took another sip from his cup and then shrugged. "I don't dislike it. It just wasn't what I was expecting. It's quite refreshing on a hot day, though."

Linda finished her sandwich while the others drank their drinks. When they were done, they walked out of the coffee shop together.

"What are your plans for the rest of the day?" Fenella asked Jack.

"We were supposed to be moving the last of my things into his house and then having dinner with his mother," Linda replied for him. "I suppose we should still do that."

"You may be too tired to have dinner with my mother," Jack suggested. "I'm pretty sure I'm too tired to have dinner with my mother."

Everyone laughed.

"What are we doing with the rest of the day?" Daniel asked Fenella as she drove out of the parking lot.

"I don't know. What do you want to do?"

"Let's go back to the hotel," he suggested. "I'm curious as to why George didn't meet Linda for lunch. I'm hoping he's drowning his sorrows at the bar at the hotel."

"I never thought of that. I'm surprised Jack didn't go looking for him."

"Jack doesn't know that George is staying at our hotel, does he?"

"Now that you mention it, he probably doesn't," Fenella replied after she'd thought back through the previous evening. "You'd taken him to get a room before George turned up in the bar."

"And then I walked Jack to his door and helped him open it," Daniel told her. "He was more than a little drunk and very upset."

Fenella nodded. "So he didn't know to go looking for George at the hotel today. Do you really think he's there?"

"I think it's a good place to start, anyway."

Fenella parked the car and switched off the engine. "I wonder what's going on over there," she said, pointing to the opposite end of the parking lot. There were half a dozen people standing around a large dumpster.

"Maybe we should find out," Daniel suggested as they got out of the car.

"I don't think so," Fenella replied with a sinking sense of foreboding.

Daniel either didn't hear her or chose to ignore her. She followed reluctantly as he walked briskly toward the dumpster.

"Stay back a bit," a man said as they approached. "We've called the police. Someone is on the way."

Fenella looked past him, into the dumpster. Only half of the lid was open, but that was enough to reveal the dead body inside. Now Fenella knew exactly why George hadn't met Linda for lunch.

✵ 5 ✵

"You said you've rung for the police?" Daniel asked.

"Yes, I did," a man replied. "I'm the manager on duty."

Daniel nodded. "I'm a homicide inspector, but I'm way out of my jurisdiction here."

"That's just as well," another voice said. "Since your girlfriend was having drinks with the dead man just last night."

Everyone in the small crowd turned to look at Fenella. She frowned at the man who'd been tending bar the previous evening.

"We both met the man earlier yesterday," Daniel said. "Beyond that, we've no comment for anyone other than the police."

"No one should be saying anything," a man in a police uniform said as he approached the crowd. "We got a call about a dead body," he added as he looked around.

As his gaze moved from person to person, Fenella felt as if he was memorizing every face.

"In the dumpster," the manager said, nodding toward the metal container.

The officer took a step forward and then frowned. "I need you all to move back at least two paces," he said. "Don't think about leaving, though. You all need to stay here."

"I should get back inside," the manager told him. "I have guests to take care of."

"Was he one of your guests?" the policeman asked.

The man nodded. "He checked in yesterday for three nights."

"Did you check him in?" was the next question.

"I did. I sometimes cover for the reception desk staff when they go to lunch or dinner. Suzy took her dinner break at five and..." He stopped when the policeman held up his hand.

"You can save your statement for the homicide detectives," he said. "You need to wait here until someone from homicide tells you otherwise."

"What about me?" the bartender asked. "I'm supposed to be behind the bar."

"Did you ever meet the dead man?" he was asked.

"I served him a few drinks last night, but we didn't talk," he replied.

"You'll have to wait as well," the policeman replied.

The bartender sighed deeply. "You don't need to talk to me. She can tell you everything you need to know," he said, pointing to Fenella. "She's the one who was having drinks with him last night."

Fenella felt herself blushing as everyone turned to look at her again.

The policeman raised his eyebrows. "As much as I'd love to ask, you can save your statement for the homicide detectives, too."

She nodded and then looked at Daniel. He took her hand and gave it a squeeze. They could hear sirens in the distance. A few minutes later, as everyone stood around in an uneasy silence, two more police cars pulled into the lot. Uniformed officers joined their colleague at the dumpster. A few glanced inside, but no one spoke.

When the black car arrived, all of the uniformed men and women seemed to snap to attention. All eyes were on the car's door as it swung open.

The woman who climbed out was younger than Fenella had been expecting. She looked no more than forty as she strode across the lot in her dark suit, her brown hair in an immaculate twist on the back of her head.

"Report," she snapped at the man who'd arrived first.

He gave a quick account of what he'd found, including everything that the manager and the bartender had told him.

Fenella found herself being scrutinized by the woman, her cool green eyes staring at Fenella for a minute longer than felt comfortable.

"Who found the body?" was the first question the woman asked.

"That would be me," a dark-haired man said. "I came to empty the dumpsters." He nodded toward the large truck that was parked a short distance away. "It's all automatic. The arm at the back lifts them and dumps them. Before the arm can lift them, though, I have to open the lids."

"So you got out of the truck to open the dumpsters?" the police-woman asked.

"Yeah, I open them and lock them open so the lids don't flap around while they're being dumped. I started to open this one and then, well, I saw the guy."

The woman nodded. "What did you do next?"

"I went inside and told the manager that he had a dead guy in one of his dumpsters. He thought I was kidding, so he came back out here with me."

"And I called the police," the manager said.

"And then a small crowd gathered?" the woman asked, looking around at the half dozen or so people who were watching with great interest.

"Something like that," the manager agreed.

"Jackson, take them all inside and get their statements. I'll speak to the manager, the bartender, and those two myself," she said, nodding at Daniel and Fenella.

"Yes, ma'am," the policeman replied. "If you'll all come with me," he said.

"I was just walking by. This has nothing to do with me," someone protested.

"Then it won't take long for you to give us your statement," the policewoman said smoothly. "I don't want to arrest anyone for refusing to cooperate with a homicide investigation."

That seemed to silence everyone. They all followed the policeman into the hotel's lobby where they were directed to sit in a small group together.

"Please refrain from speaking to one another," they were told. A moment later three more uniformed police officers arrived. They positioned themselves around the space, making it impossible for anyone to have a whispered conversation unnoticed.

Feeling as if she'd done this far too many times in her life already, Fenella sat back and shut her eyes. George was dead. The idea seemed almost impossible. It seemed highly unlikely that he'd climbed inside the dumpster deliberately, which meant he'd probably been murdered.

The list of possible suspects has to start with Jack, she thought, immediately feeling guilty for even considering the idea. She'd known Jack for a long time. There was no way he'd killed anyone, not even the man who'd threatened to come between him and his beloved Linda. *But could Linda have killed the man?*

Fenella shook her head. There was no point in going through the list of suspects now. She and Daniel could discuss them later. For now she simply had to clear her head and try not to worry about the conversation she was about to have with the homicide detective. Daniel gave her hand a squeeze, causing Fenella to open her eyes. The woman in the dark suit was approaching the group.

"Before we begin interviews, I want to get everyone's names," she said. She started with the hotel manager and the bartender before she turned to Fenella.

"I'm Fenella Margaret Woods," she said, carefully spelling Fenella. "When I lived in the US, I went by Margaret, but I use Fenella mostly now."

"What did the dead man call you?"

Fenella frowned. "I was introduced to him as Margaret, as we were introduced by people who knew me when I lived here. It's really only Daniel who calls me Fenella in this country."

The woman nodded slowly. "This must be Daniel," she said, shifting her gaze to Daniel.

He nodded. "Daniel Robinson, CID Inspector with the Douglas Constabulary on the Isle of Man."

"CID inspector?" she echoed. "Where is the Isle of Man?"

"It's a British crown dependency in the Irish Sea between England and Ireland," he explained. "Before I moved there, I worked in Liverpool in England. I primarily work in homicide."

"Interesting. I think I'll start with you, then," the woman said. "The woman at reception has given us access to one of the conference rooms. We'll talk in there."

She turned and walked away, clearly expecting Daniel to follow. He gave Fenella a reassuring smile before he walked quickly after the police woman.

An hour later, Fenella was the only one left under police guard in the hotel lobby. The bystanders had all been interviewed, as had the hotel's manager and the bartender. Fenella was entertaining herself by counting backward from a million by threes when the policewoman finally came for her.

"Ms. Woods, sorry to have kept you waiting for so long," she said, not sounding the least bit sorry.

Fenella stood up and shrugged. "I've been involved in murder investigations before. I know everything takes time."

"Indeed. If you'll come with me?" She didn't wait for a reply before she turned around and walked briskly across the room.

Fenella followed her down a short corridor and then through a door into a small conference room. There were two uniformed policemen already sitting at the table.

"Have a seat," the woman told Fenella, gesturing to the chair between the two men.

Fenella sat down and waited while the other woman took the chair across the table from her.

"I don't believe I ever introduced myself," she said as she picked up a pen and opened a notebook. "I'm Carol Gregory. I'm a homicide detective with the Buffalo police."

"It's nice to meet you," Fenella said, wincing at how stupid the words sounded under the circumstances.

"You're welcome to call me Carol. Would you prefer that I call you Fenella or Margaret or Ms. Woods or something else?"

"It's actually Dr. Woods, as I have a doctorate in history, but please call me Fenella."

Carol made a note and then smiled at her. "I've had a long conversation with Daniel. He was able to give me a policeman's version of the events from last night, which was very helpful. He's an excellent witness."

Fenella nodded. "And a very good person."

"He seemed very nice and very devoted to you. He gave me his life story and a great deal of yours as well, but I'd prefer to hear directly from you, please."

"My life story?" Fenella echoed.

"Yes, please, not everything, but enough to help me understand why you're in Buffalo right now and how you know everyone involved in my murder investigation."

"I suppose I should start with Jack, then," Fenella said. She gave Carol a brief overview of her life before Jack and then told her a bit about their relationship. "And then I inherited my aunt's estate on the Isle of Man and I took early retirement, sold my house, and ended things with Jack," she told her.

"And moved to the Isle of Man," Carol said. "I'm fascinated by everything Daniel told me about the island."

"I could bore you for hours with its history."

"I'm more interested in yours for today."

Fenella continued her story, telling the woman about Jack's unwillingness to believe that their relationship was truly over and his subsequent visit to the island to try to win her back. Then she explained how much Jack had changed during his visit and how, once he'd returned to Buffalo, he'd begun dating Linda.

"And now things get interesting," Carol murmured before Fenella continued.

She told Carol everything she knew about Jack and Linda's engagement, their wedding plans, and finally, the party the previous evening. Carol took extensive notes, but didn't interrupt Fenella's account of the party. When she was done, Fenella felt as if she'd been talking for hours.

"Daniel told me that this isn't the first time you've been caught up in a murder investigation," was the first thing Carol said as Fenella sat back in her chair.

"No, it's not. I've had a rather odd run of incredibly bad luck," she replied.

"He also mentioned that you have a knack for bumping into the people involved in the investigations while you are out and about."

"It's been known to happen, but the Isle of Man is a small island. It isn't that unusual."

"Except Buffalo is a big city, and from what Daniel tells me, you've already managed to run into one of the people from last night's party again."

Fenella nodded. "We bumped into Karl Jensen at lunch today, yes."

"Take me through that lunch, please, as close to word-for-word as you can."

"Is there any chance I can get a glass of water first?" Fenella asked. "I'm really sorry, but I don't normally talk this much."

Carol nodded. "I should have offered you something. Do you want water or would you prefer tea or coffee or a soda?"

"Water is fine."

Carol said something to the man on her left. He nodded and left the room. A few minutes later, he returned with several bottles of water, which he put on the table in front of Carol. She handed one to Fenella and opened another and took a sip.

Fenella took a large drink and then closed the bottle and sighed. "Lunch today," she began. She drank the last of her bottle of water after she'd finished recounting the conversation over lunch.

"Thank you. I'll compare your version to Daniel's later, before I interview Karl. I have officers rounding up all of the guests from last night's party as we speak. There's just one more thing to discuss, I think. Tell me what happened after lunch. Daniel said you received a text from Jack?"

Fenella told her about the text and about Linda's accidental trip to Grand Island and how they'd driven Jack to the island to help Linda get home again. "We were coming back here, to see if we could find George, when we, er, well, found George," she concluded.

Carol nodded. "It's quite a long drive to Grand Island. I'm not sure how you could end up there accidentally."

A dozen questions sprang into Fenella's head, but she knew better than to ask any of them. She and Daniel were both outsiders here. There was no way Carol was going to share any information about the investigation with her.

"Just one more thing," Carol said as Fenella fiddled with her empty water bottle.

"Yes?"

"Who do you think killed George Hawkins?"

Fenella frowned. "I've no idea," she replied, almost instinctively.

Carol nodded. "And, no doubt, he knew dozens of other people in the city who weren't at the party last night, as well, but if you limit your suspect list to the men and women who were at the party last night, which one of them had the strongest motive for murder?"

"If you simply want to talk about motive, Jack probably tops the list, but I know Jack too well to ever believe that he'd kill anyone, even a man who threatened to get between him and Linda. I suppose Linda may have had even more motive, as she had been treated badly by him for years and then had to deal with him trying to destroy her happiness yet again, but I don't think she did it."

"Why not?"

"She was badly shaken last night, upset at George's sudden reappearance. She wanted time to think and a chance to talk to George. I can't see her killing him before her meeting with him today."

"Maybe she called him and rescheduled the meeting to last night or early this morning. They met. They talked. She got angry. She killed him."

"It sounds possible, but I don't think it happened that way. I can't see Linda killing anyone."

"I believe everyone is capable of murder if pushed too far."

"I'm sure you're right about that, but I don't think George had pushed her too far, at least not from what I saw. I suppose, if they did meet again last night or earlier today, things may have escalated, but the last I knew, they were planning to meet for lunch today. I can't see Linda agreeing to anything else, even if George did call her and suggest it."

"But he had some sort of hold over her," Carol argued. "You said he kissed her and that she told Jack that the wedding might be canceled. It sounds as if she still had feelings for him."

"There was something between them, but it may just have been many years of shared history. I don't know. For what it's worth, I don't think she would have canceled the wedding in the end, no matter what George said or did."

"It will be interesting to learn if he'd actually had a vasectomy or not," Carol remarked.

Fenella frowned. "I hope Linda didn't lie to Jack. He's really crazy about her."

Carol nodded. "If she did lie about that, does that make her a more likely suspect in the murder investigation?"

"I don't know. I liked her when we met last night and I want to believe that she's a wonderful person who will make Jack happy. George managed to plant a seed of doubt in my mind, though, which worries me."

"What about Jack's mother? Can you see her as the murderer?"

"If the victim had been Linda, maybe," Fenella said dryly.

"She doesn't like Linda?"

"She doesn't like anyone coming between her and her son. She hated me because I took over Jack's laundry and his shopping and all of the jobs that she'd been doing for him since he'd been born."

Carol frowned. "How old was Jack when you started dating?"

"He was in his late forties."

"And his mother was still doing his laundry and his shopping?"

"Yes."

She made a note and then shook her head. "So Mrs. Dawson hated you?"

"I believe she still does, but I'm past caring now. She was delighted when George turned up last night. I think she thought he'd come between Linda and Jack, which would have devastated Jack."

"She wants to see her son devastated?"

"I think she wants her son to move back in with her. If Linda had ended things, Jack may have been upset enough to consider the idea, as well."

"Interesting," was Carol's reply. "Tell me about Karl. Can you think of any reason why he might have wanted George dead?"

Fenella thought for a minute. "None, although I never spoke to Karl about George, or vice versa for that matter. I got the impression that their wives were friends and they were simply dragged along to weekly get-togethers and whatever."

"What about Melanie, then?"

"She was furious with George because he'd treated Linda so badly, and because he'd come back right before the wedding. They had an intense conversation, or at least it looked intense from where I was standing, but I don't know that I can see her killing the man for Linda's sake."

"Does she know that her husband has a girlfriend?"

"I doubt it, but she did tell Linda that she and Karl were having problems. Karl said they were doing everything they could to keep Linda from finding out before her wedding that they were planning to divorce. Maybe he was telling the truth."

"It will be interesting to find out if all the things Karl has been telling Cindy are true."

"Yes, I was looking forward to asking Melanie about her health and her birthday party," Fenella said with a sigh.

"No doubt you'll be seeing her again soon," Carol said. "The wedding is only a few days away, assuming it goes ahead."

"I can't see why they'd cancel it now."

"You did say that Linda told Jack she wanted to go ahead earlier today, even before the body was found."

Fenella nodded, wondering if the woman had meant to make the words sound like an accusation or not. Was the detective suggesting that Linda had decided to go ahead with the wedding because she'd already known that George was dead?

"But where were we?" Carol asked. "Any idea why Howard or Gloria might have murdered George?"

Fenella shook her head. "I barely spoke to either of them. If one of them killed him, it must have been over something that happened back when George lived in Buffalo, I suppose."

"Yes, of course, they all have years of shared history. George's death may have nothing to do with Linda at all. It's possible that he didn't leave Buffalo to get away from her. Maybe he was running away from something else and leaving her was simply a byproduct of that escape."

"I don't envy you your job."

Carol smiled. "I love my job. Each murder is a new puzzle and I have to find the pieces, which are scattered everywhere. To be honest, most of the murders that I investigate aren't that difficult to solve. Many are drug related and those that aren't are usually domestic. Husbands and wives kill one another with shocking regularity."

"That's a terrible thought."

"That's why I'm still single."

Fenella smiled at the woman. "Maybe I shouldn't be in a rush to marry Daniel."

"He may be one of the good ones, actually. If I were you, I'd marry him quickly."

One of the men shifted in his seat. Carol raised an eyebrow and then looked back to Fenella.

"Tell me about Sue and Hazel. You seemed to lump them together every time you talked about them. Why?"

Fenella had to think about her reply. "They're always together," she said eventually. "Whenever I see them, I mean. They used to come to all of the department meetings and events together. I believe they live near each other. They were hired at the same time, about fifteen years ago, as adjunct faculty when we expanded the department. They're around the same age and they'd both done other things before deciding to turn to teaching."

"It doesn't sound as if you like either of them."

"I don't dislike them, but I always thought they disliked me. When they were first hired, they both flirted with Jack rather outrageously. Fortunately for me, he was oblivious. I understand they both tried again after I moved away, with no more success."

"I'm looking forward to meeting them both. Can you think of any reason why either of them might have killed George?"

"Not unless one of them had some shared history with the man about which I know nothing. Neither of them mentioned knowing him to me, but I don't think I spoke to them after George crashed the party."

"There were a handful of other people at the party, some of Linda's cousins and former work colleagues from the high school. Did you talk to any of them?"

Fenella shook her head. "I probably should have tried harder to meet everyone, but the cousins all stood together in a group in one corner and I'm going to assume that the small circle of men and women in the opposite corner were the friends from the high school. I never spoke to anyone from either group for more than a minute or two."

"One last question," Carol said with a chuckle. "Who told George about the engagement party?"

"He said it was a man, but that may have been a lie to try to protect the person," Fenella said thoughtfully. "Karl admitted to having spoken to him, but he denied telling him about the party."

"You think it was more likely to have been a man?"

"I don't know. If he'd called Melanie, I can almost see her telling him, just to prove to George that Linda had forgotten all about him and had moved on. I can't see her telling him where the party was being held, though."

"So Howard or Karl?"

"Yes, Howard or Karl. I barely spoke to Gloria, but she might be another option. I have to think that if it had been one of the women, that woman would have warned Linda."

"And you think the men wouldn't have bothered?"

"They might not have even thought about it. I don't know if they understood how badly George hurt Linda."

"Do you have any questions for me?" Carol asked.

Fenella swallowed the dozen questions that sprang into her head. "I don't know how much you'll be able to tell me. Daniel never discusses cases with me, especially not when I'm a suspect."

"I prefer to think of you as a witness at this point," Carol said with a smile. "I won't be telling you anything that's confidential, but that doesn't mean you can't ask."

"Are you sure he was murdered? He couldn't have, I don't know, been drunk and simply fallen in the dumpster and had a heart attack?"

"We're sure he was murdered."

Fenella sighed. "I was afraid of that."

"Anything else?"

"I assume Daniel and I can't leave the area."

"You assume correctly. You have a wedding to attend, anyway. What are your plans for the next few days?"

"I was supposed to be showing Daniel every wonderful thing about Buffalo. We were going to go to Niagara Falls and the malls and Canal-side and some of the museums. We didn't make definite plans for each day, though."

Carol nodded. "Just make sure I can find you if I have more questions."

"Of course. We won't go far. I hope Niagara Falls isn't too far away?"

"As long as you stay on the US side of the falls."

Fenella frowned. She had vivid memories of the shops and museums on the Canadian side of the falls and had been looking forward to sharing them with Daniel.

"I'm off to talk to everyone who was at the party last night," Carol said, getting to her feet. "Thank you for your time. You'll be hearing from me soon, I'm sure."

"Thank you," Fenella said, standing up. "Now I just have to find Daniel."

"He asked me to tell you that he'd be in your room," Carol told her. "No doubt he's trying to work out who killed George. I'm sure it must be frustrating for him, being on the outside of a murder investigation for a change."

"He's had some experience with that."

"I should buy him a drink one night. We could swap war stories."

"He'd enjoy that."

"I may have to wait until George's killer is behind bars. I can't imagine any reason why Daniel would have murdered George, but he is still a key witness in the investigation."

Fenella nodded. One of the uniformed men got up and opened the door for her. She walked out with her mind racing.

Daniel was napping when she got back to their room. She shut the door quietly and then carefully climbed into bed next to him. As she snuggled up against him, she surprised herself by bursting into tears.

"Hey, baby, it's okay," he said, pulling her close and rubbing her back.

"It isn't okay. Someone murdered George. Okay, he was probably a horrible person, but it still isn't okay to murder someone, especially when I'm around, trying to have a nice vacation. That's all I wanted, a nice vacation. Is that too much to ask? Clearly, it's too much to ask. Someone has to go and die every time I try to do anything. Sometimes I don't even have to do anything, but I still manage to trip over dead people. It simply isn't fair. I hate this. I just wanted to have a nice vacation with the man I love. Why can't I just have a nice vacation with the man I love? Why?"

Daniel stared at her. "Take a deep breath," he said gently.

Fenella breathed in and then held her breath and counted to ten. As she blew out slowly, she sighed. "I'm sorry. George is dead and that's horrible. This isn't about me, not at all. I was just a little overwhelmed for a minute there."

"You've every right to be upset. I'm furious that this has happened in the middle of our holiday. I was looking forward to seeing the sights and enjoying your company. Now I'm sorry we didn't decide to come over a few days later. We could have missed the engagement party and missed being there when the body turned up. We could have missed being a part of the entire investigation."

"I'm sorry," Fenella said.

"You've nothing to be sorry for," he told her, pulling her into a kiss.

"It's been a really long day," Fenella said some time later.

"It has and we haven't had dinner."

"I wasn't hungry until you said that."

"And now you're starving?"

"Pretty much."

"We could go out or we could get room service."

"Room service sounds good. With a bottle of wine, or maybe two."

"All things considered, I don't think I want to drink tonight," Daniel said.

Fenella sighed. "Sometimes I hate it when you're sensible."

He laughed and kissed the tip of her nose. "I'll have a glass of wine if it will make you happy. One glass won't hurt, even if Carol does come back to ask us more questions."

"If we get a bottle and you only have one glass, I won't be in any condition to talk to Carol if she comes back."

"We'll just have to hope she doesn't come back."

"Maybe we should go out. I had a list of a dozen different restaurants I wanted to take you to. We shouldn't let the investigation get in the way of our having fun."

"We can go out, if that's what you want."

Fenella looked at the clock. "It's six. The mall is open until nine. Let's go and have a walk around and then get dinner at one of the restaurants there."

"Okay."

"Maybe we can get dinner first and then walk around the mall," Fenella laughed as her stomach rumbled loudly.

"Whatever you want to do," Daniel said easily.

"You really are the perfect man."

"Don't you forget it."

They were both laughing as they walked out to the car. The mall was only a short drive away and by the time they arrived, they'd agreed that food was their first priority. They ate far too much at one of the mall's many restaurants before they began to wander through the corridors lined with shops.

"There's too much choice," Daniel said after a short while. "I've seen at least ten shops that sell jeans. How does anyone ever choose where to buy their clothes?"

"I've been buying the same jeans for years. I found a brand that I like and I know exactly what size fits. I just buy two or three pairs when I see them on sale. I can't get them in the UK, though. I should buy a few pairs while we're here."

"Tonight?"

"No, not tonight. I don't have the energy to actually shop tonight."

Daniel nodded. "Do you have the energy to eat a cookie?" he asked, gesturing toward the small cookie kiosk on the level below them.

"I will by the time we get there. We have to do the upstairs first."

"Why?"

"So that we don't miss any of the stores."

"Are you planning on buying anything?"

"That isn't the point. Oh, look, that store is new. Actually, there are several new stores. I can't remember what used to be in any of the spaces, though."

They were walking back through the ground floor, eating their cookies, when Fenella spotted a familiar face. "Isn't that..." she began, staring at the woman who was standing in line at the coffee shop.

"Melanie, and she looks as if she's been crying." Daniel finished her sentence for her.

6

"Melanie?" Fenella said as the woman began walking away with her coffee cup in hand.

The other woman jumped and appeared almost frightened as she looked around. "Margaret? What are you doing here?"

"Daniel and I came to get some dinner and then do some window shopping," Fenella explained. "When we saw you in the line, you looked upset. Are you okay?"

Melanie shook her head. "I'm far from okay, but I have to go and close my store. I can't talk right now."

Fenella glanced at Daniel. "If there's anything we can do..." she began.

"Come back to my store while I close," Melanie suggested. "It doesn't take long. Then you can buy me a drink or ten."

"Sure," Fenella said. She and Daniel fell into step with the woman as she walked briskly along the corridor. When she turned down one of the side hallways, Fenella looked around. As far as she could remember, none of these shops had been here when she'd last been in the mall.

"This is mine," Melanie said, stopping in front of a small storefront that looked like a trendy boutique. "Having my own store, selling my designs, was always one of my dreams. When a distant aunt died and left me a little bit of money, I decided to live my dream."

They followed her into the store.

The teenager behind the register looked up and then sighed. "Can I go, then?" she asked.

Melanie nodded. "Thanks for staying late. I wasn't expecting, well, but never mind. Thanks for staying late. I'll see you tomorrow."

The girl disappeared through a door in the back wall. She returned a moment later, carrying a large handbag. "Bye," she shouted as she headed out into the mall.

Melanie walked to the front of the store and looked up and down the corridor. "No one," she said grimly before flipping the switch that lowered the metal security gate.

"I suppose you've heard the news," she said as she walked back to the register.

"What news?" Fenella asked.

Melanie glanced at her. "George is dead. He was murdered just outside of the hotel where he was staying."

"We had heard that," Daniel told her.

"I can't stop crying. I hated him. He was terrible to Linda and I love Linda like a sister, but I still can't stop crying. I never knew anyone who was murdered before. I still can't believe it's real," Melanie said, wiping a hand across her face as a tear slid down it.

"I'm sure it's been a terrible shock," Fenella said softly.

Melanie shrugged and then punched a few buttons on the register. It beeped and then began to print out a long receipt. As it worked, Melanie leaned against the counter.

"I spent over an hour with the police, answering all sorts of questions. I had to get Jana to stay late here. When the policeman came and asked me to come and talk with them about something, I had no idea. I still can't get my head around any of this."

"You're still in shock," Fenella suggested.

"I think I am." She looked at the register and sighed. "I have to count everything," she said a bit helplessly.

"I can help," Fenella offered. "I worked retail years ago. It can't have changed that much."

"If you can count the cash, I'll check the credit card slips," Melanie told her.

It took Fenella a few seconds to recall that she was counting American money, not Manx, but once she'd remembered that dimes were worth ten cents and nickels were worth five cents, she quickly counted everything in the drawer and wrote down the total.

Melanie compared it with the register tape and then shrugged. "It's close enough. It never matches, but at least it's in the same ballpark tonight. I just have to lock the cash in the safe and we can get out of here."

A few minutes later, they all walked out of the store together.

"I need a drink, but I'm driving," Melanie sighed.

"We'll follow you back to your place and then take you somewhere for a drink," Daniel offered.

"That's very kind of you. It will work, too, if Karl isn't home."

"Is he likely to be home?"

"How should I know? He never tells me where he's going to be these days." She blinked back tears. "I'm pretty sure he has another woman, but I can't bring myself to confront him. But we can talk about that over drinks. I'm parked outside of here," she said, stopping near an exit door.

"We're on the other side of the building," Fenella said.

"I'll wait with Melanie in her car, while you go and get ours," Daniel offered.

"Okay, I won't be long," Fenella promised.

She was halfway back to her car before she realized that she had no idea what kind of car Melanie drove. A moment later, she received a text from Daniel.

We're in a small red SUV in row four. The car park is clearing fast. We'll probably be one of the last cars here when you arrive.

"Love you," Fenella muttered as she picked up her pace. Just about every store was closed now and the mall was starting to feel a bit creepy. She nearly ran to her car once she got outside. It didn't take her long to find Daniel and Melanie.

"I'm going to ride with Melanie, if that's okay with you," Daniel told her when she arrived. "She's really upset and she needs someone to keep her focused while she's driving."

"No problem," Fenella said. "Then, if I get lost, you can find me."

He laughed. "Always," he promised with a kiss.

Melanie didn't live far away. Fenella pulled in behind her car on the long driveway that led to the large suburban home. Melanie got out of her car and ran inside. She was back a few minutes later.

"Okay, let's go," she said as she climbed into the back of Fenella's rental.

"Karl isn't home?" Daniel asked.

"Nope."

"Maybe he's being questioned," Fenella suggested.

"Oh, I hope so," Melanie said. "I hope they keep him for hours and hours and ruin his plans for tonight, whatever they were."

"I don't want to pry," Fenella said slowly, "but have you two been having trouble for long?"

"Let's have this conversation over drinks," Melanie suggested.

"Where do you want to go?" Fenella asked.

Melanie suggested a nearby bar. Fenella had been there once, many years earlier, taken by a pair of graduate students to celebrate the completion of their dissertations. It was a short drive away. The parking lot was nearly empty.

"I can walk home if I have to," Melanie said as they got out of the car.

"We'll take you home," Fenella told her.

"Only if I'm ready to leave when you are," Melanie countered.

Fenella swallowed a sigh. She was already tired and had been hoping that they could have a single drink and call it a night. Daniel took her hand and squeezed it tightly.

They sat at a table in a dark corner and ordered drinks. Fenella opted for soda, since she was driving. Daniel requested a beer after Melanie ordered her whiskey sour.

"I was going to tell you about how my marriage is falling apart," Melanie said after her first sip. "This is so good," she added.

"I'm sorry you and Karl are having difficulties," Fenella said.

Melanie shrugged. "We've been married for thirty years. It's been hard work for most of them. Karl cheats now and again. I've always ignored it, but lately I've been wondering why I don't just leave."

"Why don't you?" Fenella asked.

"There's always something, you know? Christmas, birthdays, weddings, things, things that are better lived through with someone by your side. I'm too old to go to weddings on my own. I don't think I could stand the sympathetic looks and there's no way I could endure being expected to try to catch the bridal bouquet. Now, as we get older, there are funerals, too. I don't think I could have survived my mother's funeral without Karl by my side. It's just easier being married. I can't even remember what being single felt like, really."

Fenella nodded. "But now you're thinking about leaving?"

"I don't know what I'm thinking. I still care about Karl and we still have fun together, but I think he's ready to call it quits. He used to make sure he came home every night. When he didn't, he always had a very plausible excuse for why he hadn't. Now he simply doesn't bother to come home or make excuses. Maybe I should have fought harder years ago."

"As you said, we're all getting older. We're starting to get to an age where we have health concerns, too," Fenella suggested.

Melanie shrugged. "Karl and I have been lucky so far with our health. He had flu last November, but otherwise, we're both healthy, aside from some fertility issues that we dealt with years ago."

Fenella exchanged glances with Daniel. He took a sip of his drink and then grinned at Melanie. "Maybe you'll have some suggestions," he said. "I want to throw a special birthday party for Fen, er, Margaret. She hasn't had a birthday party since she was a child. Any ideas for ways to celebrate her birthday?"

"I had a huge party when I turned fifty, a few years ago. I don't expect I'll have another until I'm sixty, although I may decide not to bother by that time. My fiftieth was supposed to be a celebration of everything that was fun when I'd been five, but in the end everyone just got drunk and Karl and I had a huge fight. George had to take me home while Karl went off with Linda to complain about me for hours and hours."

"I think maybe we should just go away for my next birthday," Fenella said. "Hawaii is supposed to be nice."

Melanie made a noise. When Fenella looked at her, she shrugged. "I was just there last month, actually. It's lovely, if you like sandy beaches, beautiful weather, and endless icy cocktails. It was like a little slice of heaven for the first six hours every day. Then Karl would finish his work meetings and come back to the hotel."

"Oh, dear," Fenella said.

"He hated everything about Hawaii. It was too hot, too sandy, too bright, too happy. I was sorry I'd gone with him by the time it was over."

"Why were you there?" Fenella asked.

"The entire department from his office went. It was a working vacation for them. Six hours of meetings each day, followed by hours of team building and recreation with the wives and girlfriends included. He had to take me to everything so that he would be seen as a team player. It was as hideous as it sounds."

"Maybe you should take a proper vacation together," Fenella suggested.

Melanie shrugged. "I keep going back and forth between wanting to try to save my marriage and feeling grateful that it might finally be over. I think I need to make up my mind what I want before I do anything, really."

"Linda's wedding won't be helping you make up your mind," Fenella suggested.

"You're right about that," Melanie laughed. "Of everyone I know, Linda is my only friend who was always happily married. I never once heard her complain about George during all the years they were together. She was at his beck and call all the time and she loved it that way. She was blindsided when he left her."

"Did he just move out without warning?" Fenella asked.

"She went on a research trip to Albany. It had something to do with her dissertation. She was gone for three days and when she got back, he'd moved out. She called me in hysterics. I could barely understand what she was saying. I actually worried that she might, well, I was afraid she might not be able to survive without George."

"And now she's getting married again," Fenella said.

Melanie sighed. "I think Jack is wonderful, but I do worry that Linda's fallen for him too quickly. I don't know that she's truly recovered from losing George. His turning up here last night complicated things no end."

"What did he want?" Fenella wondered.

"He wanted to show Linda that she wasn't over him. He wanted to snap his fingers and get her back. It was all about his ego."

"Is that all?"

"I don't know. I'm just guessing," Melanie sighed. "I barely spoke to the man and when I did talk to him, all I did was beg him to leave poor Linda alone. He laughed at me, though. He didn't care who he hurt."

"Were you friends with him before he left Linda?" Daniel interjected.

She looked surprised. "Yes, I mean, I suppose so. The six of us did a lot together. There were even eight of us for a while, but you heard all of that last night, didn't you? Some of this is probably hindsight, but I feel like I always thought George demanded a lot from Linda. She didn't seem to mind. As I said earlier, she never complained about him, not once."

"So you were just as blindsided when he left?" Fenella asked.

"Maybe, although I remember asking Linda questions about their marriage on more than one occasion. I never thought it was as happy as she tried to make it appear. I don't know. I guess I felt like she was telling me about the marriage she wanted to have, rather than the one she actually had."

"Were you surprised when you heard that George was dead?" Daniel asked.

Melanie blinked several times and then sighed. "Yes?" she made the word a question. "I don't know," she added. "It was a shock, but I don't know that I was surprised. There were some people here who were really angry with him, after all."

"Who do you think killed him, then?" was Daniel's next question.

"I don't want to point fingers," she said, draining her drink.

"Let me get another round," Fenella said, getting to her feet.

The waitress waved from behind the bar. "Same again?" she called.

Fenella nodded, even though Daniel hadn't taken much more than a few sips of his beer.

"I was just curious what you thought," Daniel said casually, as he lifted his glass. "It won't go any farther than this table."

"I don't know Jack all that well," Melanie said, casting a nervous look at Fenella.

"I know him very well. He would have been devastated if Linda had canceled the wedding, but he would never have done anything to hurt George, regardless," she told her.

Melanie nodded. "I didn't think he seemed like the type to kill anyone. I could see him finding George and offering him money to go away, though."

Fenella gave the idea some thought. "Maybe, if he'd have thought of it, but it probably would have taken him a day or two to come up with idea."

Melanie laughed. "I can believe that."

"Do you think George would have taken the offer if it had been made?" Daniel asked.

Now it was Melanie's turn to think. "That depends on what he's been doing since he left Buffalo, really. As far as I know, he quit his job and left with just a few suitcases of clothes and a few thousand dollars in his personal bank account. It's possible that he needed money, maybe badly. Maybe that's what this was all about. Maybe he was hoping to guilt Linda into giving him something."

"Did she get much out of the divorce?" Fenella asked.

Melanie shook her head. "She got the house, but over the years they'd taken out a second mortgage and a home equity line of credit. They put in a new kitchen and two new bathrooms in addition to a new roof and a bunch of other things. Linda owed the bank more than the house was worth when she sold it. She and George always lived from paycheck to paycheck. She did say that she's doing better now that she's with Jack. Apparently, he's che— er frugal."

Fenella laughed. "He is cheap. It's one of his more endearing idio-syncrasies."

"If you say so. Karl and I have always lived more like Linda and

George. We won't have anything but bills to fight over if we do get divorced."

"I think we can rule Jack out as the murderer," Fenella said.

Melanie shrugged. "I'll never believe that Linda had anything to do with it, even though she probably had the strongest motive. Having said that, I can't imagine any stronger motive for anyone other than Linda or Jack."

"Maybe he'd made enemies at work or elsewhere," Daniel suggested.

"He simply wasn't that interesting," Melanie laughed. "He changed jobs every few years, doing something in middle management. I have no idea what that actually entails, but I know he made decent but not great money. He didn't talk about his job when we were all together and Linda rarely mentioned it, unless he was between jobs."

"Was he often between jobs?" Fenella asked.

"Maybe two or three times over the years. Usually, when he changed jobs, he had another one lined up to start immediately, but there were a few occasions where he had some time off between positions."

"Did he cheat on Linda?" Fenella asked.

Melanie shrugged. "Don't all men cheat?"

"No," Daniel said flatly.

"Linda never suspected him of cheating, or, if she did, she never said anything to me about it," Melanie said.

"And she would have told you if she was suspicious," Fenella guessed.

"I would hope so. I tell her every time I think Karl is cheating, which is just about all the time now."

"Is there anyone else you can think of who could have had a reason to want George dead?" Daniel asked.

"We could talk about everyone at the engagement party," Melanie replied. "He upset all of us, but I don't think anyone there, other than Jack, loves Linda enough to kill for her."

"Jack wouldn't kill for her," Fenella replied.

"If it were Linda who'd been murdered, I'd suspect Jack's mother,"

Melanie said. "She really doesn't like Linda and she really doesn't want Jack to marry her."

"She's a bit possessive of Jack," Fenella told her.

"I don't know how you put up with her for all of the years you dated Jack," Melanie replied.

Fenella shrugged. "I spent a few years trying to get her to like me. I used to remind Jack to call her, and I used to help him pick out the most perfect Christmas and birthday gifts. We had her over for dinner at least once a week. It was awful, but I really wanted her to accept me."

"How did that work for you?" Melanie laughed.

"Yeah, she hated me. But then she decided to retire to Florida. I truly believe she thought that Jack would go with her, but he opted to remain in Buffalo. She was furious, and, of course, she blamed me for persuading him to stay here. I had nothing to do with his decision, but I'm sure she felt better having someone other than Jack to blame."

"So she moved away and you and Jack were much happier," Melanie guessed.

"I was happier, anyway. Jack really missed her, but he used to go and visit her fairly regularly. I went with him only once. She put Jack in the guest room and made me sleep on the couch in the living room, which wouldn't have been so bad, except she had two other bedrooms that were fully furnished and not being used, aside from her master bedroom," Fenella told her.

"Why wouldn't she let you stay in one of the other bedrooms?" Melanie asked.

"She simply told me that I was to sleep on the couch and refused to discuss the matter further. Jack did try to reason with her, but she reminded him that it was her house so she got to make the rules. I never went with Jack again."

"I'm surprised she didn't move back to Buffalo when you and Jack split up," Melanie said.

"I think she was still hoping Jack would move to be with her. She hates snow almost as much as she hates me," Fenella replied.

"I can't see her killing George, though," Melanie mused. "George was the one thing that might have stopped the wedding."

"What about Howard and Gloria?" Fenella asked. "I barely spoke to them, but they're a part of your close circle of friends. Tell me more about them."

"They are a part of our circle, but I've never been as close to Gloria as I am to Linda. We were all pretty tight when we were first married and living in the same building, but then Howard and Gloria decided to move to the Northtowns and started having children. We only saw them a few times a year after that, although recently they've started spending more time with us again."

"How recently?" Fenella asked.

"It's probably just in the last eighteen months or two years, which has been awkward, actually, because they started wanting to hang around with us while Linda's marriage was falling apart and then when she'd first started seeing Jack. We hadn't been spending much time as a group anyway, because of all of that, and suddenly Howard and Gloria wanted to start getting together every Friday again like we did years ago."

"You can't think of any reason why either of them would have wanted to kill George?" Daniel wondered.

Melanie sighed. "There was a time, years ago, when I wondered if Gloria and George were having an affair," she said in a low voice. "I need another drink," she announced loudly.

"I'll go," Daniel said, getting up and heading for the bar.

"He makes me nervous," Melanie said.

"Daniel does? Why?"

"He's a police inspector. I don't want to say anything in front of him that might get my friends into trouble."

Fenella chuckled. "He's a police inspector back home. Here he's just as much a suspect in the investigation into George's murder as we are. You can say what you like in front of him."

She shrugged. "Gloria and I were never very close, but I don't want to cause trouble for her or for her marriage. I've always suspected that one of the reasons why she and Howard moved out of our apartment building was because Howard wanted to get her away from George, though."

"You think Howard knew they were having an affair?"

"I assume so. It was an odd time, really. We were all starting to get a bit older and Gloria and Linda were both talking about starting families. Karl and I had decided that we didn't want children, but Linda was really keen on having at least two. George seemed less enthusiastic, but that didn't seem unusual. I assumed that Linda would get her way eventually."

"But she didn't."

"There were complications," Melanie said with a wave of her hand. "But I was telling you about Gloria and George. Not that I'm certain that anything ever happened, but I had my suspicions. We were going out as a group at least once a week at that point, and sometimes more often. Things weren't always planned. One of us would call the others and we'd all go to one of the local bars, things like that. Whoever was around would go, so sometimes, if Karl was working late, I'd go on my own or maybe George would be there but Linda wouldn't. After a while, I started to notice that Gloria and George were nearly always together, already at the bar when I arrived places. It happened too many times for me to believe that it was just a coincidence."

"Here we are," Daniel said, putting another round of drinks on the table. Fenella noticed that he'd switched to soda for this round. "I'm just going to the loo," he added before walking away again.

"So you think that Gloria and George were seeing each other behind Howard and Linda's backs?" Fenella asked.

Melanie frowned and then nodded. "That was what I thought at the time, anyway. I thought about confronting Gloria or maybe George, but I didn't have any evidence. Before I'd decided what to do, Gloria and Howard bought their house and moved away. We didn't see them for a few months and the next time they did come to something, Gloria was pregnant with their first child."

"There's no chance George was the father?"

Melanie looked stunned. She sat back in her seat with a puzzled look on her face. "Why didn't I ever wonder that? I don't know how to reply to that question."

"How do you think Howard would have reacted if he'd found out about the affair?"

"Like I said, I thought he had his suspicions. I was pretty sure that was why they rushed through the house purchase. Originally, they'd said they were going to move in a year or two, but they actually went just a few months later."

"And when did Gloria get pregnant?"

"She must have already been pregnant when they moved," Melanie said. "We didn't see them for three or four months and when we did see them, Gloria was already five months pregnant. I suppose that was why they'd moved so quickly, actually. They probably found out she was pregnant and decided to move sooner rather than later."

"But at the time you thought they'd moved because Howard wanted to get Gloria away from George?"

Melanie laughed and took a long drink from her glass. "I'm getting everything muddled up in my head now," she said. "It was a long time ago and it's all running together in my memory now. I could be wrong about everything, really. Maybe they didn't have an affair. Maybe it was just me seeing things that weren't there."

Fenella wanted to press her, but she wasn't sure it would be worth the effort. Melanie was already getting confused and she was still drinking steadily. Daniel returned before Fenella could work out what to ask next.

"It's getting late," he said as he sat down. "I'm going to be ready to head back to the hotel after this round."

Melanie frowned. "You're far too handsome to be that boring," she said. "I don't ever want to go home."

"Do you need somewhere else to stay?" Daniel asked, sounding very much like a policeman.

Sighing, Melanie shook her head. "Maybe Karl will be home and we can have a screaming fight. That will liven up my evening."

She drained what was left in her glass and stood up. "Let's go, then. Take me home." Waving to the bartender and the waitress, she walked to the door at a brisk pace.

Fenella and Daniel hurried to catch up to her. The car was silent on the short drive back to Melanie's house.

"No Karl," she said as Fenella parked behind her car. "I think I'll open a bottle of wine and watch a sad movie."

"Are you okay?" Fenella asked, getting out of the car at the same time as Melanie

"I'm fine, really. Mostly, I'm struggling to process the loss of a friend. I didn't always like George and I really didn't like the way he treated Linda, but I'd known him for nearly all of my adult life and I'm going to miss him." Tears began to flow down her cheeks.

Fenella hesitated and then took a step closer to the woman. "I'm sorry for your loss," she said, reaching out to pat her arm.

Melanie nodded and then started to walk toward the house. "I'll be okay," she said softly as Fenella fell into step next to her. "You go and spend time with your gorgeous man. I just need to cry for a while, for George, for Linda, and for me. There are so many things that might have been had the circumstances been different."

"Call me if you need anything," Fenella told her.

Melanie dug out her mobile phone and carefully put Fenella's number into it. "I'll be fine, but thank you," she said, dropping her phone back into her bag and then unlocking her door. "Thank you for everything," she added before she shut the door behind herself.

"Are you okay?" Daniel asked as Fenella rejoined him in the car.

"I'm sad for her. She's lost a friend and her marriage is falling apart."

"I did wonder if you were going to tell her about seeing Karl earlier today."

"I thought about it, but tonight didn't seem like the best time to do so. I may tell Karl that I'm on to his lies, though, and tell him he needs to come clean to both Melanie and Cindy."

Daniel nodded. "But what did Melanie have to say while I was busy elsewhere?"

They were back at the hotel by the time Fenella had finished repeating the conversation she'd had with Melanie about Gloria and George. She parked as far away from where the dumpster had been as she possibly could and then she and Daniel went inside.

7

"You've found yourself in yet another mess, then," Mona said.

"What are you doing here?" Fenella demanded.

"I told you I was going to try to come to the wedding. I wanted to be at the engagement party, but I couldn't manage it. I'm really sorry that I missed it though, now that you've found yourself at the center of another murder investigation."

"I'm not at the center and how do you know about the murder?"

"I arrived in Buffalo just as the body was found. I sat in on your interview with Carol Gregory. She seems very competent, but I still think she's going to need our help."

"We aren't going to help. We're staying as far away from this murder investigation as we possibly can."

"Yes, yes, of course, but you've already spoken to two of the suspects. I don't care for Karl. Melanie would be better off without him."

"Whether I agree with that or not, we've no reason to believe that Karl killed George."

"Well, someone did. For sake of argument, let's assume it was someone at the engagement party. I heard what you told Carol about that. What didn't you tell her?"

"I told her everything."

Mona sighed. "Everything?"

"Yes, everything."

"I wish I would have arrived earlier. If I had, I might have seen someone putting the body into the dumpster."

"That's an interesting point. The body had to be have been heavy. I wonder if that rules out any of the suspects."

"Maybe someone persuaded George to climb into the dumpster and then killed him," Mona suggested.

"How do you persuade someone to climb into a dumpster?"

"I don't know, but it's a possibility."

"It seems a remote one, though."

"If he had to be lifted in, then you're probably ruling out most of the female suspects," Mona told her. "I didn't get a good look at the body. Was George a large or small man?"

"He was at least six feet tall, with broad shoulders. He looked as if he'd maybe played football when he was younger."

"So Jack couldn't have lifted him," Mona said.

Fenella laughed. "You're probably right about that. Having said that, I can't see anyone that I've met being able to lift him, especially if he was, er, dead weight."

"Suddenly my theory about him climbing into the dumpster isn't as remote," Mona said smugly.

Fenella frowned. "I still can't imagine how that would have worked."

"I'd love to stay and talk to you about the various suspects, but Daniel is about to wake up and he won't understand why you're talking to yourself. I'm going to do my best to go everywhere you go for the next few days. No doubt I'll have plenty of opportunities to meet everyone."

"We won't be seeing any of them again until Friday," Fenella protested. "That's when they're having the rehearsal dinner."

"I'll be back tomorrow night for another chat," Mona said, fading away.

"I can't believe she's here," Fenella muttered.

"Who's here?" Daniel's voice asked.

Fenella jumped and opened her eyes. "I just had the strangest dream," she said slowly.

"Do you want to talk about it?" he asked, sliding an arm around her.

She shook her head. "I want to forget it happened," she said firmly.

"What are we doing today?" Daniel asked a short while later.

"I don't know. There are museums and parks and all sorts of things that I'd love to show you, but there's also a murder investigation going on."

"We should ring Carol and tell her about our conversation with Melanie last night," Daniel said with a sigh.

"Must we?"

"Yes, but I'll do it, if you want. I'll ring her while you're in the shower. She may want to speak to you too, but I'll try to persuade her otherwise."

"I don't mind talking to her, not really. I'd just much rather put the entire thing out of my head and simply go and have some fun."

"We can do that, after we've spoken to Carol," Daniel promised.

She gave him a kiss and then headed for the bathroom. She didn't exactly dawdle, but she didn't rush, either. When she walked out of the bathroom nearly an hour later, dressed and with her hair and makeup done, Daniel was on his phone.

"She's here now," he said. He held out the device to Fenella. "Carol just wants you to tell her what was said while I was getting the third round of drinks."

"Hello?"

"Ms. Woods, good morning. Daniel has given me a very thorough account of the conversation that took place last night. I'm going to type it into a report and email him a copy. I'd appreciate it if you'd read through it and let me know if you remember anything differently."

"I can do that."

"Excellent, then I just need you to fill in what was said while Daniel was at the bar."

Fenella did her best to remember the conversation that had mostly been about George and Gloria.

"Thank you for that. I'll include it in the report that I'm going to email to Daniel later today. Let me know if you bump into anyone else, please."

"I don't expect we'll see anyone else until Friday. That's the rehearsal dinner, assuming the wedding is still going ahead."

"I'm hoping to have everything wrapped up by Friday," the homicide detective said.

Fenella tapped the button to end the call and then put the phone on a table. Daniel was in the shower, so she grabbed her phone, planning to kill some time with a game. She was surprised to see that she had a text message.

Linda and I are beyond upset. Can you and Daniel come and talk to us about the murder? Please? Jack.

She read the message twice and then sighed. Saying no would be mean and, in truth, she'd love a chance to talk to Jack and Linda about the murder, but the last thing she wanted to do was have to call Carol back and report another conversation. Sighing, she found a puzzle game that she hoped would divert her thoughts until Daniel was done.

Half an hour later, Daniel emerged from the bathroom, his hair still damp from the shower. He was wearing jeans and a T-shirt advertising the Tale and Tail pub, one of Fenella's favorite places on the Isle of Man. She pulled him into a hug and breathed in deeply. He smelled of some spicy, leather-scented soap and the pine-scented aftershave he always wore. It was a potent combination that made her head spin for a moment.

"I hope the conversation with Carol went well?" he asked after the kiss.

"We may have to call her back," Fenella replied with a sigh.

"What's happened?"

"Jack texted. He and Linda want to talk to us about the murder."

Daniel nodded. "I was expecting someone to be in touch, actually. Jack would have been my first guess, but I wouldn't have been surprised if you'd heard from just about anyone from the engagement party."

"Most of them don't have my phone number."

He laughed. "That will be why Jack is the only one we've heard from, then."

"Maybe."

"Did he suggest a time or place?"

"No. Are you happy to go and talk to them, then?"

"Happy isn't the right word. I'm willing to go and talk to them. It would be nice to see the murder solved as quickly as possible so we can get on with enjoying ourselves."

Fenella nodded. "Let me see what he's thinking, then."

A few minutes and several texts later, she looked up from her phone.

"Lunch in the faculty dining room at the university," she said. "Linda is teaching this morning and Jack has a class this afternoon, but they're both available from twelve to two."

"Sounds good," Daniel said.

Fenella sent a final text, confirming the arrangements and then looked at the clock. "We have three hours until we're due at the university. What do you want to do?"

"What is there to do?"

"I was going to show you the university, actually. I thought I could show you around the entire campus, from where I lived when I was a student there to the buildings where I taught and everything else. Only if you're interested, of course."

"I am interested. I'd love to see your old house, too, the one you sold when you moved to the island."

Fenella flushed. "If I'd known that I'd inherited a fortune, I'd have kept it. I loved that house, and I'd love to be able to stay there when I visit New York. We can drive past it and a few other places before our tour of the university."

After a short driving tour around the area, they headed to the campus. Fenella parked in a spot marked "Visitors" and then she showed Daniel around. With a bit of time to spare, they sat in the sunshine on a bench that overlooked a small pond.

"It's a large campus, but it feels like a real community," Daniel said.

"That's only because we got stopped a dozen times by people who knew me," Fenella laughed.

"I got the impression that you were very well respected as a professor."

Fenella blushed. "I was reasonably popular with the students. I worked hard to make my classes interesting and to share my absolute passion for history with them."

"Do you miss it?"

She thought for a minute. "Yes and no. I've been incredibly lazy since I've been on the island. I miss having a routine and having places that I need to be and things that I need to do, first of all. But I also miss teaching. I miss seeing young people every day and I miss their energy and their enthusiasm for life. I've been thinking about applying for a job at the island's college, but there's a part of me that doesn't want to get tied down again. I don't really know what I want to do."

He slid his arm around her. "I don't know what I'd do if I were you," he said. "You've more money than I can imagine having. You could do anything. You could travel, live on a yacht, whatever. I'd be very tempted to do one of those things or something else equally extravagant. But I also love my job and I can't imagine not doing what I do."

"I'm going to think about it more before I do anything," she told him. "They may not need history professors on the island, anyway. We should go."

It was a short walk from where they were to the building that housed, among other things, a small faculty dining room.

"We're meeting Dr. Dawson for lunch," Fenella told the woman behind the desk at the door.

"He told me he was expecting guests. Right this way," she replied before leading them across the room.

Jack was on his feet as they approached. "Hello," he said, pulling Fenella into a hug. He shook Daniel's hand and then motioned them into chairs. "Linda will be late. She's always late when she's teaching because she always stays behind to answer questions, which turn into long conversations."

Fenella nodded. "You never want to cut a conversation with a student short."

"I'm not late," Linda called as she rushed across the room. She nodded at Fenella and Daniel before kissing the top of Jack's head as she dropped into the chair next to his. "Sometimes I wonder why I wanted to do this for a living," she laughed. "Students taking summer classes are extra difficult, I think."

"The summer session must be nearly over," Fenella said.

"It is. I'm giving all of my finals on Wednesday, which is why I was so popular today. Everyone had last-minute questions about what is going to be on the exam. I told them that they simply need to have been at every lecture, read every book, and done every assignment to do well."

Fenella laughed. "You make it sound so easy."

She shrugged. "But you didn't come to hear me complain about my job."

"Ready to order?" a waiter asked.

Fenella picked up her menu and then laughed. "It hasn't changed, has it?"

Jack shook his head. "And I know exactly what you're going to order."

"I love their French dip sandwiches," she told Daniel. "It's thinly sliced roast beef and sautéed onions on a roll smothered in garlic butter and then toasted, with a cup of seasoned beef juices in which to dip the entire thing."

"That does sound good," Daniel said.

Once everyone had ordered, Jack leaned forward and took Linda's hand. "What's going to happen next?" he asked anxiously.

"What do you mean?" Fenella asked.

"With the murder investigation. What's going to happen next?" he clarified.

"The crime scene team will do their job, examining everything that was found at the scene. There will be a post mortem to determine exactly how George died. And the police will continue to question everyone who knew George in an attempt to determine who killed him," Daniel replied.

"We're supposed to be leaving on Monday for our honeymoon," Jack said. "Can the police refuse to let us go?"

"They can," Daniel replied.

"But we won't get our money back if we have to cancel because we're tangled up in a murder investigation," Jack complained.

"Maybe the case will be solved by Monday," Fenella said.

"Is that likely? You two have a great deal more experience with this sort of thing than we do. What do you really think?" Jack asked.

Fenella looked at Daniel, who shrugged. Before he could reply, the waiter brought their soft drinks.

"It's impossible for me to answer that question. I've no idea what's going on with the investigation. They may have already arrested someone, for all that I know," Daniel said as the waiter walked away.

"Oh, I hope so," Linda exclaimed. "I'm, well, scared may be the best word. I've never known anyone who was murdered before. It's quite terrifying, really."

"This is my second murder investigation," Jack told her. "The first one was terrible because I may have been in the house when the murder was committed, but at least I didn't know the victim. This time, I feel as if I could really be a suspect."

"We're both suspects," Linda said flatly. "Even in death, George is making my life miserable. I never should have married him."

"Let's not go there, not now," Jack told her. "We can have that conversation later. For now, we want to learn all that we can from Daniel and Maggie."

Linda nodded and smiled weakly. "Yes, of course," she murmured.

"One French dip with spicy fries, one with regular fries, one mixed salad, and one plain ham sandwich on white with regular fries," the waiter said, putting down the plates. "Anyone need anything else right now?"

"We're good," Jack told him.

"I'm not sure what you think you can learn from me and Daniel," Fenella said between bites.

"Jack said homicide detectives always look for three things," Linda replied. "Motive, means, and opportunity. Is that right?"

"Those are all important components in the investigation," Daniel replied.

"So if we can figure out who had those three things, we'll know who killed George," Linda said. "How hard can it be?"

"If it's easy, then someone should have already been arrested," Daniel told her.

"But Detective Gregory doesn't know everyone the way I do," Linda replied. "She may have missed something."

Daniel looked as if he wanted to argue, but after a moment he shrugged. "We can't really discuss means as we've no idea how George died."

"All the police would tell me was that he'd been found in a dumpster," Linda said. "I assume someone had a gun and ordered him to climb inside and then shot him."

Daniel looked at Fenella. "I suppose that's one possibility," he said.

She frowned. The idea had never crossed her mind. After living for such a long time in a country with strict gun control laws, she'd forgotten that many Americans owned deadly weapons.

"If that's what happened, though, maybe it was a robbery that went wrong," Jack suggested. "Why do they think that he was killed by someone who knew him?"

"The majority of murders are committed by family or friends of the victim," Daniel told him. "I'm sure Carol hasn't ruled out robbery or random violence as possibilities, but she'll keep her focus on the people who knew George unless she gets evidence that points in a different direction."

"Which is why I'm at the top of her suspect list," Linda sighed. "Even though I would never have done anything to hurt anyone."

"Of course not," Jack said, patting her hand.

"You must understand why you're a suspect, though," Fenella said. "You were angry at the man and upset that he'd come back and crashed your engagement party. I'm sure you wanted him to disappear."

"Of course I did. I wanted him to disappear. I didn't want him to die," Linda replied.

"And I have just as much motive," Jack sighed. "George was threatening to come between me and Linda."

"I wouldn't have let that happen," Linda told him.

"And yet, at the party, you said you weren't sure the wedding was still going to happen," Fenella reminded her.

She sighed. "I was upset. George had just kissed me and he'd, well, he'd threatened me. He said he'd tell Jack all sorts of horrible lies about me if I didn't agree to talk to him."

"I wouldn't have believed a word he said," Jack said stoutly.

Linda shrugged. "He could be very convincing. I didn't want to take that chance. That's why I agreed to meet him for lunch the next day, but the whole thing got me into such a state that, well, you both know what happened. I got so upset that I drove almost to Canada without thinking."

"With everything going on, you were entitled to be upset," Fenella told her.

Linda shrugged. "But I know that I didn't kill George, and I know that Jack didn't do it, either. I don't think that helps, though."

"If you and Jack didn't do it, who else had a motive?" Fenella asked.

"Maybe someone from his old job?" Linda replied questioningly. "I don't know how they would have found out he was back in town, though."

"We have no idea what George did once he got back into town," Jack said. "He may have called a dozen people and told them he was back. Maybe he told them all where he was staying and invited them all to meet him for a drink or something."

"He didn't mention that he was meeting anyone later," Fenella said.

"When did you talk to him?" Linda demanded.

"I saw him in the bar at the hotel," Fenella told her. "We're staying at the same hotel."

"I thought you had drinks with Fenella and Daniel in the bar after the engagement party," Linda said to Jack.

"I did, and then I went and got a room and went to bed," Jack replied.

"And while Daniel was helping Jack sort out a room, George came into the bar," Fenella added. "We had a short chat before Daniel came back and we left for our room."

"And George stayed behind in the bar?" Linda asked.

"Yes," Fenella said.

"I didn't know you saw him again after the party," Linda said softly. "Was he upset? What did he say?"

Fenella hesitated, not sure how much she should tell Linda.

"Let's talk about some of the other people who were at the engagement party," Daniel said. "Melanie seemed pretty angry with George."

Linda nodded. "She was furious with him on my behalf. I've known Melanie since we were children. She never liked George, although she was always perfectly polite to him when we were together. I didn't realize how much she disliked him until after my divorce, actually. That's when she told me how she really felt."

"Why didn't she like him?" Fenella asked.

"She just always thought that I could do better," Linda replied. She looked over at Jack and smiled. "It appears that she was right all along."

"So she disliked him but she never said anything until after he left you," Daniel repeated.

"Yes, and she was my rock when he left. Actually, she was my rock during my marriage, too. George and I had a few rough patches over the years and I always knew I could count on Melanie to help me get through them. She was always really careful, in those days, to not say anything horrible about George, because she knew I'd never leave him, no matter how badly he treated me."

"Why not?" Fenella demanded.

Linda flushed and looked down at her barely touched salad. "I'd promised him forever and I'd always planned to keep that promise," she said softly.

"Do you think any of the issues that caused your rough patches might have given someone a motive to murder George?" Fenella asked, trying to word the question so that didn't sound too much like prying.

"Mostly we fought when he cheated on me," Linda replied.

Jack made a noise.

"It only happened a few times," Linda said quickly. "And it wasn't anything serious, just, well, just sex, for George, anyway."

"That doesn't excuse it," Fenella said.

"That's exactly what Melanie used to say," Linda laughed. "I swear, she used to get more upset about his affairs than I did. She said it showed that he didn't respect me, but I could never bring myself to leave him, not over an occasional affair, even if we did fight about them when they happened."

"Did he ever have an affair with anyone you knew?" Fenella asked, thinking about what Melanie had said about Gloria.

Some of the color seemed to drain from Linda's face. "Someone I knew? What are you suggesting?"

"I was just wondering where he found the women," Fenella replied.

"I don't know where he found them. I never knew the identities of any of the women involved. There were things that gave him away when he was cheating. He'd start telling me that he was working late, but if I called his office, he was never there — things like that," she replied.

"Do you think Melanie was angry enough at the party to kill George?" Fenella asked bluntly.

Linda shook her head slowly. "She's the closest thing I've ever had to a sister, but I can't imagine her murdering anyone for me. It's a crazy idea. I know George treated me badly, but that was between me and George, anyway. As much as she wanted me to be happy, I can't see Melanie killing George just so that I could marry Jack."

"What about Karl?" Daniel interjected.

"Would Karl have killed George for my benefit? No," Linda replied.

"Can you imagine any other motive for Karl?" Fenella wondered.

"They were good friends before George left me. He never cared that George cheated on me or treated me badly in other ways. I suspect he cheats on Melanie, too," Linda told her.

"They both told me that their marriage is having difficulties," Fenella said.

"Oh, they both say that all the time," Linda replied, waving a hand. "They'll never actually separate, no matter what either of them says."

Although she wasn't sure she agreed, Fenella felt a pang of sympathy for Cindy Paxton, who seemed unlikely to get a happy ending, regardless.

"Tell us more about Howard and Gloria," Fenella suggested.

"I was never very close to either of them," Linda told her. "I think I told you that there were eight of us who all hung out together when we all had our first apartments in the city. I much preferred the other couple, Donald and Jennifer, to Howard and Gloria. Unfortunately, it was Donald and Jennifer who moved away, leaving us rather stuck with Howard and Gloria."

"Until they moved out to the Northtowns to have babies," Fenella suggested.

"Yes, but even after that, we used to see far more of them than I would have liked," Linda said. "I was always happy to do anything with Melanie and Karl, but, well, Howard and Gloria weren't as much fun."

"Can you think of any motive for either of them?" Daniel asked.

Linda shook her head slowly. "I really haven't seen much of them since George and I split up. We all had dinner together once or twice with Jack, after Jack and I had started dating, but we'd mostly lost touch, which was fine with me. Neither one of them could have cared less that George left me."

"What about anyone else with a possible motive?" was Daniel's next question.

"It had to have been something random. Was he robbed? He used to carry around a lot of cash. It made him feel important, I think. Maybe someone in the bar saw his bulging wallet and decided to mug him," Linda suggested.

"Did he have any family in Buffalo?" Fenella wondered.

"He didn't have any family anywhere," Linda told her. "His father died not long after we got married and his mother died about ten years later. He'd been an only child. He had an uncle, his mother's brother, I believe, but he died childless. There were a few cousins on one side or the other. George used to send them Christmas cards when we were first married, but he stopped after a few years since we never received any cards back from them."

"Do you know if he had a will?" Fenella asked.

"He had one when we were married," Linda replied thoughtfully. "We both had wills made back when we were trying for children. I didn't update mine until after the divorce. I suppose I'll have to do another one after the wedding, won't I?"

"You should," Fenella said. "But what about George?"

"You'd have to ask his lawyer. I can tell you who he used for the divorce, but I don't know if he'd have used the same firm for his will or not," she said.

"You should give that information to the police," Daniel told her.

Linda nodded. "The detective, Carol Gregory, is coming to my house to see me later. She wants to go through all of George's things, the things he left behind at the house when he left. I just put every-thing into boxes and piled them into a corner of a spare room when I moved to my new house, assuming he'd come back for them one day. He did tell me that he wanted his things, actually, that night at the party."

Fenella was tempted to suggest that she and Daniel help her go through them before the police arrived, but she bit her tongue. There was no way Daniel would let her interfere in the investigation to that extent.

"Why did he leave?" Daniel asked.

Linda sighed and then shrugged. "I've been asking myself that question since the day he walked out. We'd been having another rough patch. I'm pretty sure he was cheating again. When he didn't come home for a few days, I just assumed he'd gone off with his other woman for a short vacation. It was unusual behavior, but he'd done it once or twice before."

"I'm sorry," Fenella said softly.

"I remember calling Melanie, wanting to cry on her shoulder, but she was travelling for work," Linda continued. "I told Karl all about what was happening, and he said I shouldn't worry, that men like him and George always went home again after a bit of fun. It was weirdly reassuring, even though I hated that he'd basically admitted that he'd cheated on Melanie."

"But George didn't come home?" Fenella asked as Linda pushed her food around her plate.

"Oh, he came home, but when he did, he packed up all of his things. Well, most of his things. He was sitting in the living room with his suitcases when I got home from school that day."

A tear slid down her cheek. Jack reached over and brushed it away. "You don't have to tell her anything," he whispered, shooting Fenella an angry look.

"It's fine," Linda replied. "I'm nearly at the end, anyway. When I got home, he told me he was tired of being married and that he wanted something different for the rest of his life. He gave me the name and address for his lawyers and told me that I was welcome to file for divorce if I wanted one. Otherwise, he'd get around to it one day. And then he left."

"Did he say where he was going to go?" Daniel asked.

"He said he didn't want me to know anything about his plans. That's why he gave me the information for the lawyers, so I wouldn't need to find him. He left his mobile phone behind, although I assume he got another one right away."

"Who filed for the divorce?" Fenella wondered.

"I did, less than a week later. I wish I could say that I was doing so because I'd realized I had to be strong or something like that, but I really did it hoping that it would scare him into returning. He signed the papers immediately, though, and that was the end of that." She burst into tears and rushed out of the room.

8

"I didn't mean to upset her," Fenella said.

"She didn't get this upset when she told me the story," Jack said. "I think it's just harder because George is dead now."

"I should go and find her," Fenella said after a moment. "She's probably in the ladies' room."

"I have a class to teach," Jack said, glancing at his watch. "Tell her that I love her, please."

Fenella watched him walk away and then looked at Daniel. "Do you want to wait here?"

"I've nothing better to do."

She sighed. "I'm sorry."

"Don't be. The pudding menu was incredibly tempting."

She laughed and then kissed him lightly before heading for the bathrooms just outside the dining room. Fenella found Linda sitting on the couch in front of the mirrors. She was redoing her makeup, her eyes still puffy and watery.

"I didn't mean to upset you," Fenella said as she sat down next to the woman.

"I know. I didn't think I'd get that upset, or I might have refused to answer. I've been able to talk about the divorce without tears for over a year now. I suppose George's death has upset me more than I'd realized."

"That's understandable. Murder is always horrible."

Linda shuddered. "I still can't quite believe that he was murdered. Maybe he was drunk and he simply fell into the dumpster and, I don't know, had a heart attack or something."

"That's for the police to work out."

"Yes, of course." She sighed. "Has Jack gone?"

"Yes, he had to get to a class. He asked me to tell you that he loves you."

"He would. He's such a dear and wonderful man. Sometimes I can't quite believe how lucky I am to have him in my life. He'll never cheat on me. I'm positive about that."

"He's a good man."

"What did George tell you about me when you saw him after the party?"

"What makes you think he told me anything?"

"He would. I'm sure he said something to try to get you on his side. He'll have defended his decision to leave me, blamed me for the marriage ending, something."

"He said something about you rewriting history to suit yourself or something," Fenella muttered.

Linda frowned. "That's just vague enough to be believable," she sighed. "I can't even defend myself against it, because don't we all rewrite history to suit ourselves? History is written by the winners, after all, and we all want to be the winners in our own stories."

"I asked him about his vasectomy and he suggested that it never happened," Fenella blurted out.

Linda looked shocked. "Jack told you what I'd told him about George having had a vasectomy without telling me? I never imagined that Jack would repeat such a thing."

"He was simply trying to explain to me how badly you'd been treated by the man," Fenella told her, feeling as if she was making things worse.

Linda sighed. "I may not have told Jack the whole story. In that instance, I suppose I could be accused of rewriting history in order to make myself look better."

"I'm sorry. I'm not trying to pry."

"But you don't know what to believe, do you? George managed to plant some doubt in your mind and now you're worried that I might not be a good person or the right person for Jack."

"I trust Jack to make up his own mind."

She sighed. "You don't have children, do you?"

Fenella shook her head. "When I was younger, I had an unplanned pregnancy that resulted in a miscarriage. That miscarriage left me unable to have children."

Linda took a deep breath. "My story isn't that dissimilar, except when I found myself pregnant unexpectedly at nineteen, I found a place to help me get rid of it. They botched the abortion, but they didn't tell me. I didn't know I couldn't have any more children until years later, when George and I were trying and I couldn't get pregnant."

"I'm sorry," Fenella said, patting the woman's arm as tears flowed down her cheeks.

"I felt like such a failure. No, I felt like a horrible person. I couldn't have children and it was my fault. I'd made a terrible mistake and then I'd compounded it with an even bigger one. In a way, I came to feel as if I didn't deserve to be a mother. Of course, I had to tell George everything. He was upset, but he forgave me and he stayed with me. I was so grateful to him for that. I couldn't imagine trying to find someone else, not when I was so badly damaged."

"Lots of women can't have children for lots of different reasons. You shouldn't have felt as if you were damaged in any way."

"Maybe not, but I did. When George cheated on me for the first time, it wasn't long after we'd found out that we'd never have children. I was shocked and hurt, but I wasn't really surprised. I couldn't blame him for wanting a real woman, one who wasn't, well, damaged."

"Presumably, he didn't want children with anyone else, though."

Linda nodded. "I found out, about ten years later, that he'd just had a vasectomy. That felt like a huge betrayal, because I knew he'd had it so that he couldn't get his mistresses pregnant, but it wasn't to keep me from getting pregnant. I may have mixed up those things when I told Jack about the vasectomy, though. I didn't, well, I didn't want to admit to him that I was damaged."

"You need to stop thinking of yourself as damaged," Fenella said firmly.

Linda shrugged. "I'm too old now to make babies. I feel less horrible about the whole thing now."

"I suppose that's something," Fenella muttered.

"I'm sorry. I didn't intend to tell you all of this. I'm sure you think I'm all wrong for Jack now."

"Not at all. As I said, I trust Jack to make his own decisions."

"I love him dearly. He's completely different from George and that's exactly what I wanted. I know we'll be very happy together."

"Are you truly over George, though?" Fenella asked the question that had been bothering her.

"I am, although I know it probably doesn't look that way. I wasn't going to take him back, no matter what he'd said, but he could have ruined things between Jack and me, anyway. As I said before, he threatened me and I didn't know what to do."

"You said he threatened to tell Jack lies about you," Fenella remembered.

Linda hesitated and then nodded. "Lies, half-truths, whatever," she said with a wave of her hand.

"And there are probably things you haven't told Jack that you'd rather he not know," Fenella suggested.

"Of course there are. I'm fifty-three. I have a past. I've not done anything criminal, but there are things in my past that I'm not proud of, things that I'd rather not discuss with Jack. My abortion is one of those things."

"I won't repeat any of this conversation to Jack," Fenella promised. Of course, she was going to tell Daniel everything that was said, but she was hoping to persuade him that there were things that Carol Gregory didn't need to know.

"Thank you."

"You might want to tell him, though," Fenella added.

Linda sighed. "I suppose I should. Does he have any deep dark secrets in his past?"

Fenella laughed. "If he does, they're from before I met him and he's never shared them with me. I think Jack is an open book, though."

"I wish I knew why George came back. He'd started a new life somewhere else. We were divorced. Why come back?"

"Maybe his new life wasn't going well."

"I hope the police are investigating that. Maybe someone from that new life came here with him or followed him here. There had to be a woman in his life. They should find her."

"I'm sure they're looking."

"I wish I'd had a chance to talk to him, really talk, not just the five minutes I gave him at the party. I have so many unanswered questions and now I'll never get the answers."

"You might not have gotten any answers, even if you'd had more time to speak to him."

Linda nodded. "He would have only told me what he wanted me to know or believe. It just all feels so unfinished."

"Maybe you'll find out more once the police work out who killed him."

"I hope so. There's another thing bothering me. Who told him about the engagement party? Karl admitted to speaking to him and telling him that I was getting married, but he claims he didn't tell George about the party. Who did?"

"Maybe, like Karl, whoever it was didn't want to upset you, so he or she didn't tell you what was happening."

"I'd much rather have had some warning."

"I'm sure the person didn't realize that George was going to decide to come and crash your engagement party."

"It was a very George thing to do, of course. He loved being the center of attention and there was nothing he enjoyed more than upset-ting me." She sighed. "I shouldn't say that. For many years we had what I thought was a good marriage. We both had decent jobs and we lived comfortably. We never worried about saving money, because we knew we wouldn't have anyone to inherit it, so we spent nearly every penny we made. We traveled and we had a big house and new cars every few years. Aside from him cheating now and again, I thought things were good for a long time."

"What happened?" Fenella asked.

She shrugged. "I don't know how to answer that. It was gradual. So gradual that I didn't really notice until, well, until after George left, really. Over time George started being less nice. It's hard to explain. It was just a bunch of little things, things I barely noticed while it was happening."

"I don't understand."

"And when I try to explain, it all sounds crazy." Linda sighed. "It was just little things, like less thoughtful presents for Christmas and my birthday. When we were first married, he used to buy me the most wonderful things, things that he'd clearly thought about and made an effort to find. On our last Christmas together, he bought me a gift certificate to my hair salon."

"At least it was your hair salon."

Linda chuckled. "Yes, okay, but it was clear he didn't put any thought into it. He just went to the place he knew I used and bought a gift certificate. And now that I think about it, he probably asked Melanie where I went. He may have even asked her to get the gift certificate."

"So he wasn't putting as much effort into the relationship."

"He wasn't putting any effort in by the end," she sighed. "Like I said, it was so gradual, that I barely noticed. Melanie spotted it before I did, but I didn't want to listen to her when she started pointing things out. There were so many little things that I wanted to ignore. I shouldn't have been surprised when he left. Melanie kept telling me my marriage was in trouble, but I didn't want to see it."

"Did you try talking to George about it?"

"Once or twice, but he would just look at me like I was crazy. It was such small stuff, like forgetting that we had dinner reservations somewhere once in a while or maybe leaving his car on the driveway so I couldn't get out of the garage without moving it. Just dumb little things, but they were things that he'd never have done when we were first married."

"Sometimes, over time, people start to take one another for granted."

"Of course, and that's what I tried to convince myself was all that it was. I told myself that we'd been married for a long time, so of course we weren't leaving little notes under each other's pillows or sending random cards to one another. It was only natural that George and I both had lots of other things on our minds. That's what George always told me whenever I said anything to him, anyway."

"And it was all little things right up until he left?"

"Actually, I was starting to think that things were getting better," she sighed. "I'd always done all of the cooking and cleaning and taking care of the house, even though I'd always worked full-time. It was a struggle, once I was also studying for my doctorate, but I was careful not to complain. Melanie used to complain on my behalf, quite regularly, but that's another matter."

Fenella laughed. "That's what friends are for."

"Anyway, in the last year or so of our marriage, George started cooking once in a while. I'd come home from one of my classes and he'd have dinner ready for both of us. It was really sweet and I truly believed that things were getting better. I thought he was finally starting to properly appreciate how hard I worked. Now I think he was just practicing for when he was going to be living on his own."

"And he left to live on his own? He didn't move in with another woman?"

Linda looked surprised and then frowned. "I've no idea. He left Buffalo and just left me with his lawyer's contact information. Now that you've said that, I can't imagine why I've always assumed that he moved away on his own. He may have taken someone with him or he may have moved in with someone about whom I know nothing."

"The police should be able to find out where he went."

"If there was another woman, I don't want to know."

Fenella nodded. "I can understand that."

Linda looked at her watch. "We've been talking for ages. I'm sure you have better things to do."

"I left Daniel having dessert. He's probably done by now, though."

"Thank you for coming and finding me. I thought I was going to hate you, because I know Jack still has feelings for you, but you've been nothing but wonderful to me."

"I'll always love Jack, but I haven't been in love with him for a very long time. We were more like brother and sister than anything else by the end of our relationship."

"That surprises me," Linda giggled. "He's amazing in bed."

Fenella felt her jaw drop. She swallowed hard before she could say something stupid. A buzzing noise startled them both.

"Mine," Linda told her, digging out her mobile phone. "It's Melanie."

Linda typed out a reply and then looked up at Fenella. "She's curious about what we should expect to happen next with the murder investigation. So is Karl, and I'd be willing to bet Howard and Gloria feel the same way. If I arrange something, could you and Daniel come and explain it all to everyone?"

"We've no experience with murder investigations in the US," Fenella protested.

"But you have a lot more experience with murder investigations in general than any of us. That's especially true for Daniel, of course. He's a very reassuring person, too. I think all of my friends would feel better if they had a chance to talk to Daniel about the investigation."

Her phone buzzed again. She looked down at it and then up at Fenella. "How about tomorrow night? There's a nice little restaurant not far from here that has a small private room. I'm sure I can reserve it for tomorrow. Melanie is willing and she's said she'll bring Karl. Even if Howard and Gloria can't make it, you and Daniel can talk to Melanie and Karl."

"Sure," Fenella said, hoping Daniel wouldn't mind.

Linda surprised her by giving her a hug. "Maybe, between us, we can work out what actually happened to George," she said excitedly. "Is there anyone else you think we should invite?"

Fenella thought for a minute. "Not really. Everyone who was at the engagement party is on the suspect list, but most of the other guests didn't really know George, did they?"

"Not really. My cousins had all met him at various events over the years, but I'm not close to any of them and I'm not even sure they all knew we'd gotten divorced. I invited them to the engagement party because they're all the family I have left, but I didn't really expect any of them to come."

"Were you surprised that they came?"

"No. I'd say they came out of a sense of obligation, but really, I think they all came for the free food and the open bar. They'll all be at the wedding for the same reason."

"Who else was at the party?" Fenella asked.

"Hazel and Sue from work, but they didn't know George. I didn't meet them until after the divorce."

"Unless one of them knew George from somewhere else," Fenella said thoughtfully.

Linda frowned. "I didn't think of that."

"That seems unlikely, though. Buffalo is a big city. It's unlikely that George ever crossed paths with either of them."

"I should ask them. I am going to ask them, actually. Of course, if one of them killed him, she won't admit to having known him, will she?"

"Maybe you should leave the questioning to the police."

"I'm going to see them later today. I may say something, just casually, and see what they say. Maybe I'll even invite them to dinner tomorrow night."

"That's up to you."

"And then, of course, Jack's mother was at the party."

Fenella frowned. "As much as I'd love to see her go to prison for something, I can't see why she'd have murdered George."

"She was incredibly pleased to see him. She hates me. I think she actually thought that Jack was going to move back in with her at some point in the future."

"I can't see Jack ever doing that."

"No, me either. As much as he loves being taken care of, he no longer wants his mother doing the job. He told me you did a lot for him when you were together. I try to encourage him to do more for himself, but that's just because I did so much for George."

"That's better for Jack, too."

"Not according to his mother. She was shocked when he

mentioned that he'd been a few minutes late getting to the airport to pick her up because he'd been ironing. She wanted to stay with him, you know, but I told Jack that I wouldn't stay with him if she was there. She makes me uncomfortable. He ended up getting her a hotel room."

"You can invite her tomorrow night if you think she might have something to contribute."

"I can't imagine that she will, but I may have to invite her anyway. She'll complain if she doesn't get to spend any time with Jack tomorrow and he's teaching for most of the day."

"I'm surprised you're both teaching summer classes, especially since you were planning a wedding."

"We're both teaching summer classes because of the wedding," Linda laughed. "Actually, we're both teaching summer classes because of the honeymoon. Jack didn't want to spend any money on a honeymoon. I suggested that I could teach a few summer classes and we could use that money for the honeymoon, since it was, effectively, bonus money. In the end, he opted to teach a few classes as well, so we'd have enough to have a really wonderful trip."

"Jack told me you were going to Europe."

"We're going all over Europe. It's going to be amazing. I just hope we'll still be allowed to go, even if the murder isn't solved. Can the police really keep us here?"

"I believe so, but that's a question for Carol, really. The rules in the US might be very different to the ones on the Isle of Man."

Linda nodded. "Let me see what I can arrange for tomorrow night. Plan on meeting at least some of us around six, okay?"

"I'll call or text Jack if we can't make it for some reason."

"Great, thanks."

Fenella dug out her comb and ran it through her hair as Linda exited the room. She counted slowly to one hundred before she followed, not wanting to have to talk to the woman any more for the time being. Daniel was still sitting at the table, sipping coffee.

"I'm so sorry," she said as she sat down opposite him.

"I hope you learned something interesting after all that," he replied.

She shrugged. "She wouldn't stop talking, but I don't know if anything she said was interesting."

"Let's take a walk," he suggested. "I had two puddings while you were gone. I need to burn off a few extra calories."

"What did you have? No, wait, don't tell me. I'll just be jealous that I didn't get any."

As they slowly made their way around the campus again, Fenella repeated everything she could remember from her conversation with Linda.

"Tomorrow night?" Daniel asked when she was done.

"I hope you don't mind too much."

"I was hoping for lots of romantic dinners, just the two of us," he sighed. "But since we're already hopelessly entangled in a murder investigation, I'm all in favor of anything that might help get the case solved more quickly. A chat with all of the major suspects certainly fits that description."

"You think one of Linda's friends killed George?"

He shrugged. "I don't know anything about George's former work colleagues. I also know nothing about where he went when he left Buffalo. There could be dozens of suspects from either or both of those places about whom I know nothing. Linda's friends are my main suspects, because they're the only suspects that I've met."

Fenella nodded. "I want to believe that the killer was at the engagement party. That rules out George's former work colleagues and anyone he knew in his new life."

"Of course, there could have been some overlap between his old life and his new life."

"What do you mean?"

"I mean, he was clearly in touch with someone here, someone who told him about Linda's engagement party. Maybe he'd kept some of his old friends when he moved."

"Do you think it's possible that he had an affair with Gloria?"

"That's something I'd be looking at if I had Carol's job."

"Maybe they were still involved or maybe they got involved again after George and Linda split up," Fenella said thoughtfully.

"Or maybe George stayed in touch with Karl or Howard," Daniel said. "I think tomorrow night we need to try to work out who told George about the engagement party."

"No one is going to admit to that."

"Probably not," Daniel agreed. "But I feel as if it could be important."

"It would be better to know who knew where George was staying."

"Yes, of course, but I can't see anyone admitting to that, considering the man was murdered there."

Fenella sighed. "Or maybe we could just go up to Niagara Falls tomorrow and stay there until the wedding."

"Or after the wedding?" Daniel muttered.

She stopped. "I'm sorry," she said softly.

He pulled her into a tight hug. "You've nothing to be sorry for, unless you killed George." He pulled back and gave her a hard look. "Did you kill George?" he asked, his tone mock-serious.

She giggled. "I won't confess, not ever."

"You'd have to persuade me that you had a motive."

"That's a good point. Why would I want to kill the man?"

"Maybe you really want Jack to be happy."

"I do really want Jack to be happy, but not enough to murder someone for him."

Daniel frowned. "Maybe you and George had some secret history. Maybe you knew one another years ago."

"Of course that's true for everyone involved in the investigation, even you."

"Except I've never been to Buffalo before. There's no way I could have met the man."

"Maybe he'd been to the UK," Fenella suggested. "Maybe you encountered one another once when you both happened to be in London or somewhere. Maybe he did something truly awful and you vowed to kill him if you ever saw him again."

"Maybe you've been reading too many weird books."

Fenella laughed. "I know it's all very far-fetched, but it's remotely possible. I feel sorry for Carol."

"It's remotely possible, but I'm fairly certain that this murder is going to turn out to have been committed by someone we've met, someone with a significant shared history with the man."

"Do you think Linda might have done it?"

"She's not at the top of my list, but she's definitely on it." He sighed. "I need to ring Carol and tell her about lunch and your conversation with Linda. After that, do you think maybe we could talk about something else?"

"Of course we can," she replied quickly.

Daniel nodded and then pulled out his phone. He dialed the number he had for Carol and then put his phone into speaker mode. Fenella was surprised when the woman answered.

"It's Daniel. Fenella and I had lunch with Jack and Linda. I thought I should share the conversation with you."

"When you said that Fenella made a habit of bumping into suspects, I didn't really believe you," Carol replied.

"Jack asked us to have lunch with them. He wanted to talk about the investigation," Daniel explained. "And then Linda asked us to have dinner with her and her friends tomorrow night for the same reason."

Carol sighed. "I didn't warn you to stay out of the investigation or to stay away from the suspects. I knew you'd be seeing them at the wedding, at the very least. This is something else altogether, though."

"We don't need to have dinner with them tomorrow if you'd rather we didn't," Fenella said.

"Tell me what was said over lunch while I think about tomorrow," Carol suggested.

Daniel repeated the conversation they'd had over lunch and then Fenella added the highlights from the conversation she'd had with Linda in the bathroom after lunch. She'd told Daniel everything, but she chose not to share Linda's secret with Carol.

"I don't think anything there will solve the case, but I do think you're getting some valuable information that's helping me build up a fuller picture of the parties involved. Call me tomorrow night after your dinner. I want to hear everything that gets discussed."

A loud click told Daniel and Fenella that the woman had ended the call.

"I guess that means she doesn't mind if we have dinner with Linda and her friends tomorrow," Fenella said as Daniel put the phone in his pocket.

"I think she minds a great deal, but she also knows that we're finding out things that people aren't telling her. A murder investigation is like a huge jigsaw puzzle. Right now, all we're doing is helping fill in the background, but at some point we might just find one of the more important pieces."

Fenella sighed. "Now what?"

"Now we stop talking about murder and George and Linda and Jack and just spend some time together," Daniel said, pulling her into a kiss.

"We just have to find something fun to do." Fenella checked her phone and then grinned at him. "I know just the thing," she said.

"Where are we going?"

"I'm not telling."

They walked back to the car and Fenella drove them down into the city. She parked near the water and they walked along Canalside, enjoying the summer sunshine.

"It's beautiful down here," Daniel said.

"I hope you're in the mood for some music," she told him.

A short while later, she'd bought their tickets for the evening's concert. They grabbed food from one of the food trucks and then sat on the grass and enjoyed the music with the crowd.

"That was a wonderful way to spend the evening," Daniel said as they walked back to the car.

"Canalside has seen a huge revival," she told him. "They weren't doing concerts in the park ten years ago down here. Now they have activities here all year-round."

They drove back to the hotel in a companionable silence. Fenella parked and then they walked inside.

"One drink at the bar before bed?" Daniel suggested.

"I'd like a drink," she agreed. "I really wanted a glass of wine at the concert, but I know better than to drink and drive with a policeman in the car."

He laughed. "I don't have any jurisdiction here," he reminded her.

"And yet Linda still wants you to talk to her friends about what to expect from the investigation."

"I'm happy to talk to them. You know I'm hoping to get more out of them than I tell them."

She nodded. At the bar, they ordered drinks and then sat at a table as far from the one they'd sat at previously as they could get.

"What should we do tomorrow morning?" she asked him as she rested her head on his shoulder.

"What would you like to do?"

"We won't have time to get to Niagara Falls, or rather, we won't have time to see much if we do go. What about going around a couple of art museums? We have two excellent ones."

"I'd like that, as long as we don't have to rush out of bed early."

"No rushing," she agreed. "If we have time for only one museum, well, we can save the other for another day."

They finished their drinks and then headed up to their room. As they reached it, Fenella's phone beeped.

"It's Jack," she sighed. "We're all set for tomorrow night at six. He and Linda will be there, as will Karl and Melanie, and Howard and Gloria. Jack's mother will be there, too."

"And won't it be nice to see her again," Daniel muttered as he shut and locked the door behind them.

9

"**O**uch," Daniel's voice shocked Fenella awake.

She sat up and looked around the dark room. "Are you okay?" she called into the darkness.

"I'm fine," Daniel replied.

She watched as his shadowy figure walked out of the bathroom.

"I thought the sink was a few paces further from the door than it actually is and I walked right into it. I didn't want to turn on any lights and risk waking you. It was much better to stand in the bathroom and shout," he explained.

She laughed. "What time is it?"

"Nearly eight. I woke up at seven and couldn't get back to sleep. I've been lying in bed, trying to decide what do to ever since."

"You should have woken me."

"We agreed last night that we weren't going to rush off anywhere today."

"Well, I'm awake now. Let's get ready and go down for some breakfast."

"That sounds like a plan."

After breakfast, they headed back downtown. This time, their destination was the Albright-Knox Art Gallery. They spent two hours enjoying the art before making the short journey to the nearby Burch-field Penney Art Center.

"I think our first stop should be the café," Fenella said as they entered the museum.

"They have a new menu," the girl behind the ticket counter told her. "Everything is really good."

"I'm ready for lunch," Daniel agreed.

A few minutes later, they were sitting together at a table for two in the small café.

"And your luck continues," Daniel said, nodding toward the door.

Fenella looked up and then sighed. "What are they doing here?"

Hazel looked over and then said something to Sue. A moment later, the pair headed straight for Daniel and Fenella.

"Fancy seeing you here," Hazel said.

"Hello," Fenella replied.

"We should get a table together," Sue suggested. "We didn't have a chance to catch up properly at the party the other night. We barely even got introduced to your new, um, significant other."

Fenella looked at Daniel, who shrugged.

"I'm sure no one will mind if we take that table over there," Sue said, gesturing toward a larger table nearby.

The café was nearly empty, but Fenella was painfully aware that everyone in the place was staring at them.

Hazel seemed to be doing her best to ensure that they'd remain the center of attention as she loudly said, "And we can talk about murder," as Fenella and Daniel got up from their table.

"I'd rather not," Fenella said flatly as she took a seat the new table.

"Oh, don't be that way," Sue said. "I've never been involved in a murder investigation before, but Daniel is a homicide investigator. I'm sure he can tell us everything we need to know about the case."

"I don't know anything more than you do," Daniel protested. "I'm as much on the outside of this case as you are."

"I don't believe that," Hazel told him. "If nothing else, you must be a much better judge of character than we are. You'll have spoken to hundreds of murderers over the years. You can probably spot them as soon as you see them now."

"I wish it were that easy," he replied.

Fenella thought he looked amused.

"I told Hazel, after the disaster that was that party, that I wouldn't be surprised if someone ended up murdered," Sue said in a loud whisper.

"You said no such thing," Hazel snapped.

"Yes I did. You just don't remember. It was when we were leaving, after that man turned up and caused all that trouble. You don't remember because you'd been drinking," Sue replied.

"I had three drinks over three hours. That's not enough to trouble my memory," Hazel told her.

"Then it must have troubled your hearing," Sue muttered.

"You were worried that someone might get murdered?" Daniel asked.

"It just seemed likely, that's all. I mean, Linda was terribly upset with George, but then she went and kissed him. It was quite the kiss, I thought," Sue replied.

"I thought it looked as if George kissed her, not the other way around," Fenella said.

"I can't see the difference," Sue replied. "She didn't stop him and then she said she might want to cancel the wedding."

Fenella opened her mouth to object, but Daniel took her hand and squeezed it.

"Who did you think was going to get killed?" he asked Sue.

"Well, the man who did get killed, of course. It was like something out of a movie, really, one of those made for television movies, not a proper one, but still. There we all were, celebrating together, and then that man crashed the party. As an aside, I've never been to a party that was crashed like that before. Have you?"

Fenella shook her head.

"It was a first for me," Daniel told her.

"I was at a wedding that was crashed once," Hazel said.

"You were?" Sue demanded.

"Years and years ago now, when I was still in college, working on my first degree. One of my friends from high school was getting married. She'd only been dating the guy for a few months, but she told me she was sure he was the one."

"And someone crashed the actual wedding?" Sue asked.

"His former girlfriend turned up. She was, well, visibly pregnant and absolutely furious. She didn't even wait for the part where the minister asks for objections. She followed the bride down the aisle, screaming and shouting about Jackie stealing her man."

"Jackie was your friend?" Sue checked.

"Yeah, sorry. Jackie was my friend. I don't think I ever found out the name of the former girlfriend. Anyway, she screamed and shouted at the groom for over half an hour, crying and sobbing about how she was having his baby and how he'd dumped her because of it. He kept saying that it probably wasn't his kid, which just made her cry harder. It was horrible but no one could look away," Hazel continued.

She was interrupted by the waiter, who took their drink order.

"What happened in the end?" Fenella asked as the man walked away.

"Oh, eventually, the groom's mother talked the ex-girlfriend into leaving with her. They went outside and talked for a short while and then the groom's mother came back in alone. As soon as she was back in her seat, the minister flew through the service at a ridiculous speed. People were already arriving for the evening prayer service, you see, so he had to rush through it."

"And did the marriage last?" Fenella had to ask.

"They split up at the reception," Hazel told her. "Actually, they split up before the reception in the car on the way from the church to the reception hall."

"Was the baby his, then?" Sue asked.

"I have no idea. That isn't why they split up. When they got into the limousine after the ceremony, Jackie accidentally sat on the best man's lap. Apparently, once she'd sat down, she'd decided she was quite comfortable there, and had refused to move over. The best man didn't complain and by the time they'd reached the reception, the pair were making out like, well, newlyweds."

"In front of Jackie's new husband?" Sue demanded.

"And the best man's girlfriend," Hazel told her. "It was all a huge mess, really."

"Where are they all now?" Daniel asked.

"Jackie ended up marrying the best man once her divorce was finalized. They were married for something like twenty years before they went their separate ways. The groom left town and I've no idea what happened to him. His former girlfriend was from the next town over. I have no idea what ever happened to her, either."

"And the best man's girlfriend?" Fenella asked, trying to keep up with the story.

"Oh, that was me. I counted my lucky stars that I'd found out that my boyfriend was the cheating kind before we'd gotten serious, and then I went back to college determined not to waste any more time on men until I'd finished my degree."

Sue sat back and frowned at Hazel. "I'm not sure I believe any of that actually happened," she said.

Hazel shrugged. "I have pictures and the article from the local paper about the wedding that very nearly didn't happen. It was the talk of the town for about twenty-four hours."

"But we were talking about the man who crashed the party the other night," Sue said. "I was sure he was going to get himself murdered after the way he'd behaved at the party."

"And who did you think was going to kill him?" Daniel asked.

Sue frowned. "I didn't really give that much thought. I mean, he seemed like a horrible person, trying to destroy Linda's happiness like that. I'm sure he must have had a lot of enemies."

"Had either of you ever met him before?" Fenella asked.

"Of course not," Sue said.

"I had," Hazel said quietly.

Sue stared at her for a moment. "You're full of surprises today," she muttered.

"You had?" Daniel asked.

Hazel shrugged. "I knew Linda back when she was studying for her degree. I shouldn't say that I knew her. I'd met her. She got her doctorate at a different university, but we work in a similar area. When she started doing her research, she sent me an email and asked me about some of the research that I'd done on a particular topic. After a handful of emails back and forth, I suggested that we have lunch one day to discuss her dissertation proposal."

"Is that typical?" Daniel asked.

"It's something I do probably at least once a year," Hazel replied. "There are a number of colleges and universities in the Buffalo area, and more in Rochester and beyond. I'm always happy to talk to students who are interested in my research. Usually, I limit myself to emails, but Linda was considering working on a topic that's especially interesting to me, one that I'd love to dig into further if I simply had more time, so I was actually eager to speak to her, to encourage her to pursue that line of study."

"And did she?" Fenella wondered.

"Partly," Hazel told her. "We met again, once or twice, while she was writing her dissertation. At one of those meetings, she had car trouble and she called her husband to come and pick her up. That's when I met George. The next time I saw Linda, George had just left her and she was thinking about giving up on her doctorate. I hope I was able to help convince her to keep working. When she finished, I wrote her a letter of recommendation for the job with us."

"What did you think of George?" Daniel asked.

"I didn't care for him, and that isn't just hindsight talking. As I said, Linda had had car trouble. She called him and practically had to beg him to come and help. I told her that she should have emergency breakdown coverage. I've had it ever since I got my first car. She said she probably should since George wasn't the most reliable man in the world."

"Did you get a chance to talk to him at the party the other night?" Fenella asked.

Hazel shook her head. "I didn't make any effort to speak to him, either. I wasn't any more impressed with him on Saturday than I'd been the first time I'd met him."

"Did you suspect that he might get murdered, too?" Sue asked.

Hazel stared at her for a moment and then shook her head. "Murder is something that happens on television or in movies or books. People don't get murdered in real life. Not in my real life, anyway."

Fenella frowned. "They get murdered in my real life," she muttered.

Daniel squeezed her hand. "And murder is my job," he said.

Hazel nodded. "Of course, and I realize that perfectly ordinary people get killed every day. It just wasn't something I was expecting to happen to someone that I'd met, even only just in passing."

"Had you ever met any of the other guests?" Fenella asked.

"One of Linda's cousins once took one of my classes," Hazel replied. "I barely remembered the man. He was a business major, but he took my introductory class to meet his core requirements. He made a point of speaking to me at the party, mostly to complain that I'd given him a 'B' instead of the 'A' he thought he'd deserved."

"The cousins all looked to be in their forties or fifties. When did he take your class?" Fenella asked.

"More than twenty years ago," Hazel told her.

Fenella shook her head. "And he's still angry about his grade?"

"He tried to sound as if he were joking, but yes, I do think he's still angry about his grade," Hazel replied.

"What did you say back?" Sue asked.

"That I always prided myself on grading my students fairly, and that if he had concerns about his grades, he should have addressed them with me at the time," she said. "He muttered 'whatever' and walked away."

"And I missed it all," Sue said.

"It was when you were speaking to the man who'd brought the present," Hazel told her.

"Ah, Howard Keller," Sue said. "He was the only person at the party that I'd met before."

"How do you know Howard?" Daniel asked.

"I sometimes talk to prospective students and their families. He brought his son to tour the university a few years ago. We started talking and discovered that we live fairly near one another. He has a history degree, too, but just an undergraduate degree. He's never worked in the field, but he was hoping his son might want to follow in his footsteps and study history," Sue explained.

"His wife didn't come with them?" Fenella asked.

Sue flushed. "She did not. At the time, I believed that he was, well, unattached."

Fenella gave the woman a curious look. "Did he ask you out?"

Sue turned an even brighter shade of red. "We had lunch together, not just the two of us, but in a small group. We talked a great deal, just the two of us, though. He seemed very interested in my research and also in my job with the university. At the time I thought he was curious about life as a university professor because it was something that his son was considering as a future career, but I later started to wonder if he was more interested in finding out how much influence I had with the department's scholarship committee."

"You never saw him again after that day?" Daniel asked.

She shook her head. "He asked for my number, just in case his son had any additional questions. I gave him my card, with my office number and my email on it, but I never heard from him again."

Fenella thought she could hear disappointment in the woman's tone. "What did he say when you spoke to him at the party?"

"That his son had decided to go to a college in Ohio and that he was studying physics," Sue told her.

"Sorry this took so long," the waiter said as he delivered their food. "It's a new menu and the kitchen is still struggling with it a little bit."

"It's fine," Fenella assured him.

"Except I have an appointment this afternoon," Sue complained as she looked at her watch.

"You've plenty of time," Hazel told her. "It's been ages since we've had a proper chat with Margaret. Tell us more about your new life," she said to Fenella.

"I think I told you everything interesting the other night," Fenella said, trying to remember the conversation they'd had at the party.

"Then, Daniel, tell us about fighting crime," Sue said. "You told us a few stories at the party, but we want to hear about murder now that we're tangled up in a case of our own."

Daniel looked at Fenella and then shrugged. "Why don't I tell you about one of the cold cases that Fenella helped me solve?" he asked. "It wasn't long after we'd met, actually."

While he talked, Fenella concentrated on eating while wondering if Howard had ever cheated on Gloria. Melanie had suggested that Gloria and George had had an affair. Maybe everyone in the world was having affairs with everyone else and she was the one who was missing out. She reached over and took Daniel's hand, squeezing it tightly. Whatever the rest of the world was doing, she had no intention of cheating on him and she trusted him to be faithful to her, as well.

"Oh dear, look at the time," Sue said as Daniel finished telling them about the case. "I really must go. Where is the waiter? I need my check."

"I'll get lunch," Fenella told her.

"Are you sure? That's very kind of you," Sue replied.

"I'm sure," Fenella replied.

"In that case, maybe I have just enough time for dessert," Sue said, waving to the waiter. She had him tell them the dessert options and then ordered a slice of apple pie.

"Anyone else?" he asked.

"I can't resist chocolate cream pie," Fenella told him.

"I don't know that I've ever had chocolate cream pie," Daniel said. "I'll try that."

"Make it three," Hazel laughed.

Sue frowned. "Now I'm the odd one out," she said as the waiter walked away.

"I'm sure the apple pie is delicious," Fenella said.

Sue shrugged. "I wish I'd known that you were all going to get the same thing."

"We didn't plan it that way," Hazel told her. "It just sounded so good when Margaret ordered it."

Sue shrugged. "Whatever."

"Tell us about another case," Hazel said to Daniel as the waiter returned with their slices of pie.

"I'd rather hear more about you," he replied. "I know you both have your own special areas of interest. Tell me about them."

"I'll go first," Sue said. "I do have to leave very soon, after all."

Fenella found herself struggling to stay awake as Sue spent the next fifteen minutes droning on and on about European economics in the seventeenth century.

"Fascinating," Daniel said when she finally stopped talking.

"If you truly think so, I must get you a copy of my most recent book," Sue told him. "It's an in-depth study of the French and German economies over just a ten year period. I may have a few extra copies somewhere. If I can find one, I'll bring it to the wedding."

"That's very generous of you, but I'm sure you have better uses for the books," Daniel replied.

"I may not even be able to find them," she replied. "But now I must go. I'll see you at the wedding on Saturday."

Fenella felt guilty for feeling relieved as the woman left the room.

"Imagine how bored her students must be," Hazel whispered.

Fenella and Daniel both laughed.

"I'm being unfair, because she's quite brilliant and some of her work is incredibly interesting. She has a way of drawing unexpected conclusions and then presenting her evidence in ways that are very convincing, but she isn't always the best at sharing her ideas when speaking. I'm always trying to find excuses to miss her lectures when she gives public ones."

"What about your research?" Daniel asked.

Hazel gave him a wicked smile. "I've been working on something new lately. I've been chronicling the lives of prostitutes during the seventeenth and eighteenth centuries in America and England. It's fascinating."

"It certainly sounds a good deal more interesting than what Sue's been doing," Fenella laughed.

"I started out studying family life in the US, but over the years and decades, I started to get more interested in the roles of working women within society. I've studied everything from the first female doctors and lawyers to women working more traditional jobs over the centuries. Researching prostitutes is my newest obsession, though, and it's proving quite a challenge. As you can imagine, there isn't a lot of original source material with which to work."

They talked more about Hazel's work while they finished their desserts and Fenella paid the bill.

"And now, I should get back to work," Hazel said. "It's been really nice seeing you again."

"Likewise," Fenella said.

They all walked through the building together before Hazel left and Fenella and Daniel started their tour of the galleries. A few hours later the pair had toured the entire building.

"I can't remember the last time I went to an art museum before today," Daniel said as they walked back to the car.

"Me either, and I really enjoyed today's visits. Of course, the island doesn't have an art museum, just the gallery at the Manx Museum."

"Which has a lot of art for such a small island," Daniel suggested.

"What should we do now?" Fenella asked as she headed the car back toward the hotel.

"This is going to sound odd, but can we go grocery shopping?" Daniel asked.

"Grocery shopping?" Fenella echoed. "What do you need?"

"I don't need anything, but you always see American grocery shops on television or in movies. They're huge and full of things we don't have in the UK. I'd like to see one for myself."

Fenella laughed. "We can go grocery shopping," she said. "We'll start at one store and, if that isn't enough, we can try another. There are several large grocery stores near the university, along with a mall and tons of other stores."

A few minutes later, she parked in the parking lot for what had once been her favorite grocery store. It was nearly two hours later when they finally emerged with just enough time to get to the restaurant for their dinner with Linda and the others.

"Too much choice," Daniel said as he slumped in the passenger seat. "An entire aisle of nothing but breakfast cereal. We don't have that on the Isle of Man."

Fenella laughed. "When was the last time you went to the big ShopFast in Douglas? They just expanded, you know. I think you'd be surprised at how many different varieties of cereal they offer now."

"I never go down the cereal aisle, actually. Most of it is full of sugar. I tend to stick to toast and fruit for breakfast. Not that I have time for breakfast most mornings."

"Breakfast is important. You should make more of an effort to eat in the mornings."

"Yes, well, I've been eating breakfast every morning since we've been here. I think I'm gaining weight."

"You can't blame breakfast for that. You've also had dessert at just about every meal since we've been here."

Daniel laughed. "But it's easier to skip breakfast than skip pudding."

"And now we have to go and meet everyone for dinner."

"Don't let me get pudding."

"Actually, they do really good desserts," she told him. "At least, they used to do really good desserts. I hope they still have the melting middle cookie. I always used to get a small meal so I would have room for the cookie."

"I might be able to save room for a cookie."

"It's a large cookie," she warned him. "It's served warm and it has a big, gooey, melted chocolate center."

"I'm going to have to start going running in the mornings."

"When we get home."

"I could start now."

"There aren't any sidewalks around the hotel. Wait until we're home."

"Will you still love me if I put on a stone while we're here?"

"How much is a stone?" she teased.

"It's fourteen pounds, and I may have already gained that much."

"I doubt that very much. You've probably gained only a few pounds. I know I have, as well, but we're on vacation. If you don't gain a bit of weight on vacation, you haven't properly enjoyed yourself."

"In that case, I'd better get the cookie thing," Daniel said as she pulled into the restaurant's parking lot.

Fenella laughed. "That's the spirit."

"We're meeting Linda Hawkins for dinner," Fenella told the man at the door.

"Ah, yes, she's in the private dining room," he told her. "It sounds fancy, doesn't it?" he added with a wink. "It probably was when the place was first built, but the wife and I aren't interested in having special events in there. Anyway, Linda's back there with her fiancé, waiting for her friends. Do you need me to show you the way?"

Fenella shook her head. She'd eaten there enough to know where she was going. The entrance was obvious, anyway, being halfway along the wall at the back of the restaurant. It had a sign that said "Private" on it. Fenella and Daniel crossed to it and Fenella knocked before she opened the door.

"Fenella, hello," Linda called. "And Daniel, you look extra handsome tonight. What have you two been doing all day?"

Fenella glanced at Daniel.

"She's been drinking," he murmured in her ear.

"We went down to the art galleries," Fenella replied.

"I love our art galleries," Linda told her. "I love everything about Buffalo. You know what else I love? This guy," she said, pointing to Jack, who was frowning and staring at the table.

"How are you?" Fenella asked as she sat down next to Linda.

"I didn't get any lunch. I don't think I had breakfast either. I had dinner last night, didn't I?" she asked Jack.

He nodded.

"Anyway, I haven't eaten lately, and as soon as we got here, I started drinking. It's all gone right to my head, and now I want to hug everyone, and I feel like I might burst into tears at any moment," she continued.

"Maybe you should stop drinking," Fenella suggested as Linda picked up the glass in front of her.

"Jack's way ahead of you," Linda said in a loud whisper. "He took my wine away from me and gave me this glass of water. I'm just waiting until everyone else gets here. I'm sure Melanie will get me a glass of wine, even if Jack won't."

"I'll get you a glass of wine, if that's what you want," Jack said tightly. "I just don't want you to say or do anything you'll regret later."

Linda shrugged. "I'm tired of being careful. I'm tired of being good. I want to drink too much and behave badly and be wild and crazy, just for a few hours. My ex-husband was murdered a few days before my wedding. I think I'm entitled to be wild and crazy, just for a few hours."

"I won't disagree," Jack replied. "But I'm not sure that tonight is the night for wild and crazy. We're supposed to be talking with all of your friends about what happened to George."

"Maybe I don't really care what happened to George," Linda nearly shouted. "He was murdered. It was probably something random. He was probably in the wrong place at the wrong time. It's probably nothing to do with me or with you or with anyone we know." She sighed dramatically. "Don't get me wrong. I'm devastated that he's dead. I loved him dearly and he'll always have a place in my heart, but I'd moved on. I'm getting married again. I'm tired of talking about George."

"Maybe we should go home," Jack said.

"We can still have dinner with my friends. We don't have to talk about George. We can talk about other things," Linda argued.

"You invited them all to come and talk to Daniel about what they could expect from a murder investigation," Jack reminded her.

"Well, that was silly of me," she said. "What was I thinking?"

"Maybe it would be best if we rescheduled this for another time," Daniel suggested.

"But we don't have another time," Linda objected. "Tomorrow night Hazel is giving a lecture and Jack and I both have to be there. The next day we have to grade all of the final exams from our summer classes so that we're done before we go away. Then it's the rehearsal dinner and then it will be our wedding day, the Sunday brunch after, and then our honeymoon. We are going to get to go on our honeymoon, aren't we?"

"You'd have to ask Carol about that," Daniel said.

Linda shook her head. "I shouldn't drink," she said softly. "I thought it would help me forget about everything that's happening, but it's not working."

As she began to cry softly, Jack looked at Fenella. "I'm going to take her home," he said.

She nodded. "I think that's for the best."

"But what will my friends think?" Linda sobbed.

"We'll stay here and have dinner with them," Fenella told her.

"Daniel can answer all of their questions. We'll tell them that you weren't feeling well."

"I'm not feeling well," she agreed.

Jack helped her up and then put his arm around her. "We'll go back to my house," he said softly. "You can have more wine if you want, and I'll make you some dinner. If you need a good cry, you can do that in my arms."

"I love you," Linda said.

"I love you, too," Jack replied.

Fenella blinked back tears as she watched the pair disappear though the door.

"They seem well suited," Daniel said as the door shut behind them.

"I never thought I'd see Jack taking care of someone else like that."

"And now we're stuck with Linda's friends," he sighed.

"Where is Jack?" a voice in the doorway demanded.

Fenella looked up and forced herself to smile. "Mrs. Dawson, hello," she said, swallowing a sigh.

10

"Where's Jack?" Mrs. Dawson repeated.

"Linda wasn't feeling well. He's taken her home," Fenella explained.

"Wasn't feeling well? What was wrong with her?" was the reply.

"I'm not sure," Fenella said, looking at Daniel for help.

"It hardly matters," he said. "You're more than welcome to stay and have dinner with me and Fenella and Linda's friends. I believe they want to discuss the case and murder investigations in general."

"Yes, of course, because you're a homicide detective, aren't you?"

"I'm a CID inspector," he replied. "Shall I tell you some of the differences between policing in the US and UK?"

Mrs. Dawson seemed to give the question some thought. "That might be interesting," she said after a moment.

"Sit here," Daniel suggested, patting the seat next to his. "Fen, can you get us all some drinks?"

"Sure, what do you want?" she asked.

"Lager," he replied.

"A glass of the very best dry white wine they have," Mrs. Dawson said.

Fenella nodded and then left the room. The man who'd been at the door was standing behind the small bar in the back corner of the main dining room.

"I saw Linda leaving. Are you staying for dinner?" he asked when she'd reached him.

"Linda's friends are still supposed to be coming. I'm not sure what's keeping them, actually," she replied.

"Linda told me that everyone else would be coming around six thirty," he told her. "She and Jack came early to make sure they could use the room."

"She told us six," Fenella sighed, glancing at her watch. Could she survive twenty-two more minutes with Jack's mother before the others arrived?

"Did you want drinks, then?" the man asked.

"Yes, please, one beer, one glass of a dry white wine, and I'll have a soda because I'm driving."

"Any white wine?"

"Whatever you have, but if anyone asks, I ordered the most expensive one you have available."

He laughed. "We only have one white wine that we sell by the glass and we only have a handful of bottles of wine on the menu. Our customers aren't typically wine drinkers."

"I'll warn you now that I'm going to complain to everyone else that I was charged an absolute fortune for this glass," she told him as he poured the wine out of a huge jug.

He nodded. "This is for that older woman, isn't it? She's going to be very demanding, isn't she?"

"I suspect so. The last time I had dinner with her, she sent her meal back three times."

"I knew I should have bought that lawn care business," he sighed. "My wife thought having a restaurant would be more fun. Fun? Ha! You see how much fun it is? She isn't even here. She decided after the first month that she couldn't take the 'fun' anymore and went out and got a full-time job."

Fenella laughed. "I'm sorry. I can't imagine. How long have you owned the restaurant?"

"Nearly a year now and in spite of everything, I mostly love it. You won't believe me when I tell you that we actually get quite busy sometimes."

Fenella glanced around the empty dining room. "I believe you."

"It's a Wednesday night. We're usually pretty empty on a Wednesday, although this is even worse than normal. I think it's because it's such a nice day outside. No one wants to be indoors tonight, do they? Not when they can barbeque at home."

Fenella nodded.

"Don't you worry, though, the chef is in the kitchen and I have two waitresses coming in any minute now. You and your friends will get excellent service and great food."

"I used to eat here when I lived in Buffalo years ago. Have you changed the menu much?"

"Not much, and I've kept the same chef, so if there's something you used to enjoy that isn't still on the menu, he can probably make it anyway."

"All I really want is the cookie," Fenella admitted.

He laughed. "You and everyone else who comes in. I wouldn't dare take that off the menu. We'd go out of business."

"That's the best news I've had all day," Fenella said. "And now I'd better get back in there and rescue my boyfriend."

"He looks as if he'd be able to charm the old dear."

Fenella nodded. "I hope so."

Carrying the drinks, she walked across the room, setting down her soda so that she could open the door.

"...all over the sidewalks," Mrs. Dawson was saying as Fenella walked back into the room.

"That's terrible," Daniel replied.

"It's very upsetting and I simply don't know what to do about it," she said.

"Here we are," Fenella said, passing Daniel his drink. She put Mrs. Dawson's glass down and sighed. "That better be delicious. It was very expensive," she said.

Mrs. Dawson smiled thinly. "Thank you, my dear. Danny was telling me that you inherited a great deal from your aunt. I'm sure you can afford to buy an old woman on a fixed income a drink or two."

Danny? Fenella swallowed a dozen replies and then took a large drink from her soda before she could blurt out anything she might regret later.

"You're very lucky to have found him," Mrs. Dawson continued. "He's very smart and funny and charming."

"Now, Rosalie," Daniel said. "That's quite enough."

Mrs. Dawson shook her head. "I can't imagine what you see in Margaret, really, unless it's her fortune, but I don't think you're the sort of person who would date someone simply because they're wealthy. What is the attraction, Danny?"

Daniel looked at Fenella and cleared his throat. "Fenella is beautiful, smart, funny, sweet, kind, and she fascinates me more than any woman I've ever met before," he said.

Fenella swallowed the lump in her throat. "Thanks," she muttered.

"Well, I suppose I'm happy for both of you, although I do rather wish that Margaret had seen fit to share some of her good fortune with Jack. They were together when she inherited the money, you understand. If they'd been married, he'd have been entitled to half of her inheritance. I do think she should have given him some portion, maybe a quarter."

Don't say anything, Fenella ordered herself. She started counting to ten, but quickly found that wasn't nearly a large enough number. When the door swung open, she was thrilled at the interruption.

"Where's Linda?" Melanie demanded from the doorway.

Fenella stood up and smiled at her. "She wasn't feeling well. Jack has taken her home."

Melanie looked at Karl, who was right behind her in the doorway. "We should just go," she said.

Karl shrugged. "I thought you wanted to talk to the policeman."

"Can you tell us anything useful?" Melanie asked Daniel.

"Probably not," Daniel replied.

Melanie stared at him for a moment and then laughed. "At least he's honest. Linda seemed to think that you'd be able to tell us how a murder investigation works."

"I can tell you how a murder investigation works when I'm the one conducting the investigation. I've no idea how Carol does things, though," Daniel told her.

"It's better than nothing," Karl muttered.

"Is it, though?" Melanie challenged.

"Hello, hello," Howard said as he walked up behind the pair who were still standing in the doorway. "Gloria isn't here yet?"

"Not yet," Fenella told him.

"She said she was going to come straight from work. I wonder what's keeping her," he said.

"Linda wasn't feeling well," Melanie told him. "She's gone home."

"Oh? Does that matter?" he asked. "I thought she'd set this up so that we could talk to, um, the policeman from England. She said it would be our best chance to talk to someone who could explain how murder investigations work. Isn't that why we're here?"

Melanie sighed. "I suppose so. I was just looking forward to spending some time with my best friend, that's all."

"I'm late," Gloria said loudly as she rushed up to join Howard.

"Just a few minutes," he replied. "Why?"

She shrugged. "Traffic was heavy getting out of the city."

He frowned and then nodded slowly. "Maybe we need to talk about that."

"We don't need to talk about anything," Gloria countered. "It's fine."

"It's not fine. I'm not certain it's acceptable," he replied.

"I'm not quitting my job," she said tightly.

"But you're already working more than you're supposed to be. This isn't what I agreed to when you wanted to go back to work," Howard said.

"You do realize that I don't need your permission, don't you?" Gloria snapped.

Howard flushed. "I thought we agreed that it was important that your working didn't negatively impact the rest of the family."

"I'm five minutes late. I'm sorry if you're negatively impacted," Gloria said, her cheeks red with anger.

"You've been late every night this week," Howard replied. "It's not like this is an isolated incident."

"Drinks," Daniel said loudly. "Everyone needs drinks. Menus would be good, too. Let me go and see if I can find a waiter or something."

As he stood up, the four people in the doorway walked farther into the room. Karl and Melanie took seats at the table while Gloria stormed through the room to go and stand in the corner farthest from the door. After a moment, Howard followed her. As Daniel left, the pair began what was obviously a heated whispered argument.

"Danny shouldn't have interrupted," Mrs. Dawson complained. "It was just getting interesting."

"Would you like me to start a fight with Karl for your amusement?" Melanie asked.

"I'd prefer that to discussing that poor man's murder," Mrs. Dawson replied.

"That poor man broke Linda's heart. I have very little sympathy for him," Melanie replied.

"I thought he seemed like a lovely person," Mrs. Dawson said. "He was here to try to win Linda back. Surely that was a good thing."

"He didn't deserve her," Melanie snapped. "She's much happier with Jack and much better off, as well."

"It almost sounds as if you're happy he was murdered," Mrs. Dawson said.

Melanie gasped. "Of course I'm not happy he was murdered. I'm not sorry he died, but that's a very different thing. All things considered, though, I'd much prefer it if he'd simply had a heart attack or been in a tragic car accident. This murder investigation is difficult for all of us."

"Here we are," Daniel said from the doorway. He walked back into the room with the owner on his heels.

"I'll take your drink order after I tell you about today's specials, if that's okay?" the owner asked.

Everything sounded good to Fenella who felt as if she'd had lunch far too many hours earlier.

"Wine," Melanie said. "Anything white."

"You're driving," Karl reminded her.

"You can drive," she told him.

"We came in separate cars."

"So we'll go home in your car and I can come back for mine tomorrow."

"I wasn't planning on going home tonight."

"Who is she?"

"That doesn't matter."

"Of course it matters," Melanie shouted. "You're having another affair. That doesn't surprise me, but you could at least wait until after Linda's wedding before you abandon me altogether."

"I'm not abandoning you altogether. I was just going to stay with a friend tonight. I need to get my mind off murder, that's all."

"And staying with me reminds you of murder?" Melanie laughed bitterly. "Tell me about your friend, then. What's his name?"

Karl shook his head. "We aren't having this conversation right now. Have a drink. Have ten drinks. I'll make sure you get home safely."

Melanie glared at him for a minute and then nodded. "Wine," she said loudly. "Just bring me a bottle of something drinkable."

The owner made a note and then looked at Karl. "Sir?"

"Whiskey, neat," he replied.

"You're driving," Melanie said mockingly.

"One won't hurt."

"Except you never stop at one."

"If you're worried, you can get a taxi home."

"Maybe one of my friends will take me home," Melanie suggested, looking at Gloria.

"I'd rather not get involved," Gloria told her.

Melanie began to laugh. "Of course not. You've never been there for me. You weren't there for Linda when her marriage fell apart, either."

"I tried to help," Gloria protested. "Linda never wanted to see me."

"She never wanted to see me, either. I went to her house anyway. I camped out on her doorstep until she finally gave in and let me in. I was there when she couldn't stop crying, when she insisted that her life was over, when she seriously considered ending her life. That's what friends do for one another."

Gloria flushed. "I did my best. I called her every day for a month, and I listened to her endless babbling about what a wonderful man

George had been and how much she'd loved him. I could have argued. I could have told her what I really thought of George, but I didn't."

"What you really thought of him? What did you really think of him?" Melanie demanded.

"Did anyone else want a drink?" the owner asked a bit desperately.

Fenella ordered another soda, while Daniel asked for a second beer. Mrs. Dawson requested more of the same wine. After a long pause, Gloria asked for a soda and Howard requested tap water.

"Why don't you all sit down?" Daniel suggested as the man went to get their drinks.

As soon as everyone was seated, he was quick to speak again. "When Linda invited me to come tonight, she suggested that some of you had some questions about how murder investigations are typically conducted. I'm afraid I can't tell you anything about how such matters are handled in Buffalo, New York, but I'm happy to walk you through the basic steps that I follow when I conduct a murder investigation, if anyone is interested."

"I want to know how the police work out who's a suspect," Gloria said. "I mean, we were all questioned, but we can't all be suspects. I didn't have any reason to kill George."

"If it was my investigation, you'd all be suspects," Daniel replied, earning himself a scowl from the woman. "I always start with the widest possible pool of suspects and then do what I can to eliminate people from consideration. In this case, anyone who knew George could be considered a suspect."

"But there must be hundreds of people who knew the man. He lived in Buffalo for many years," Karl protested.

Daniel nodded. "So then I would look at which of his former friends and acquaintances knew he was back in the city. Obviously, you all qualify."

"Would you go out and question everyone he knew, though? That would take a long time," Gloria said.

"If I were at home, I'd put a constable on that job. He or she would start with George's former employers and do his or her best to talk to everyone who used to work with the man. Actually, I'd probably put two or three constables on the task, as we're talking about a number of years and several different jobs. The constables would be trying to find people who'd kept in touch with George after he'd left."

"But no one is going to admit to that," Melanie laughed.

Daniel shrugged "Of course, that's always a risk."

"So who else is on the suspect list?" Karl asked.

"I'd have someone investigating where George went after he left Buffalo," Daniel told him. "I'd want to know everything about his life over the past two years."

"I can tell you all of that stuff," Howard said.

Fenella stared at the man. "You can?" she asked.

Howard shrugged. "George and I talked once in a while. We were friends, had been for years."

"Here we are," a pretty blonde woman said as she walked into the room carrying a large tray. "Drinks for everyone." Once she'd passed out the drinks, she took their food order and then disappeared again.

"So, where had he been?" Melanie demanded.

"Pittsburgh," Howard told her.

"Why?" Karl asked.

"He'd met a woman through work. She lived there," Howard explained. "She worked for a different division of the company and they'd talked on the phone and emailed each other a lot when they were working on a project together. When he got sent down there, in the final stages of the project, they finally met and he, well, he fell for her."

"Fell for her?" Melanie echoed. "What does that mean?"

"At the time, he told me that he'd fallen in love," Howard replied. "He'd changed his tune recently, though. When I last talked to him, he said he'd been bewitched by her charms and mistakenly believed himself in love."

"So it didn't work out?" Fenella asked.

"He called me about three months ago to tell me that they'd split up. He had a new address and a new phone number. Apparently, she'd been blowing up his old phone with constant messages begging him to come back."

"So he dumped her?" Melanie asked.

"That's what he said, but, well, he may have lied. He obviously wouldn't have wanted to admit that he'd been dumped."

Melanie nodded. "What do you know about the woman?"

"Not a lot. He said she had the sexiest phone voice he'd ever heard. Apparently, when they first started talking, he was worried that she'd turn out to look nothing like she sounded."

Melanie looked impatient. "Name? Age? Occupation?"

Howard shrugged. "Let me think. I don't remember him ever telling me her name, but he used to talk about her. It may have been Jennifer. I seem to remember him calling her Jenny or maybe Janey."

"It was Jenny," Karl said.

Melanie froze. "You knew about her, too?"

"Only in the early days," he replied. "When they first started talking, he said something to me about a woman at work with an amazing phone voice. He even had me call her, just to hear her voice."

"What did you say to her?" Melanie demanded.

"Nothing much. George called her and then put me on the phone. I just said something like 'nice to meet you' and she said something polite back."

"And did she have a sexy phone voice?" Melanie asked angrily.

Karl chuckled. "She did, actually." He looked at his wife and sobered instantly. "I had no idea that he was thinking of leaving Linda for her. Like I said, this was in the very early days, right after the first few times he'd spoken to her. I had no idea that it was going to lead anywhere."

"And you never spoke to her again?" was Melanie's next question.

Karl flushed. "Just once, about a year ago," he muttered.

"Oh, this should be good," Melanie snapped. "Go on."

"Do you remember when we were looking for a good plumber? I thought maybe George could suggest someone. He and Linda had had new bathrooms installed in their house, after all. Anyway, I called George, but Jenny answered. We only talked for a minute or two, just long enough to establish that George wasn't home. I asked Jenny to have him call me back. That was it."

"And did George call you back?" Daniel asked.

Karl nodded. "A couple of hours later, he called with the name of the plumber he and Linda had used."

"Why didn't you just ask Linda?" Fenella blurted out.

Karl shrugged. "I didn't think she'd know who they'd used. George handled all of their finances and everything."

"I didn't know you had a number for George," Melanie said.

"He called me right after he left Linda," Karl told her. "He gave me his new number and asked me to stay in touch. I only ever called him the one time, though. I knew you'd be upset if you thought I was speaking to him regularly."

"I'm upset that you spoke to him at all," she replied.

He shrugged. "You have to admit that the plumber did a great job."

"And that makes everything okay?" Melanie asked. "The man left his wife for another woman, but as long as he knows a good plumber, all is forgiven?"

"I didn't have a problem with George. What happened between him and Linda was, well, between him and Linda. I'd have probably tried harder to stay in touch with him if I hadn't known it would upset you," he replied.

"You didn't speak to him again after the conversation about plumbers?" Daniel asked before Melanie could speak.

Karl looked at him and then shook his head. "Not until the day before the engagement party. I didn't know that he and Jenny had split up, and I didn't think that he was serious about coming back to Buffalo. I've already admitted that I told him Linda was getting remarried, though."

Daniel looked at Howard. "George called you to tell you that he and Jenny had split?"

"Actually, he called to invite me to a football game and to give me his new number. He only mentioned the breakup when he was explaining why he had a new number," Howard told him.

"Did you go to the football game?" Fenella asked.

He shook his head. "He'd gotten some tickets at the last minute and I was in the middle of a big project at work. I couldn't take time off for a football game on such short notice."

"When did you next speak to him?" Daniel wondered.

Howard sighed. "That was the last time we spoke before he turned up at the engagement party. When we spoke three months ago, he didn't say anything about coming back to Buffalo and we didn't discuss Linda at all."

"You didn't tell him about the engagement party?" Daniel asked.

"I did not," Howard replied firmly.

"But George said it was a man who'd told him," Melanie protested. "It had to have been either Karl or Howard who told him about the engagement party."

"There are other men in the world," Howard said.

"And George may have lied," Karl pointed out.

"Gloria, did you ever speak to George after he left Buffalo?" Daniel asked.

Gloria flushed. "Once, but it was around six months ago. He called the house and I answered. He asked for Howard and I said that Howard wasn't home. As he was apologizing for disturbing me, I recognized his voice. I, well, I said a few things to him about how he'd treated Linda. He tried to argue, to explain, whatever, but I told him I wasn't interested in his distorted version of events and then I hung up on him. I, er, never told Howard that he'd called."

"Thanks," Howard muttered.

"Melanie, what about you?" Daniel asked. "Did you ever speak to George after he left Buffalo?"

Melanie sighed. "I was so angry at him, if I had spoken to him, it would have simply turned into a shouting match. I'm still mad at him, really."

Daniel nodded. "So we still don't know who told George about the engagement party."

"Why does it matter?" Mrs. Dawson asked.

"It may not matter at all," Daniel told her. "It's all part of working out exactly what happened to George, though. It would be helpful to know to whom he was speaking regularly and why that someone told him about the party. Did that person expect George to crash the party? Maybe the person was trying to convince George that Linda had moved on and that there was no point in him coming back to Buffalo.

There are lots of possibilities and the more we know, the closer we get to finding the killer."

"I can't imagine that George stayed in touch with anyone else in Buffalo," Melanie said thoughtfully. "He'd quit his job and I don't think he was particularly friendly with anyone at his office, anyway."

Howard nodded. "He said something to me once about having lost touch with everyone in Buffalo, aside from me."

"But someone told him about the engagement party," Daniel said.

Melanie frowned. "I don't like to say this, especially as she isn't here, but is it possible that Linda told him? Maybe he called her out of the blue and she wanted him to know that she was happy and in love. I'm sure she never expected him to turn up at the party, of course."

"Surely George would have said as much at the party," Fenella suggested.

"Maybe he didn't want to get Linda into trouble with Jack," Melanie suggested. "And now Linda doesn't want to admit to having spoken to him because she's afraid that Jack will be angry."

"He should be, as well," Mrs. Dawson said. "Linda had no business discussing anything with her former husband. If he did call her, she should have simply put the phone down."

"This is all speculation," Fenella reminded her.

"But it makes sense," Mrs. Dawson replied. "Maybe George had decided that he wanted Linda back, so he called her, but she surprised him with the news that she was getting married. Maybe they had a fight and she didn't want to tell Jack and risk upsetting him. It's all very plausible."

"But still speculation," Fenella insisted.

"It's the only thing that fits, though," Melanie said. "No one here told him, that just leaves Linda or Jack."

"Or one of the dozen or so other guests," Fenella suggested.

"George didn't get along with Linda's family when they were married. He would never have called any of them now," Melanie told her. "And the other guests at the party were Jack's friends. George didn't know any of them."

Fenella opened her mouth to argue, but Daniel put a hand on her arm.

"Let's move on," he said. "The police are going to do what they can to work out where Jenny was on the night that George died. They'll also look at her family and friends and anyone who worked with George in Pittsburgh. He must have made some new friends there. They'll all be considered as possible suspects."

Before anyone could reply, the door opened and the waitress walked in with a tray full of food. Once she'd distributed everything and taken refill requests for drinks, she left again.

"Why would anyone from Pittsburgh come all the way to Buffalo to kill the man?" Mrs. Dawson asked. "Surely it would have been easier for them to kill him there."

"Maybe they thought they'd never be a suspect so far from home," Karl suggested.

"So what else are the police doing, besides chasing shadows?" Melanie asked.

"They'll be working to trace George's movements from the time he left Pittsburgh until his death," Daniel told her. "They'll try to find everyone he spoke to, from taxi drivers and waitresses to everyone who was at the party and then at the hotel after the party."

"Surely if anyone saw anything useful, he or she would have told the police, and the police would have already arrested the killer," Mrs. Dawson said.

"Sometimes people see things that they don't recognize as significant," Daniel told her. "If it was my investigation, I'd be making a point of interviewing all of you again in another day or two, taking you back through your statements, trying to get each of you to remember more about the party, about the things that George said, about what was going on around you at the time."

"Maybe someone should 'remember' something helpful," Melanie suggested, putting air quotes around the word "remember."

"If you're suggesting that someone should make something up, I'd advise against it," Daniel said.

"While they're doing all of this stuff, the police are still looking for street thieves and muggers, right? I mean, maybe someone was simply trying to rob George," Karl suggested.

"That's a possibility, and yes, the police will be looking at those possibilities, too. The whole thing will take time, of course, and may prevent Jack and Linda from taking their honeymoon as scheduled," Daniel said.

Melanie frowned. "That's awful."

"And yet, at the party, Linda did threaten to cancel the wedding," Mrs. Dawson said. "I do wonder if that's still a possibility."

"I don't think so," Melanie replied. "When I spoke to Linda earlier today, she sounded very happy about the wedding."

Mrs. Dawson frowned. "There's still time for her to change her mind," she muttered.

"Maybe you should be trying to get Jack to change his mind," Howard suggested.

"Don't think I haven't," Mrs. Dawson muttered darkly. "He's unwilling to listen to me. I don't think he understands that I have his very best interests at heart."

The waitress brought in the second round of drinks and the group began to ask Daniel more general questions about murder investigations. As they ate, Fenella found herself wondering how Gloria would have answered Melanie's earlier question. What did Gloria really think of George? More importantly, had she had an affair with him?

"This has been interesting," Melanie said as she put down her empty wine glass. "I think I need to go home and go to bed."

"I'll put you in a taxi," Karl said.

"Take me home," Melanie replied. She stood up and when Karl did the same, she pulled him into her arm. "Take me home," she whispered loudly in his ear. "You can leave me tomorrow, but for tonight, let's pretend we're still in love."

Karl frowned. "I'll have to send a quick text," he told her.

"Send it. Tell your girlfriend that your wife needs you tonight. She can have you tomorrow."

Karl pulled out his phone and quickly sent a message.

Fenella felt a pang of sympathy for Cindy, assuming that was who was getting the message. It seemed entirely possible that Karl had other women in his life besides his wife and Cindy, though.

As the pair left the room, Howard stood up. "Thank you for an interesting evening," he said to Daniel. "You ready to go?" he asked Gloria.

She shrugged and then looked at Daniel. "We should talk," she said quietly before she got up and left the room with her husband.

"What was that about?" Fenella asked as the door swung shut behind the couple.

"She knows something that she wants to tell someone, but she isn't ready to share it yet," Daniel said with a sigh. "I'm going to have to tell Carol to have another talk with her."

"Or you could take her out for a drink," Mrs. Dawson suggested. "I'm sure Margaret wouldn't mind. It would be work, after all, not personal. Although, I must say, Gloria is quite attractive, don't you think?"

Daniel raised an eyebrow. "She isn't my type," he said flatly. "Are you ready to go?" he asked Fenella.

She nodded. At the bar, she paid for everything, as everyone else seemed to have forgotten about the bill. Mrs. Dawson walked out while they were at the bar. She was getting into a taxi as Fenella and Daniel left the building.

"I don't suppose I can persuade you to frame her for the murder," Fenella said as she and Daniel walked back to the car.

"Don't tempt me," he laughed.

11

"What are we going to do today?" Daniel asked the next morning.

"I feel like we need to track down Gloria," Fenella said.

"That's a job for Carol, not me," he told her. "I told her everything that was said last night. She's going to be talking with everyone again today."

"Including us," Fenella sighed.

"But not until four o'clock. We have the whole day ahead of us. What do you want to do?"

"We don't really have time for Niagara Falls," she sighed. "We could drive up and take a quick look, I suppose."

"Let's leave it for another day. We have another week after the wedding. That can be for sightseeing."

"So what do you want to do today?"

"Can we go to a movie?"

"I suppose so. What do you want to see?"

"I don't know, but I'm sure we can find something we'll both enjoy."

They found a movie theater showing a superhero movie they were both interested in seeing. After a late breakfast, they ate too much popcorn at the movies.

"It was better than I was expecting," Daniel said as they exited the theater.

"It was much better than I was expecting," Fenella told him. "But now it's noon and I should be hungry for lunch and I'm stuffed full of popcorn."

He laughed. "We can have a late lunch. Then it won't matter if we end up talking to Carol until six or later."

"I hope it won't take that long. Why does she want to talk to us?"

"For the same reason that she's talking to everyone again. She'll be going back over statements, hoping people might remember more or be more willing to talk to her now."

"Especially Gloria."

He chuckled. "Maybe, although we've no idea what Gloria wanted to talk with me about. It may not be anything to do with the murder. Maybe she wanted to ask me about getting a job with the police."

"Or about moving to the Isle of Man," Fenella suggested.

"Realistically, it could have been anything. We just want to believe that she knows something that's relevant to the case."

They went to a nearby shopping mall and wandered through the shops, looking at everything, but buying nothing.

"I think I'm happier with our rather more limited shopping options at home," Daniel said as they left.

"Of course, we can always get what we need online if the local shops don't have it."

"That's true. I would imagine shopping on the island was more frustrating even ten or fifteen years ago."

"It can still be very frustrating if the ferries don't sail."

Daniel nodded. "That's the downside of life on a small island."

"One of them, anyway."

"What are some of the others?" he asked.

"Everyone knows me."

He laughed. "You're Mona's niece. Mona was a legend."

Fenella nodded. "I can't really complain, can I? Where are we meeting Carol?"

"At the hotel. She was supposed to be interviewing everyone from the engagement party again today and then going to the hotel to talk to the staff there. I told her we'd meet her in the lobby at four."

"So we need to hurry," Fenella said. "And we never got any lunch."

"You did have a big soft pretzel."

"You ate half of it."

"But it was your pretzel."

Fenella laughed. "It was our pretzel and it was delicious."

"It was delicious, but I'm not sure it was a suitable substitute for lunch."

"If you factor in our early breakfast and that giant tub of popcorn, it's closer."

Daniel chuckled. "I know you're right, but now that we're talking about food, I'm getting hungry."

"We'll have to talk to Carol quickly."

"Unfortunately, I don't think that will be up to us."

Carol was sitting on one of the couches in the lobby when they arrived.

"Good afternoon," she said, getting to her feet as they approached. "I'll start with Fenella, if that's okay with you both?"

"Sure," Daniel said. "I'll just wait here."

Fenella frowned. She'd been expecting that they'd all talk together, although she wasn't sure why.

Carol turned and walked across the room. Fenella rushed to catch up to her as Carol opened the door to a small conference room.

"We're in here today," she told Fenella, gesturing for her to step into the room.

Inside the room, there were a few chairs around a long rectangular table. Carol had left paper and a pen on the table, along with several bottles of water.

"Help yourself to water if you want some," she told Fenella as she sat down. "And have a seat."

Fenella sat down and took a water bottle. She drank a sip while she waited for Carol to begin.

"Let's work backwards," Carol said after a moment. "Daniel's given me his account of the various conversations you've had with the men and women involved in the case since the murder. I'd like to hear your version of all of those conversations. Start with last night, unless you've seen anyone today?"

Fenella shook her head. "We went to a movie."

She'd finished her water by the time she'd worked her way backward through the last few days. Carol let her stop when she got back to when she and Daniel had first arrived in Buffalo.

"Thank you," Carol said, putting down her pen. "Your accounts match Daniel's almost exactly. That might make me suspicious, if I wasn't aware that you've both had a good deal of practice at this."

Fenella flushed. "I'd be quite happy to have this be the last murder investigation in which I'm ever involved."

"Because I know that you've been through this before, I want to ask you to share your thoughts with me," Carol told her. "This is all strictly off the record. It won't go into your statement or even into my notes, but I'm curious. Tell me what you think of each of the people you've met over the last few days."

"What I think of them?"

"Let's start with Linda. Do you like her? Are you happy that she's marrying your former lover? Do you think they'll live happily ever after?"

Fenella took a deep breath. "I'm not sure how to answer all of that," she said.

"As I said, this is off the record. I'm simply interested in your opinion."

"When I first met her, I liked her a lot. She seems to make Jack happy and she seems to be genuinely in love with him. Since that first meeting, well, she hasn't been at her best."

"So you like her less now than you did at first."

"I have more concerns about her now than I did at first," Fenella corrected her. "Some of that has to do with what George said about her having her own version of events. I want to like her and I want to believe that she and Jack will be happy together, but I will admit to being more worried about their future now than I was before George arrived."

"Did her behavior last night upset you?"

"I wasn't thrilled that she got drunk and then left before anyone else arrived, but I can understand how she felt. If I hadn't been driving, I might have had a drink or two myself."

"Tell me about the incident on Grand Island again."

"I don't know what I can tell you. Apparently, she was upset because George hadn't met her for lunch as planned and that caused her to get a bit lost when she was meant to be on her way to our hotel to meet Jack."

Carol nodded. "And when you arrived on Grand Island, how upset did she seem?"

"She was actually quite calm, but she'd had some time to pull herself together."

"Is it possible that she'd exaggerated just how upset she was when she spoke with Jack?"

"Maybe."

"Did she ever cheat on George?"

Fenella blinked several times. The question had surprised her. "I have no idea," she said eventually.

"She's on record as saying that George cheated on her. If you knew your husband was cheating, wouldn't you be tempted to cheat as well?"

"If I knew my husband was cheating, I'd throw him out and file for divorce."

"But Linda never did that. Why?"

"I don't know. Maybe because she was in love with George? Maybe because she felt as if they belonged together, even if he did cheat now and then? I don't know and I don't understand it because I would never let a man treat me that way, but that doesn't mean I can't sympathize with her."

Carol nodded. "Do you think she cheated?"

"No, I don't. I think she was faithful to him, but that's just my impression of her as a person. I could be wrong."

"Do you think she killed George?"

Fenella took a deep breath. "No, not really. I hate to sound horrible, but I can't see her being brave enough to do it or clever enough to get away with it."

"What do you think of Melanie?"

"I feel sorry for her, because I know her husband is cheating on her. I keep thinking I should tell her, but then I think I probably shouldn't get involved."

"Do you think she's had affairs, too?"

"Maybe," Fenella said after a moment. "I think she's more likely to have done so than Linda, anyway. I don't understand why she stays with Karl anymore than I understand why Linda stayed with George, though."

"Maybe she loves Karl," Carol suggested.

Fenella frowned. "Regardless, I can't see them staying together for much longer. I suspect they'll separate after the wedding."

"And do you think that's a good thing?"

"They don't seem to be making each other happy when they're together, so maybe splitting up will be good for both of them. I feel rather sorry for Cindy, Karl's girlfriend, though, as I can't see him staying with her in the long term."

"Any other thoughts on Melanie before we talk about Karl?"

"She seems to be a truly devoted friend to Linda. She was furious with George on Linda's behalf. That doesn't mean that I think she killed him, though. That's probably pushing friendship too far."

"Would she have helped Linda cover up the murder, if Linda had killed him?"

"Yes, I think so," Fenella said, giving the matter some thought. "Like if Linda met him for a drink and then, I don't know, stabbed him to death in the parking lot, I can see her calling Melanie and asking for help in getting rid of the body."

"Give me your opinion of Karl, then."

"I don't like him," Fenella said flatly. "He cheats on his wife and I suspect he has more than one other woman in his life. Cindy seemed like a nice woman and if I ever see her again, I'm going to tell her that she can do much better."

"Can you see him being the killer?"

"I don't know that he had a motive, but if he did, then, maybe."

"Gloria?"

"She knows something or thinks she knows something. Melanie thought she'd had an affair with George years ago. She and Howard were fighting last night about her job. I know all of those things, but I've barely even spoken to the woman and I really haven't had a chance to form an impression of her."

"Did you see or hear anything at the engagement party that gave you the impression that she and George were more than friends?"

"I don't remember seeing them interact at all, which isn't to say that they seemed to be avoiding one another."

"Can you see her as the killer?"

"I don't know her well enough to answer that. I can't imagine a motive for her, unless she did have an affair with George years ago. Maybe he treated her badly and she was just waiting for a chance to get revenge on him."

"If Linda needed help getting rid of a body, would she call Gloria?"

Fenella shook her head. "Melanie is her best friend. She and Gloria haven't been close in years, at least that's how I understand it. I mean, maybe, if she was truly desperate, but I don't think she likes Gloria very much."

"What about Howard? What do you think of him?"

"Again, I've barely spoken to him. I didn't like his attitude last night when he and Gloria were talking about her job, but I know I heard only a tiny snippet of their argument, so I won't hold it against him, too much."

Carol grinned. "Not too much? Lucky him."

Fenella shrugged. "I know very little else about him."

"Can you see him as the killer?"

"Again, I don't know what motive he might have had. I suppose if his wife did have an affair with George, he might have wanted to kill him."

"He'd had a great many years in which to do so before last Friday."

"Maybe he just found out about the affair," Fenella suggested. "Maybe Gloria just told him or maybe he found out another way.

Maybe George got in touch with Gloria to let her know that he was coming back to Buffalo. Perhaps Howard overheard a conversation between the two and realized that they'd been a couple in the past. I suppose it's possible that Gloria and George kept on seeing one another for years and years and that Howard finally found out."

"What about Jack? How deeply in love with Linda is he?"

"He seems crazy about her. He's definitely more in love with her than he ever was with me."

"Crazy enough to kill for her?"

"This is going to sound odd, but I think he might be crazy enough to kill for her, but only if the idea occurred to him and he'd given it a lot of thought. Jack doesn't rush into anything. I think it would have taken him several days to decide to kill George and then at least as long again for him to plan the murder and then work up the nerve to actually do it."

"How long have he and Linda been together?"

"Not long," Fenella admitted. "I was shocked when he proposed so quickly, but even so, I can't see him killing George the same night that he met the man."

"They were staying in the same hotel. What if he went outside to get some fresh air and found George doing the same thing? Maybe they argued and Jack killed him accidentally."

"I suppose that's remotely possible, but I think it's unlikely. If nothing else, if Jack had killed him, I can't imagine him doing anything other than panicking completely as he stood over the body."

"Maybe he called a friend and that friend came and helped him get rid of the body."

"Maybe," Fenella said, not bothering to hide the doubt in her tone.

"Next question, would he have helped Linda get rid of the body?"

"If she called him, I'm sure he would have tried, but he's not at his best in an emergency. He was badly shaken when Linda called him from Grand Island and I had to distract him to get him over the bridge. If I were Linda, Jack is the last person I'd call if I needed help hiding a body."

"If you were Linda, who would you call?"

Fenella thought for a minute. "I suppose I'd call Melanie. She's Linda's best friend and she seems like the type to stay calm in a crisis."

"What about Jack's mother? Would she be any help in a crisis?"

"Jack's mother could murder someone in cold blood and hide the body without batting an eyelash. She'd be an excellent person to call in a crisis, except I wouldn't trust her in the slightest. If Linda called her for help, I can see her blackmailing Linda into canceling the wedding as a consequence."

"So if the wedding gets canceled, I should take another look at Mrs. Dawson."

"I really hope the wedding doesn't get canceled."

"Even though you have doubts about Linda?"

"Whatever my doubts, assuming she didn't kill George, I think she and Jack will be happy together."

"And if she did kill George?"

"Then I hope Jack won't marry her, but he might still go ahead, because he truly is crazy about her."

The pair chatted for a bit longer about the case, but Fenella didn't think they were getting anywhere. Eventually, Carol looked at her watch and sighed.

"I'm taking up far too much of your time and I still need to talk to Daniel. Would you mind telling him to come in now? If I were you, I'd go and sit at the bar and drink steadily until he's done."

Fenella laughed as she got to her feet. "A drink sounds awfully good right now," she admitted.

"She's ready for you now," she told Daniel, who was playing a game on his phone when she reached him.

"Great. I'm losing, anyway," he said.

"I'll be in the bar," Fenella added as she walked away.

"Ah, good evening," the bartender said as Fenella slid onto a stool. "You were here the other night, weren't you? Having a drink with the man who, um, the man we, um, you know what I mean."

Fenella nodded. "I was here when George came in for a drink on Friday night and I was also in the parking lot right after his body was found."

The man frowned. "I hope he wasn't a good friend of yours."

"I'd only just met him that night and we'd barely spoken."

"It's still really sad, of course."

"Yes, of course."

"I spent another hour with the police this afternoon, going back over everything that I could remember from Friday night. It wasn't much, I have to say, and it isn't like I can suddenly remember more now that some time has passed."

Fenella nodded. "I just spent an hour with Carol Gregory."

"In that case, your first drink is on me," he laughed. "You were drinking soda the other night. What can I get you tonight?"

"How about a screwdriver? I can pretend it's healthy, because it's mostly orange juice," she replied after some thought.

"Sure, coming right up."

He walked away and Fenella watched as he filled a glass with ice and then added orange juice and vodka. "Here you are," he said a moment later, putting the drink in front of her.

"Thank you very much."

"When I talked to the police again today, I didn't get the feeling that they were ready to arrest anyone. It felt very much like they were still casting around rather desperately, looking for clues," he said as she took her a sip.

"Murder investigations are complicated," Fenella told him. "Unless it's immediately obvious who the killer is, the police have to put a lot of time and effort into their investigation."

"You've been involved in murder investigations before?"

"Yes, once or twice," she said with a sigh. "And my, er, boyfriend is a police inspector where I live now. I know more about murder investigations than most people."

"Any idea when they'll solve this one, then?"

"None whatsoever. You know as much as I do about the investigation, really, although I have seen some of the suspects since the murder."

"You have? I don't even know who the suspects are."

"The man who was killed, George Hawkins, used to live in Buffalo. He'd moved away, but he'd come back to try to persuade his ex-wife, Linda, to give him another chance. Linda is getting married on Saturday, which is why I'm in Buffalo. I came for the wedding." Fenella knew that everything she was telling him had been in the local Buffalo newspaper. Surely the man had read the coverage?

"Wow, so you're friends with Linda?"

"Yes, although I just met her on Friday, as well. The groom invited me to the wedding. He and I are old friends."

"Got it. So are both of them suspects?"

"Everyone in Buffalo is a suspect," Fenella said. "Or nearly, anyway."

"Surely I'm not a suspect. I didn't know the man."

"You served him a drink or two. Did you talk to him at all?"

The man shrugged. "Yeah, actually, after you left, he came and sat at the bar. We talked a bit between customers."

"What did you talk about?" Fenella had to ask.

The bartender looked at her and laughed. "I probably shouldn't tell you, but we talked about women. He said something about not being able to trust any of them. I, well, I thought he was talking about you, really, since he'd rushed over to talk to you as soon as he saw you."

"He definitely wasn't talking about me."

"Whatever, he said women couldn't be trusted and I agreed. My wife and I have been having a lot of trouble lately and I think she's cheating. I told George that, and he nodded and told me that women always cheat. Then he laughed and said that men always cheat, too. That's who the women are cheating with, after all. And then I said that one of my ex-girlfriends had taken up with another woman."

"And then what?" Fenella asked when the man went silent.

"Oh, he laughed and said that our lives would be a lot easier if women would all take up with one another and leave us alone. I'll be right back." The man walked to the other end of the bar. The man sitting there had been waving for a minute or two, trying to get the bartender's attention.

Fenella sipped her drink and tried to decide if anything she was hearing was important.

"Of course it's important," a voice said in her ear.

Fenella jumped and then glared at Mona, who'd slid onto the barstool next to her.

"Don't say anything," Mona told her. "Just think really hard and I should be able to work out what you want to say."

"Why are you here?" Fenella thought.

"No, I'm not getting it. Think harder," Mona told her.

"How am I supposed to think harder?" Fenella thought. *"This is ridiculous."*

"I was hoping the murderer would be behind bars by now," Mona said. "Clearly the Buffalo police need my help in solving the case."

"I'm sure they'd be delighted if you'd offer. Go and talk to Carol Gregory. She's in charge," Fenella thought, taking a sip of her drink to try to stop her lips from moving.

"No need to be sarcastic," Mona replied. "Ms. Gregory can't see or hear me, otherwise I might do just that. As it is, I have to work with what I have, which is you. When the bartender gets back, get him to tell you about the rest of the conversation. I'm especially interested in what happened at the end. Why did George leave? Did he say where he was going?"

Fenella opened her mouth to reply as the bartender returned.

"Ready for another drink?" he asked, gesturing toward her half-empty glass.

"Yes, please," she replied, quickly finishing what was in her glass while he made her another.

"You were telling me about your conversation with George," she reminded him when he put the fresh drink down in front of her.

He flushed. "I'd rather not repeat the next part of the conversation," he said. "George made a few comments about why women are useful and about, well, women doing things with other women. It was just guys talking, if you know what I mean."

Fenella shrugged. "And then what?" she asked.

"He pulled out his phone and sent a few text messages, all the while muttering about how women weren't worth the trouble. About ten minutes later, he got a text back. I don't know who it was from or what is said, but it made him smile."

"He didn't say anything about it?"

"He said something about some women being reliable, even after they'd been treated badly. As he was getting up, he added that women who were cheating were the best to cheat with, or something like that."

"You've told the police all of this, haven't you?"

"Yeah, sure. The detective I spoke to didn't seem all that interested, though."

Fenella took a sip of her drink while she tried to think.

"What did George do next?" Mona demanded.

"And that's when George left?" Fenella asked.

"Yeah, he said that thing about women cheating and then he headed for the door. He was halfway there when he looked back at me and said something about seeing me in half an hour. He said: 'Pretend I haven't already been in, okay? Wouldn't want her to know that I've already been drinking,' and then he left."

"So he was going to meet a woman," Mona said.

"He was going to meet a woman," Fenella said. "I'm sure the police were interested in that fact."

The bartender shrugged. "They didn't act interested in anything, but maybe they did that on purpose so I wouldn't know what mattered."

"Quite possibly," Fenella told him.

"Surely a woman didn't kill him," the bartender argued.

"Women are quite capable of murder," Fenella replied.

He shrugged. "Whoever killed him had to have lifted him into that dumpster. I can't see a woman managing that."

"Unless she talked him into climbing into the dumpster before she killed him," Fenella replied. "And before you ask, I've no idea how she might have done that, I'm just saying it's possible."

"How would you talk someone into climbing into a dumpster? I can't even imagine," he replied.

"Guns can be very persuasive," Fenella suggested.

"I suppose," he replied, sounding doubtful.

"How many drinks ahead of me are you?" Daniel asked as he slid onto the barstool next to Fenella.

She hid a smile as Mona quickly faded away before he could sit on her. "This is my second," she told him. "But I feel as if I want quite a few more."

He nodded. "I'll have a gin and tonic," he told the bartender. "Should we get a table?" he asked Fenella.

"Yes, let's," she agreed, eager to tell him everything that she'd learned from the bartender.

They took their drinks to a table in the corner. It didn't take long for Fenella to repeat the conversation she'd had with the man behind the bar.

"Interesting. So George left the bar to meet a woman," he said when she was done.

"And it sounds very much as if it was a married woman," Fenella suggested.

"Or one who was otherwise involved," Mona said as she sat down opposite Fenella. "Which means Linda is still very much a possibility."

Fenella bit her tongue before she could accidentally reply to Mona.

"Married or at least involved with someone else," Daniel said thoughtfully. "Of course, the woman in question may not have had anything to do with the murder."

"But she probably did," Fenella said.

"Of course she did," Mona insisted.

Daniel shrugged. "If it were my case, I would be very careful about jumping to conclusions. As it isn't my case, I'm happy to agree that whomever George left the bar to meet was probably involved in his murder in some way."

"Do you think she might have been setting him up for someone else?" Fenella asked.

"I'm not certain what to think. The bartender was right about how difficult it would have been to get the body into the dumpster. I suppose it's just possible that someone managed to get him into the dumpster while he was still alive, though."

Fenella finished her drink and looked at her watch. "It's getting late and we haven't had dinner."

"Let's go upstairs," Daniel suggested. "We can order from room service and get a bottle of wine, too."

"That sounds wonderful," Fenella replied. She looked over at Mona. *"Feel free to stay down here,"* she thought hard.

Mona laughed. "I've no interest in getting in the way of your romantic evening. I'll stay down here and see if I can learn anything else about the night George died."

"*Stay out of trouble*," Fenella thought as she followed Daniel toward the door.

"I'm already dead. I can't possibly get into trouble," Mona replied with a laugh.

❧ 12 ❧

Fenella rolled over and looked at the clock. It was three in the morning and she should have been fast asleep.

"Come into the en suite so we can talk," Mona whispered in her ear.

"I want to sleep," she muttered.

"You can sleep later. Don't wake Daniel."

Fenella sighed as she slipped out of the bed and walked over to the bathroom. She sat down on the side of the bathtub and glared at her aunt who'd floated in behind her.

"My goodness, you do look cross," Mona said.

"I'm tired. You woke me up. This better be important."

Mona shrugged. "Never mind. I'll go."

"Wait, don't go. What did you learn?"

"I learned that the bartender is married, but he isn't happy. He was flirting with two different women for most of the evening, but he went home alone in the end."

"Is that all?"

"Not entirely. I also learned that the front desk manager who works in the evenings spends most of his time napping in the office behind the desk."

"The man who was working the night George died?"

Mona nodded. "I wandered out to the desk and there wasn't anyone there. It only took me a minute to follow the sounds of his snores and track him down, though."

"So he may have missed seeing George with his killer."

"I'm pretty certain he did miss seeing George with his killer," Mona replied. "He probably told the police that he was working on paperwork in the office or some such thing, but I think it's far more likely that he was fast asleep."

Fenella frowned. "While that's interesting, I can't see that it helps with the case in any way."

"Maybe the man could be persuaded to tell a few of the suspects that he saw them with George that night," Mona said thoughtfully. "Or rather, maybe you should tell a few of the suspects that the manager mentioned to you that he had seen them with George that night. When one of them tries to kill the manager, we'll know who killed George."

Fenella stared at her aunt for a minute and then slowly shook her head. "I'm going to assume that this is all a bad dream," she said eventually. "There's no way you'd ever suggest setting someone up for a murder attempt."

"We wouldn't let her get away with it, of course," Mona said. "Whichever her it turned out to be."

"What makes you so certain it was a woman?"

"The bartender said George left to meet a woman, and a married woman at that. The killer has to be have been either Melanie or Gloria, therefore."

"Unless one of their husbands followed them here and then killed George," Fenella suggested.

Mona frowned. "I suppose that's possible, but regardless, if you tell the two women that the manager saw them the night of the murder, one of them will admit to having been here."

"Unless she helped her husband kill George or helped him get rid of the body. Why am I even arguing with you? It's a stupid idea. That sort of thing could get someone killed. Murderers are not the kinds of people with whom I want to play silly games."

"But we could help the police solve the case and put the killer behind bars."

"Or we could get another man killed. Or you could be completely wrong about who George was meeting and we could end up just complicating things. If one of the women goes to Carol and tells her that I've been putting words into the manager's mouth, Carol might just arrest me for something."

"Who else might he have been meeting?"

"I've no idea. There are quite a few married women in Buffalo, though. Maybe he was seeing someone from work or one of his old neighbors or something."

"Where did he used to work?"

"I don't know. I don't really know anything about the man."

Mona frowned. "In that case, I'm going to assume that either Melanie or Gloria killed him. If I have to pick one, it would be Gloria. Melanie said she had an affair with George, after all."

"Melanie said she'd had some suspicions, years ago. She may have been wrong and, regardless, it was a long time ago."

"Maybe they'd kept seeing one another in secret."

"Maybe, or maybe they never had an affair at all."

"What about Melanie?"

"What about her?"

"Maybe she had an affair with George."

Fenella shook her head. "She's Linda's best friend. She wouldn't do that."

"A woman I'd once considered a very dear friend tried to take Max away from me. Of course, she didn't succeed, and that was the end of our friendship, but some women simply don't value their female friends as much as they should."

Max was Maxwell Martin, the man with whom Mona had fallen in love at eighteen. He'd moved her into a room in one of the luxury hotels he owned and he'd showered her with gifts and funded her extravagant lifestyle until his death decades later.

Fenella sighed. "I don't know who killed George Hawkins and, at the moment, I'm too tired to care. I'm going back to bed. We have another day of sightseeing to get through and then the next day is the rehearsal dinner. I need some sleep."

"I may just go and visit Melanie," Mona said. "Maybe she'll be standing in her bathroom, trying to wash her hands clean of the blood that she spilled."

"Or maybe she'll be asleep," Fenella said. She shook her head as she walked back to the bed. *At least I can sleep late in the morning*, she thought as she slid under the covers again.

❧

"Good morning," Daniel's voice whispered in her ear.

Fenella opened one eye. "What time is it?" she asked.

"Seven," he replied. "I'm wide awake. I thought I might go for a run. I haven't done any running since we've been here."

"Sure, go," Fenella said, shutting her eyes tightly.

"I just didn't want you to wake up and wonder where I'd gone," he explained. "I'll be back in an hour or so. We can get breakfast."

"Yes, great," she muttered, rolling over and pulling the covers over her head. She could hear Daniel chuckling as he left the room.

Five minutes later, she sighed and sat up. "Now I can't get back to sleep," she grumbled. After a moment's thought, she reached for her mobile phone to try to find something for her and Daniel to do with their day. When he got back from his run, she was showered and dressed and ready to go out.

"I'm going to need a quick shower," he told her. "And then we're going to talk about American drivers."

She laughed. "Was it awful?"

He just shook his head and then disappeared into the bathroom. When he came back out, his hair was wet and smelled of the hotel's soap and his aftershave. Fenella pulled him into a kiss.

"I love that aftershave," she told him.

"I'll start wearing it more often," he laughed. "Ready for some breakfast?"

"I thought maybe after breakfast we could go antiquing," Fenella said as they took the elevator to the lobby.

"Antiquing?"

"There's an antique mall in Clarence, which is one of the North-town suburbs," she explained. "It's not so much a mall as a bunch of shops and storage units, but it's always an interesting place to spend a few hours."

"Northtown?" Daniel asked.

"The outskirts of the city are divided into the Southtowns and the Northtowns, based on whether they're, well, north or south of the city," Fenella explained.

He nodded. "Antiquing could be fun, but I don't know how we'd get anything home if we buy anything."

"It isn't just furniture, though, there are units full of books and CDs and just about anything and everything you can imagine. I wasn't planning on buying anything anyway, but if I do, it won't be furniture."

"In that case, let's go."

"After breakfast," she said as her stomach grumbled.

Fenella ate far too much breakfast, and then she drove them out to Clarence, where they spent several hours wandering through antique shops, looking at everything from old comic books to large items of furniture, and stained-glass windows from an old church.

"Lunch?" Fenella suggested as they left the last store.

"Yes, please. I've been hungry for the last hour, but I didn't want to miss anything."

"What did you think of it all?"

"It was an odd mix of car boot sales, market stalls, and antique shops. I've never seen anything quite like it."

"So it was an experience, even if all you bought was a few books."

"I'm very excited about my books. One is a book I've never actually read by one of my favorite authors, and the other is a book I've read a dozen or more times before but don't actually own. I lent my copy to a friend, actually, and I never got it back. And I only paid a dollar each for them. They were quite a bargain."

Fenella nodded. "There's a delicious Italian restaurant out here. Let's go there for lunch."

"Sounds great."

After a wonderful meal, they walked back out to the car.

"And now we should go back to the hotel and have an early night," Fenella suggested.

"We've gone all day without seeing anyone involved in the case," Daniel replied as they got into the car.

"Hasn't it been wonderful?" Fenella said with a sigh. "We won't be as lucky tomorrow. Tomorrow is the rehearsal dinner."

Back at the hotel, they had a drink in the bar.

"It's a different bartender tonight," Fenella remarked as they took seats at one of the tables.

"Does it matter?" Daniel asked.

"Not at all," she replied.

❧

"I'm going down to the gym," Daniel said in her ear the next morning.

"The gym?" she muttered, trying to work out where she was and why Daniel was there.

"It has to be safer than trying to run outside again," he told her before he left the room.

Once he'd left, Fenella again found that she couldn't get back to sleep. By the time Daniel returned, she was ready for the day.

"I'll shower quickly," he promised. "What are we doing today?"

"Want to walk around some old boats?"

"The ones we could see when we walked along Canalside?"

"Those are the ones."

"Sure, why not?"

They toured the Buffalo Naval Park and then had lunch in the city before heading back to their car.

"We've only a few hours before the rehearsal dinner," Daniel said. "What do you want to do?"

"I've no idea. We could go to another mall, or we could just go for a long drive, or, I don't know, something."

He chuckled. "Do you think anyone would mind if we turned up at the actual wedding rehearsal?"

"I don't know. We aren't needed, as we aren't in the wedding party. Why did you want to go to the rehearsal?"

"Because I'm interested in seeing the various suspects again, but I don't think we should tell Jack and Linda that."

Fenella laughed. "I could ask them if we can come so that you can get a sneak peek at an American wedding. You'd hate to do something wrong tomorrow, after all."

"I would, at that. Are American weddings vastly different to British ones?"

"I've never been to a British one, so I don't know."

"Now I'm worried about doing something wrong tomorrow."

"I'm sure you'll be fine," Fenella said. "But I can ask Jack if we can go to the rehearsal anyway. With which of the suspects did you want to speak again?"

"All of them, really. What the bartender told you has raised my interest in Melanie and Gloria, and also in their husbands."

"You think George was meeting one of them the night he died?"

"Maybe, and maybe a jealous husband followed whichever of them it was that George was meeting."

"You think a man killed him?"

"I don't know, but I don't want to narrow down my list of suspects to just those two women."

"Of course, George could have been meeting anyone in the city. We know nothing about his former work colleague, for example."

Daniel nodded. "I may be grasping at straws, but I was really hoping to have a relaxing and enjoyable holiday with you and that's not going to happen while we're caught up in a murder investigation."

"So you want to do your own investigating."

"So I want to talk to the sus, er, let's call them witnesses, actually. I want to talk to the witnesses."

"Melanie thought that Gloria had had an affair with George, but years ago."

"And maybe it never ended," Daniel suggested.

"Or maybe Melanie had an affair with George."

"Also a possibility, although I'd feel terrible for Linda if that proved to be the case."

Fenella nodded. "I can't imagine doing that to a friend."

"So, before we drive away, text Jack and see if we can, um, crash the rehearsal."

She sent the message and then tapped on the steering wheel while she waited for a reply. It arrived after a few minutes.

"You and Daniel are more than welcome at the rehearsal. We're meeting on the lawn at three," she read out.

"That doesn't give us much time," Daniel said. "Maybe we should go back to the hotel and get changed."

Jack was pacing back and forth across the grass in front of the building that housed the university's history department when Fenella and Daniel arrived.

"Well, at least you're here," he muttered as they approached him.

"Who isn't here?" Fenella asked.

"Everyone else," Jack snapped. "Linda had car trouble, but she should be here soon. Melanie had trouble getting away from work, but she's on her way, or so I'm told. No one seems to know where Karl is, but I'm told that isn't unusual and that he'll turn up eventually. But what if eventually is too late? We get just one chance to walk through everything before tomorrow. What if he misses the rehearsal and doesn't know what to do tomorrow?"

"Are he and Melanie your wedding party?" Fenella asked.

Jack nodded. "Obviously, Linda wanted Melanie as her, well, to stand up with her. I don't really have anyone that I wanted to ask, so it seemed easiest to just have Karl do the same for me."

"And that's it?" Fenella checked.

"For the actual wedding party, yes," Jack replied. "We've invited Howard and Gloria to dinner later tonight because Linda felt funny about leaving them out since Melanie and Karl were going to be there. Linda said something about having all of her nearest and dearest around her on the night before the wedding."

"And us," Fenella laughed.

Jack nodded. "You're one of my nearest and dearest."

Fenella flushed and blinked back a tear. "Thanks. Who else will be at dinner?"

"My mother, of course, but she's supposed to be here, too. Oh, heck, I forgot about her. She was going to come in a taxi, because I was teaching until half an hour ago. Where is she?" Jack fretted.

"Why don't you call her?" Fenella suggested.

Jack nodded and pulled out his mobile. He punched in numbers as he walked a short distance away.

"This is awkward," Daniel murmured. "I was expecting more of a crowd."

"I never really thought about the wedding party," Fenella told him. "Now that you mention it, though, it does seem as if there should be more of one."

"Jack, come and help me this instant," a voice shouted.

Fenella turned and spotted Jack's mother making her way down the sidewalk. She was limping slightly as she wobbled forward on heels that were clearly too high for her to walk in comfortably.

"I'll go," Daniel said as Jack gestured toward his phone.

"Danny, what a dear, sweet man you are," Mrs. Dawson gushed as Daniel let her take his arm. "The taxi driver insisted that he couldn't get any closer to this building than a parking lot that was half a mile away."

"There isn't any parking for this building," Fenella told her. "All of the parking is in central locations, but he shouldn't have had to leave you half a mile away, either."

Mrs. Dawson sighed. "I'm quite certain that he hadn't the first clue where anything was on this campus. If I hadn't objected, he would have left me at the front entrance and I would have had to walk for miles and miles."

"Well, you're here now," Fenella said brightly.

"And we'll drive you from here to the dinner," Daniel added. "Assuming you don't want to ride with Jack and Linda, that is."

Mrs. Dawson made a face. "I'd much rather ride with you, Danny," she said, smiling up at him. "Jack has far too much on his mind. He'd probably forget all about me and leave me behind."

"He is getting married tomorrow," Daniel said. "I remember being incredibly nervous the night before my wedding."

"You've been married before, then? I do hope you weren't left a widower, but I can't imagine anyone not wanting to be married to you. Your first wife must have died. I'm so sorry," Mrs. Dawson said.

Daniel shook his head. "My first wife inherited some money and decided that she wanted to leave me and travel the world."

"My goodness, she sounds just like Margaret. Of course, you didn't meet Margaret until after she'd inherited her fortune, but the similarities are uncanny. Margaret always used to talk endlessly about wanting to travel. No doubt, now that she's worth a fortune, one of these days soon she'll decide to take a cruise or spend a month in Australia or something."

"Are you planning on going somewhere?" Daniel asked Fenella.

She was relieved to hear that he sounded amused, rather than upset by what Mrs. Dawson was saying. "Maybe we should run away together," she replied in a teasing tone.

"Mother, come and sit down," Jack said, gesturing toward the chairs that were being quickly set up on top of a large rectangle of white cloth.

"I'm fine here," she replied. "Danny is looking after me."

"You will sit down once the rehearsal starts, won't you?" Jack demanded.

"Are you going to sit down?" she asked Daniel.

He nodded. "I wanted a chance to see how the ceremony differs from a typical British wedding so that I don't make any horrible social blunders tomorrow," he told her.

She patted his arm. "You're far too sophisticated to make any blunders, but I'm awfully glad you came tonight. I was quite worried that I'd have to sit all by myself."

"I'm so sorry," Linda called as she approached, nearly running. "I had to take my car to the garage because it was making this really strange noise, but they couldn't get it to make the noise, and then...but you really don't want to hear all of that," she laughed. "I'm here now, ready to practice for tomorrow's big day."

Jack pulled her into an embrace. "I was getting worried," he said softly.

Mrs. Dawson made a noise.

Jack flushed and then looked around. "We still need Melanie and Karl," he said. "And the minister isn't here, either."

"We have plenty of time," Linda told him. "They're still practicing setting up the chairs and the arch."

Fenella looked over and watched the team of four people who appeared to be trying to wrestle a large, white wooden arch into place on the white cloth.

"They thought it would take them less than half an hour to do everything," Linda said. "But if they actually started at two thirty like they were supposed to, they've already taken forty-five minutes and they aren't done yet."

Jack sighed. "They were here when I arrived, putting down the white carpet and then setting up the chairs. They told me that they had it all timed to perfection."

Linda glanced at her watch and then winced as the workers stepped away from the arch and it fell over backward.

"I think I need to go and speak to them," she said with a sigh.

"Do you need me?" Jack asked. He trailed along behind Linda as she walked across the grass.

"I wanted Jack to get married in a church, of course," Mrs. Dawson said. "He was raised properly. We went to church every Sunday from the time he was a baby until he left home. I wish I knew when he'd lost his way." She glared at Fenella, seemingly blaming her for Jack's lack of faith.

"By the time I met him, he hadn't been inside a church in years," Fenella said defensively.

"Yes, well, I do think you could have done more to encourage him to go back to the church," Mrs. Dawson replied.

"Is Linda terribly angry with me?" Melanie asked as she joined them.

"Not at all," Fenella said. "Jack said you got held up at work."

"My most reliable employee, the one who is supposed to be managing the shop today and tomorrow so that I can relax and enjoy my best friend's wedding, didn't show up for work this morning,"

Melanie explained. "I called her house and her mobile and didn't get a reply. I had to call half a dozen other employees before I could find someone to come in for this afternoon and evening. I'm not sure what I'm going to do about tomorrow."

"You can't miss the wedding," Fenella said.

"No, of course not. I'd shut the shop before I'd miss the wedding. I just hope it doesn't come to that."

"I'm late," Karl announced cheerfully as he crossed the grass toward them. "I'd forgotten that I was even supposed to be here, and then my phone started buzzing and beeping. My lovely wife set an alarm for me. Otherwise, I'd have missed the entire thing."

"I knew you'd forget," Melanie said. "I hope my alarm didn't interrupt something important."

"Nothing is more important than being a part of Linda's special day. She's your best friend, after all," he replied, sliding an arm around Melanie.

Fenella looked at Daniel and raised an eyebrow.

"They're still sorting out the chairs," Melanie muttered after they'd all watched Linda talking to the four workers who'd left the arch on the ground and returned to setting up chairs.

"It wasn't supposed to take more than half an hour," Fenella told her.

"I hope they figure something else out before tomorrow. It's supposed to be hot. No one is going to want to be outside any longer than they have to be," Karl said.

"We'll need a large tent," Mrs. Dawson said. "They'll have to set up a large tent over the entire space. I can't sit outside in the hot sun for any length of time."

"You won't be in the sun for long," Jack told her as he rejoined Fenella and the others. "It's going to be a very short ceremony."

"I saw the loveliest little church yesterday," Mrs. Dawson told him. "It was the perfect place for a small wedding."

"We're getting married here, on the lawn," Jack said firmly. "Now, if you'd like to take your seats, we can get started on the rehearsal."

Daniel helped Mrs. Dawson walk across the uneven grass to the first row of chairs.

"I suppose it doesn't matter where I sit today," she said, dropping heavily into the first chair in the row.

"Sit anywhere," Jack said to Fenella and Daniel. "We're all supposed to come out from the building, so we need to practice that."

Fenella thought seriously about sitting as far from Jack's mother as she could get, but she didn't want to cause a scene and risk upsetting Jack and Linda, who obviously had a lot of other issues with which to deal.

The arch was still lying on the ground. Clearly, the work crew wasn't going to bother fixing it for today's rehearsal. Karl and Melanie followed Jack and Linda into the building.

"But what about the minister?" Mrs. Dawson asked.

A moment later, the assistant dean of the history department emerged from the building and then stood blinking in the sunlight. After a minute, he shook his head and then walked over and stood in front of the fallen arch.

"Who is that?" Mrs. Dawson demanded.

"He's the assistant dean of the department," Fenella told her.

"And the minister for the wedding," the man said loudly. "When Jack asked, I couldn't say no. Anyone can get ordained to perform weddings these days, you know. All you have to do is fill out a form online."

Fenella swallowed a laugh as Mrs. Dawson turned bright red. "You aren't a real minister," she nearly shouted.

"I'm legally able to marry Jack and Linda. That's what matters," the man told her.

"I can't believe this is happening. I blame you," she told Fenella.

"Me?" Fenella gasped.

Daniel put a hand on her shoulder as Mrs. Dawson nodded vigorously.

"He was never the same after he met you," she said bitterly.

"He seems very happy now," Fenella said. "I believe he and Linda are madly in love."

"That's beside the point," Mrs. Dawson snapped.

"And here we go," the dean said loudly.

Jack and Karl emerged from the building and walked over to the dean.

"Karl, you'll stand here," the man told him. "And Jack, you'll stand right in front of me, under the, er, arch that isn't actually standing right now."

Jack nodded.

"And then my wife will start the music," the man told them. He nodded toward a woman who'd slipped into a chair on the opposite side of the lawn. She tapped something on her phone and music began to play through the two small speakers that Fenella could see on either side of the white carpet.

"This is ridiculous," Mrs. Dawson hissed. "I would have happily paid for a proper wedding."

"And then the ladies will come out," the dean said, looking toward the building.

A moment later, the door opened and Melanie walked out. She strolled slowly toward the men gathered near the arch. Linda followed her, walking a few paces behind.

"And now, Melanie, you'll stand here," the dean gestured. "And Linda, you'll join Jack in front of me."

Melanie took a step to the side as Linda moved to stand next to Jack.

"Very nice," the dean said. "And we'll begin." He dug around in his pocket and pulled out a sheet of paper. "I have the notes from when we discussed what you wanted. Did you want to change anything?"

Linda and Jack looked at one another and then they both shook their heads.

"Traditional vows are fine," Jack said.

"But I do want to add a sentence or two of my own," Linda added.

"You do?" Jack asked.

Linda flushed. "Just a few words, really. You don't have to do the same."

"But it will seem odd if you add something and I don't," Jack argued.

"I just want to say something special, something extra," Linda explained. "I want this day to be our special day and not exactly like, well, like the last time I got married."

"It's nothing like the last time you got married," Melanie said. "You and George got married in a big church with over a hundred guests. You wore a big white dress and George wore a tuxedo that didn't fit quite right."

Linda smiled at her. "It fit fine, except for the pants. They were at least two sizes too big and he had to pin them into place. I'd nearly forgotten about all of that. It was such a long time ago."

"Darling, if you really want to say something extra, that's fine," Jack said. "But I don't have any idea what I should say."

"So don't say anything," Linda replied. "We'll do our vows and then I'll just whisper my little thing to you and then we'll carry on."

Jack shrugged. "Maybe I'll be able to think of something by tomorrow afternoon."

"I didn't mean to make this so complicated," Linda told him. "I just wanted to warn you that I was going to add something, just a little something. I was going to surprise you with it. I should have done that."

"I'm glad you told me," Jack said. "I just wish I had more time to prepare the perfect thing."

Linda laughed. "What I want to say isn't going to be perfect, but it is going to be heartfelt." She blinked back tears and then sighed. "I love you, Jack Dawson."

"And I love you, Linda Hawkins, almost Dawson," he replied, pulling her close.

After a moment, the dean coughed loudly. "That part comes later," he said as the pair ended their kiss.

Everyone laughed and then the dean continued with the rehearsal.

"And then, finally, I'll present you to the guests," he concluded at the end. "Everyone will cheer and you can share your first kiss as husband and wife."

Fenella felt a tear slide down her cheek as she watched the happy couple practice that first kiss.

Daniel slid an arm around her. "They seem very happy together," he whispered in her ear.

"I'm happy for them. I just wish the murder was solved. They may have to cancel their honeymoon if the killer isn't caught before Monday," she whispered back.

"And that's the end of that," the dean said. "I'll talk to the work crew and make sure that they're going to have things set up properly tomorrow. I'll be more appropriately dressed, as well," he said, gesturing at his jeans and his sweatshirt with the university logo across it.

"I don't care what you wear," Jack told him.

"Hurumph," Mrs. Dawson said.

"And now, let's all go and have a nice dinner," Linda said. "Dean Smith, you and your wife are welcome to join us."

He shook his head. "Thank you, my dear, but I have a class to teach tonight and Mrs. Smith is watching the grandchildren while our son and his wife have a night out. Nothing is more important to Mrs. Smith than spending time with the grandchildren."

"Danny, you are taking me with you, aren't you?" Mrs. Dawson asked plaintively.

"Yes, of course," he replied. "Although Fenella is doing the driving."

Mrs. Dawson frowned. "Why?"

He laughed. "I've not had a go at driving on the wrong side of the road yet. I'm sure it isn't too complicated, but I much prefer to leave the driving over here to Fen. She's had a lot more experience than I have."

"But I'm sure you're a much better driver," Mrs. Dawson said.

"If you'd rather, I'm sure someone else could take you to the dinner," Daniel replied. "Everyone is going to the same place, after all."

"I'm not," Melanie said. "Or rather, I am, but first I'm going home. We're both going home," she added, grabbing Karl's hand. "We're going to take our cars home and then come back in a taxi. We've even gotten a room at the hotel for the weekend. We'll be able to drink as much as we like tonight and tomorrow before we have to go home on Sunday after brunch."

"It's a wedding, not an excuse to drink too much," Mrs. Dawson said tightly.

"It's both," Melanie laughed as she and Karl turned to walk away.

"I suppose I shall have to come with you then," Mrs. Dawson said to Fenella, frowning deeply.

"Mother, you're more than welcome to ride over to the hotel with me," Jack interjected. "I'm just going to follow Linda home and then she's going to ride with me too. We're all staying at the hotel tonight and tomorrow night too, of course. Linda needs to get her suitcases."

"I'll go with Danny," Mrs. Dawson replied. "We'll see you there."

❧ 13 ❧

Mrs. Dawson held Daniel's arm tightly as they walked across the campus to the parking lot where Fenella had left the car. The older woman spent the entire walk complaining about everything from the state of the sidewalks to the minister who wasn't really a minister to the idea of having to sit in the sun for the brief ceremony. Fenella was tired of the woman's voice by the time they'd reached the car.

"Everyone else is going to take ages to get to the hotel," Mrs. Dawson said as she settled into the passenger seat. "Whatever will we do while we wait?"

"Fenella and I have to go back to our room and ring a few people," Daniel told her from the backseat. "I have to ring the Chief Constable back on the island for a briefing, and Fenella needs to talk to the woman who's keeping her cat, just to make sure that everything is okay."

"I should have ridden with Jack, then, shouldn't I? This is terribly inconvenient. I suppose I shall have to come back to your room with you, then, so that I don't have to sit alone in the restaurant."

"I wish you could," Daniel told her. "Unfortunately, my conversation with the Chief Constable will be confidential. I'm probably going to have to make Fenella stand in the corridor while we talk. You can wait in the lobby, though. That might be less awkward than sitting on your own in the restaurant."

Mrs. Dawson sighed deeply. "I shall sit by myself and try to work out a way to get this entire unfortunate event canceled, then."

"What unfortunate event?" Daniel asked.

Fenella swallowed a giggle. Daniel knew exactly what the woman was talking about, of course.

"This sham of a wedding, of course," Mrs. Dawson snapped. "I don't know why I care, as I imagine the marriage won't be legal anyway, not with a history professor officiating. I still find it all terribly upsetting, though. I do think, if Linda wanted to marry my Jack, that she could have made more of an effort to get to know me."

"Perhaps she felt that Jack is old enough to make his own decisions," Daniel said.

Mrs. Dawson frowned. "I don't generally interfere in Jack's decisions, of course, but choosing a life partner, well, that's a very serious decision, indeed. Jack has never chosen his partners wisely. I've never cared for a single woman that he's dated, not once. Actually, that isn't entirely true. When he was in high school he very briefly dated a lovely young woman, but she wanted to marry a doctor, the medical type, and Jack wasn't interested in studying medicine, not even to win her heart. She was the only woman he ever dated who was worthy of him, though."

Fenella stopped at a red light, shut her eyes, and counted slowly to twenty-five. The car behind her honked as the light turned green while she was still counting.

"I'd feel ever so much better if you were driving," Mrs. Dawson said to Daniel.

"Fenella is one of the safest drivers I know," Daniel countered. "And we're here, anyway."

Pulling the car into the first available parking spot, Fenella sat back and took a deep breath. Daniel jumped out of the car and helped Mrs. Dawson out of the passenger seat.

"Let's get you inside and get you settled somewhere," he suggested.

Fenella grabbed her handbag and followed the pair into the building.

"Why don't you sit at the bar and have a glass of wine?" Daniel said as they crossed the lobby. "The bartender will keep you company, and you'll enjoy a nice cold drink after being out in the hot sun for so long."

Mrs. Dawson pressed her lips together and then nodded. "I do believe you're right. I could do with a cold drink."

"I'll see you in the room," Fenella said as Daniel began to lead Mrs. Dawson toward the bar.

"I'm rather shocked and disappointed to hear that you two are sharing a room," Mrs. Dawson said loudly.

Fenella fled to the elevators, feeling only slightly guilty about leaving Daniel with Mrs. Dawson. When she got to their room, she opened the minibar and pulled out a ridiculously overpriced miniature bottle of wine. After taking a swig straight from the bottle, she sank down in the chair at the end of the bed.

"My goodness, how classy," Mona said sarcastically.

Fenella jumped, nearly spilling her wine. "If Jack's mother ends up dead, I'm guilty," she said.

Mona chuckled. "She is rather difficult, isn't she? Daniel is very good with her, though."

"That's because Danny is just the nicest man ever," Fenella snapped.

"And he's here, so I should go. Don't be too late to the dinner, though. You might miss something important." Mona faded away as Daniel walked into the room.

"You need this as much as I do," Fenella said, holding out the wine bottle.

He raised an eyebrow. "Not bothering with a glass?"

"It didn't seem worth the effort."

He laughed and then took a sip of wine. "Come here, then. Let me make you forget about Rosalie for a minute or two."

"That's another thing," Fenella exclaimed. "Jack and I were together for over ten years and she never let me call her Rosalie."

Daniel held out the wine and waited while she'd had a drink before he pulled her into his arms. "I love you," he whispered before he kissed her.

"We're going to be late for dinner," she said some time later.

He shrugged. "I had to talk to the Chief Constable."

"Oh, that's right. You said you needed to call him," she said. "I'm sorry I forgot."

"I may have been exaggerating slightly," Daniel admitted. "I don't actually have to call him, although I should check in with him in the next few days."

"You lied to Jack's mother."

"I did," he agreed. "I couldn't stand the thought of having to sit with her for half an hour or more while we waited for everyone else to arrive. Besides, I thought being alone with you would be a good deal more pleasant. I was correct, as it happens."

She laughed. "You lie very well. It's a bit worrying."

"It's not something I do routinely, but this was an emergency. There was smoke coming out of your ears and I was afraid that you might kill her if you had to spend more time with her."

"I thought about it."

He chuckled. "So I was stretching the truth only in order to save a life."

"Which is entirely justified, of course."

"And now, we'd better get downstairs."

"Because we still have a murder to investigate."

Fenella fixed her hair and makeup and then she and Daniel rode the elevator back to the lobby. When they reached the restaurant, the host greeted them with a smile.

"Ah, yes, the wedding rehearsal dinner. Right this way," he said.

He led them to a small room in the corner. The door was open and Fenella could see everyone gathered around a small bar along one wall.

"There you are," Melanie said loudly. "We were just talking about sending a search party."

"I had to ring the Chief Constable back on the island," Daniel replied. "Obviously, he was very interested in hearing about the investigation here."

"And now you're done with that, and you can have a drink and celebrate," Melanie said.

"Yes, indeed," Daniel agreed.

He ordered drinks for both himself and Fenella as they greeted the
others.

Mrs. Dawson was frowning at a glass of wine. Howard and Gloria
were holding hands, but not looking at one another. Jack and Linda
had taken their drinks and moved over to sit at the table where they
seemed to be having a serious conversation. Melanie walked from the
bar to where the others were standing. She stopped next to Karl and
slid her arm around his waist. Then she leaned against him and whispered something in his ear.

"We should order food," Jack said after a minute. He got to his feet
and crossed to the bar. "Menus are here," he said, holding up a stack of
papers. "We have to order from the event menu, but I think you'll all
find something on it you'll enjoy."

Daniel grabbed two copies from him and passed one to Fenella.
She read down the fairly short list of options and shrugged.

"There are two or three things on here that sound good," she said.

"I thought the same. Want to share two meals?" Daniel asked.

"If we can agree on the same two things," she laughed.

"There's nothing on here that I'll eat," Mrs. Dawson announced.
"And this wine isn't up to my standards, either."

Jack flushed. "I'll sort out the wine. I thought you might like the
chicken dish."

"I don't care for heavy sauces," she replied.

"What if they put the sauce on the side?" Linda suggested. "Then
you can eat or not to suit yourself."

Mrs. Dawson pressed her lips together and then nodded slowly. "As
there doesn't seem to be any alternative, I suppose that will have
to do."

"Thank heavens for that," Melanie muttered. "Poor Jack."

"Are you all ready to order?" the man behind the bar asked.

A few people nodded, so he picked up the phone on the wall and
pushed a number. A moment later, a waiter walked into the room. It

didn't take him long to get everyone's requests. As he left, Jack waved at the table.

"Let's all sit down," he suggested. "I've ordered several appetizers for us all to share. They should be here soon."

"I wish I'd known that," Mrs. Dawson complained. "I would have simply eaten those and skipped the main course."

"You may not like any of the appetizers," Melanie suggested.

"That's very true," Mrs. Dawson agreed, sitting back with a smile on her face.

Clearly, she's looking forward to complaining about the appetizers, Fenella thought.

Daniel took a seat as far from Mrs. Dawson as he could get. Fenella sat down next to him, and the others took the rest of the chairs around the table. Melanie sat next to Karl and then slid her chair as close as she could to his and rested her hand on his knee. Howard and Gloria sat on either side of Mrs. Dawson.

"Does anyone need a drink?" the bartender asked.

"I think we're all okay for right now," Jack told him.

"I'll be back in ten minutes," he replied. "I'm just going to get some more ice and that better bottle of wine you requested."

Jack nodded. They were all silent as the man left the room. He shut the door behind himself.

"So, what shall we talk about?" Howard asked as the door swung shut.

"Weddings," Melanie suggested. "Today's rehearsal reminded me of my own wedding. It was such a magical day."

Karl made a noise that he turned into a cough. "It was magical," he agreed after a moment.

"If I remember correctly, you were rather drunk when you turned up at the church," Linda said.

"I wasn't drunk. I may have been a bit hung over, but I'd had my bachelor party the night before the wedding and we'd had a good time," Karl defended himself. "We should take Jack out tonight," he said, looking at Howard.

"No, thank you," Jack said quickly. "I've no interest in going out drinking tonight. Tomorrow is going to be the most important day of my life and I want to remember every minute of it."

Mrs. Dawson sniffed audibly.

"You can go out with them if you want," Linda told him. "I truly won't mind."

Jack shook his head. "Thank you, but I'm really not interested in drinking more than a glass or two of wine and having a nice meal tonight. I want to feel and be at my best tomorrow."

"It's your last night as a single man," Howard said. "You should celebrate."

"I'm celebrating with the woman I love. Why would I want to do anything else?" Jack countered, taking Linda's hand.

She smiled at him. "George went out and got totally plastered the night before our wedding. He almost didn't make it to the church the next day. Luckily, Melanie and the best man went and found him."

"We probably don't need to talk about that," Melanie said with a laugh.

Linda looked confused for a moment and then laughed. "Sorry," she said. "George's best man was a guy called Dominic. He was George's best friend at the time. Because Melanie was my maid of honor, the two of them ended up spending a lot of time together in the days right before the wedding."

"And I wasn't terribly fond of Dominic," Melanie added. "He thought he was a good deal more attractive than he actually was and he thought I should fall into bed with him and be grateful for the opportunity."

Linda laughed. "For what it's worth, he also suggested that I go to bed with him the night we met. George and I had just gotten engaged and he suggested that I should have one last fling with him. I just laughed and then I told George."

"And what did George say?" Melanie asked.

"That I could have one last fling if I really wanted to. Of course, I didn't. I was madly in love with George and I wasn't at all attracted to Dominic."

"Whatever happened to Dominic?" Fenella asked.

Linda frowned. "Once George and I had gotten married, I didn't really want him going out with Dominic any longer. A few weeks after the wedding, George and I had a huge fight about him going out so frequently, and he agreed to stop going out on his own for a month. It was just supposed to be a trial, but by the end of the month, Melanie had started seeing Karl, and we'd begun doing things as a foursome, and that seemed to keep George happy. Then we got our first apartment, and then Melanie and Karl got married and moved into the same building, and Dominic just sort of faded out of our lives."

"Maybe he killed George," Howard suggested. "Maybe he was angry that he'd been cut out of George's life so he killed him."

"All of this happened decades ago," Linda laughed. "There's no way the man was still angry with George. They didn't fight or anything, anyway. They simply drifted apart. Their lives moved in different directions. I doubt Dominic ever got married. He's probably still out there somewhere, trying to sweet talk women into his bed every night."

"He's not," Melanie told her.

"No?" Linda asked.

"We're friends on social media," Melanie explained. "He sent me a friend request about five years ago, and I was just curious enough to accept. He got married about seven years ago, and he and his wife have three kids under the age of five."

"Wow, he's a bit old to have children that young," Linda said.

"She posts pictures of them all the time and tags him in the photos. He looks like the kids' grandfather in most of them, although his hair is still jet black," Melanie told her.

Linda laughed. "He did have great hair. I'll give him that."

"Why are you friends with him on social media?" Karl asked Melanie.

"Why not?" she replied. "He reached out to me and, as I said, I was curious as to what had happened to him since I'd seen him last. He's living in Wyoming, so it isn't as if we'll ever see each other again in person."

Karl frowned. He started to say something, but he was interrupted by the arrival of the appetizers.

Large platters of food were passed up and down the table, and everyone helped themselves to fried cheese, chicken wings, loaded potato skins, fried ravioli, and more. Mrs. Dawson gave each platter a critical look before passing it along untouched.

"It's a good thing you ordered dinner, then," Melanie said to her as the last platter was passed.

"Yes, indeed," Mrs. Dawson replied.

"Tell us about your wedding," Linda said to Howard. "We didn't meet you until after you were married. Did you have a big church wedding?"

Gloria looked at Howard and blushed. "We eloped," she said after a minute. "We ran away to Las Vegas, actually."

"Las Vegas? How romantic," Mrs. Dawson said sarcastically.

"My parents didn't approve of Howard," Gloria explained. "He is five years older than I am, and I was only seventeen when we started dating. He'd already graduated from college, and I was still in high school. My parents wanted me to go to college, but then I fell in love and decided that I'd rather be with Howard."

"That's romantic," Linda said.

Gloria shrugged. "It all seemed incredibly romantic and daring, running away together to get married in Vegas." She looked at Howard and shrugged. "I'm still not a hundred percent certain that our marriage was legal, but Howard has always insisted that it was."

There was a short, stunned silence around the table before Melanie started to laugh.

"You mean you two may not actually be married? That would make getting a divorce a lot easier, wouldn't it? You wouldn't even need a divorce. You could just leave Howard and start a new life somewhere else," she said.

"I don't have any intention of leaving Howard," Gloria said. "We've talked once or twice about renewing our vows, making sure everything is done properly this time, but I don't know that it matters. We feel married, anyway."

"And that's enough of a life sentence," Karl said gloomily.

"Hey," Melanie snapped.

"I'm just kidding," Karl told her.

"Everything is delicious," Daniel said.

Melanie stood up. "I need another drink," she said, heading for the bar.

The bartender hadn't returned yet, so Melanie walked behind the bar and began to look through the bottles on the shelf.

"You aren't allowed to do that," Jack said, getting to his feet. "The bartender will be back soon."

"But he isn't here now, and now is when I want a drink," Melanie replied, reaching for a bottle.

"Come on, Mel," Linda said. "Don't get me and Jack into trouble. This is all costing us a fortune as it is."

Melanie looked over at her and sighed. "How long have we been friends?"

"Forever," Linda replied.

Before Melanie could speak, the door opened and the bartender walked back in, carrying a tray with an ice bucket and a bottle of wine on it. He looked at Melanie and grinned.

"Did you want to help me behind the bar, then?" he asked.

Melanie looked him up and down and then sighed. "I'm with my husband tonight," she said. "Maybe another time."

The bartender, who was probably no more than twenty-five, blushed.

"I'm right here," Karl said loudly.

Melanie laughed and then stepped out from behind the bar. "I'm only teasing and you know it," she called to Karl. "But I am dying for another drink," she told the bartender.

He quickly fixed her drink and then opened the bottle of wine and poured out a glass for Mrs. Dawson.

"You should find this much more to your liking," he told her as he handed her the glass.

She took a sip and then nodded. "That's much better," she told him. "Thank you."

"Thank your son. He's the one who's paying extra for it," the man replied.

Mrs. Dawson looked at Jack. "I would have thought you'd want to provide the very best for your rehearsal dinner. It is your last meal as a single man."

"We're having a champagne toast with dessert," he told her. "We've ordered the most expensive champagne they have. I'm sorry the wine didn't meet with your approval."

She shrugged. "This is adequate."

Jack smiled tightly. "What were we talking about?" he asked.

"We were discussing the fact that Howard and Gloria aren't actually married," Melanie said. "That means, of course, that their children are illegitimate, but I don't suppose that matters all that much anymore, does it?"

"I'm quite certain our marriage was legal," Howard said. "Which means the children are fine."

"There are ways to find out," Daniel told them. "You could probably do so with a single phone call."

Gloria looked at Howard and shook her head. "I think not knowing helps keep the spark in our relationship. I'm always wondering if he's really my husband or just a man I've been living in sin with for twenty-something years. I'm sure he looks at me the same way."

Howard laughed. "Is that what you're thinking when you stare at me?" he demanded. "I know you mention it now and again, but I've never once questioned the legitimacy of our marriage. We have a marriage license, after all."

"Yes, but the witnesses are Elvis Parsley and Marilyn Munhoe. I'm pretty sure those weren't their real names," Gloria said.

Daniel and Fenella exchanged glances.

"Maybe we should talk about something else," Karl suggested.

"Why didn't you want a nice church wedding this time?" Mrs. Dawson asked Linda.

She looked at Jack. He patted her hand and then took a sip of his drink before he replied.

"Linda and I talked about a number of different options for our wedding, and in the end, we decided on a ceremony that we both felt suited us and our beliefs. Having met at the university and having been introduced to one another by Dean Smith, asking him to conduct the ceremony simply felt right. I don't expect you to understand or to agree, but it's what Linda and I want," he said.

"We had a big church wedding," Melanie said. "I wore this huge white dress that barely fit down the aisle. I had half a dozen brides-maids and Linda was my matron of honor. I made her wear fuchsia."

Linda laughed. "It was a hideous dress, but the bridesmaid dresses were worse. The color wasn't as bad, but the style was dreadful."

"I didn't want anyone upstaging me," Melanie said with a shrug. "There were six of them and they all had very different body types. Do you have any idea how long it took me to find a dress that looked terrible on all of them?"

Everyone laughed. "I want to see pictures," Fenella said.

"They're all in albums in the attic," Melanie told her. "I should dig them out and go through them one day."

"What about you?" Linda asked Daniel. "Have you ever been married?"

Daniel nodded. "I was married, but it didn't work out."

"Did you have a big wedding?" Melanie asked.

"No, we had a fairly small wedding, just family and close friends," he said. "Money was tight and neither of us minded."

"Are you and Maggie going to get married one day?" Jack wondered.

Daniel flushed and looked at Fenella. "I don't think this is the time or the place for that conversation," he said tightly.

Fenella squeezed his hand. "Do you want another drink?" she asked.

He nodded. She got to her feet and walked to the bar. While she was getting their drinks, the waiter arrived with the food. When she returned to her seat, her main course was waiting for her.

"It looks delicious," she said.

"Don't forget that half of it is mine," Daniel told her.

She glanced at his plate and made a face. His didn't look nearly as appealing.

"I saw that face," Daniel laughed. "You don't have to share if you don't want to."

"We agreed though, and maybe yours will taste better than it looks," she replied.

"It's actually very good," he told her after his first bite.

"And this is rather bland, really, although it looks lovely," she admitted.

As they happily shared their two meals, Fenella sat back and waited to see where the conversation would go next. After a minute, Daniel broke the silence.

"I'm not certain I understand when everyone met everyone else," he said. "Linda, you said that you and Melanie went to school together?"

Linda nodded. "We met in middle school. I was around eleven or twelve and she was a bit older."

"Thanks for bringing that up," Melanie said wryly. "I had some health issues in third grade that meant that I ended up missing nearly half a year of school. The school decided that it would be best to have me repeat third grade, since I'd missed so much. That meant I was a year older than most of the other kids."

"Which meant she was way cooler than the rest of us," Linda laughed. "I was in awe of her for the first half of the year. It was one of my other friends who finally worked up the nerve to speak to her."

"And then Linda and I quickly became almost inseparable." Melanie took up the story. "We used to study together after school just about every night."

Linda laughed. "Except mostly we sat and talked about boys, not math or science. Just about every boy in school asked Melanie out between middle school and high school."

"And I went out with all of them," Melanie laughed.

"All of them?" Karl asked with a frown.

Melanie shrugged. "Just to a movie or out for ice cream. It wasn't anything serious, but I didn't see any reason to turn anyone down, aside from one or two of the, well, stranger boys."

"You even went out with most of them," Linda teased.

"That's rich coming from you," Melanie replied. "You dated Jason Jones for almost three months."

Linda flushed. "He was a bit strange," she admitted. "But he was also very nice and he helped me with my math homework every night. For three months, I got good grades in math."

"At least you got something out of it," Melanie said. "He was a lousy kisser."

Linda stared at her for a minute. "How would you know that?" she asked.

Melanie laughed, but she sounded uncertain. "I'm sure you told me that," she said. "We told each other everything in those days."

Linda nodded, but she didn't look convinced. "Anyway, I've known Melanie since school, but we lost touch after high school graduation. We went to different colleges and then she settled in Pittsburgh for a while. We didn't see each other again until she moved back to Buffalo just a few weeks before my wedding."

"Linda asked me to be maid of honor, and when I came back to the city to go dress shopping with her, I realized how much I missed Buffalo," Melanie explained. "I decided to move back on something of a whim."

"So you didn't get to know George until right before the wedding?" Daniel asked.

"I met George about three days before the wedding," Melanie told him. "Between moving and trying to find a job and also planning a bridal shower for Linda, we simply never crossed paths until just before the wedding. Linda insisted that I meet her and George and Dominic for a drink."

"I was worried that she wouldn't like George," Linda laughed. "But they hit it off right away. She was less fond of Dominic, but we've already talked about him."

"I met Karl a few weeks after the wedding," Melanie said. "After we got married, we moved into the same building as George and Linda. It wasn't long after we'd moved in that Howard and Gloria arrived, newly married, or maybe not married."

"We're married," Howard said. "We were the last to arrive and the first to leave that building, but here we are, all these years later, still friends."

"Is there dessert?" Mrs. Dawson asked.

"Yes, of course," Jack said. "You may have chocolate mousse, vanilla ice cream, or a chocolate chip cookie with ice cream on top."

"I'd prefer something lighter," Mrs. Dawson replied.

"Chocolate mousse is just about the lightest dessert ever," Melanie said.

Mrs. Dawson shrugged. "I suppose that will have to do."

"Did you have a big wedding?" Gloria asked Mrs. Dawson.

"I had a lovely wedding," she replied. "I'm sure you don't want to hear all of the boring details."

No one spoke. Fenella stared at her empty plate, hoping the bartender or the waiter would interrupt. After a moment, Mrs. Dawson continued.

"Well, if you insist, I'll tell you a little bit about the second most wonderful day of my life," she said.

While she droned on and on, the waiter cleared the table and then took their dessert orders. Mrs. Dawson was still talking about flowers and music when the desserts and the promised champagne arrived, and she managed to keep talking in between bites of chocolate mousse until everyone else was finished with their final course.

"My junior bridesmaid was only seven," she said as the waiter began to clear the table. "She was the younger sister of one of the other bridesmaids. You'll remember that I told you about..."

"Mother, as fascinating as this is, we need to move the conversation elsewhere," Jack interrupted. "I suggest the bar."

A chorus of "yeses" greeted his words and everyone seemed to get up very quickly from the table. They were all heading for the door when Karl touched Fenella's arm.

"Can I have just a few minutes of your time?" he asked hesitantly.

❧ 14 ❧

"Of course," Fenella replied.

"Maybe we could stay here while everyone else goes to the bar," Karl suggested. "I'd like to include Daniel in the conversation, too, if you don't mind."

Fenella looked around and spotted Daniel near the door. She caught his eye and nodded toward Karl.

He stopped and then stepped backward to let everyone else out of the room. As they exited, Daniel walked back to where Fenella and Karl were standing.

"I just wanted a minute to try to explain," Karl said. He looked around at the men and women who were clearing the table and taking down the bar and then shrugged. "Maybe we should go out into the lobby or something. I don't want to be in the way here."

The lobby was mostly empty. Karl sat on one of the couches and waved Fenella and Daniel into chairs next to him. "I'm sorry. I won't keep you long, but I was afraid that you'd gotten the wrong idea about things the other day," he said.

"The other day?" Fenella repeated.

"When you saw me having lunch with Cindy," he explained. "She's just a friend, although she'd like to be more, but that isn't going to happen."

"It's not?" Fenella asked.

Karl sighed. "I'm sure it looked as if we were having an affair, especially because of some of the things that Cindy said, but she wasn't being entirely truthful. Regardless, I've ended my friendship with her and I've told Melanie all about her. As I said, we were just friends, but I've realized that our friendship could damage my marriage."

"You said you were going to leave Melanie for her," Fenella reminded him.

"Melanie and I had just had a huge fight," Karl told her. "I was angry and, well, being with Cindy made me feel better. She said all the right things about how much she cared about me and how much happier she could make me than Melanie does. I was just upset enough with Melanie to go along with her for a short while."

"But you weren't really planning to leave Melanie?" Fenella asked.

"I can't leave Melanie. She's my entire world. I love her dearly and I can't imagine my life without her. Like I said, I was angry with her, but that's really no excuse. I never should have agreed to meet Cindy for lunch, and I certainly shouldn't have encouraged her to believe that we had a future together."

"You've ended your relationship with Cindy, then?" Fenella asked, feeling nothing but sympathy for the woman who seemed to have been caught up in some sort of game that Melanie and Karl were playing.

"I have. It was awkward, but it's over now and I feel much better. Melanie and I have some work to do to repair our marriage. We've both been taking each other for granted, and that has to stop. We're both ready to work hard to make sure that we're together forever," he said.

Fenella nodded. "I hope you mean that."

"I do," he said firmly. "And now I must go and buy my lovely wife a drink, I think."

Fenella and Daniel watched as the man walked away.

"That was weird," she said as he disappeared into the bar.

"He went too far," Daniel said. "If he'd have just said that he'd realized he still cared for Melanie and that they were going to try working on their marriage, I might have believed him, but he went over the top."

"Poor Cindy would be crushed if she knew how he was talking about her now."

Daniel nodded. "Why the lies, though?"

"Because they think they'll be less likely to be suspects in the murder investigation if they seem happily married?" Fenella guessed.

"I can't see why the state of their marriage has anything to do with the murder investigation."

"Unless Melanie had an affair with George," Fenella suggested.

Daniel frowned. "I'm going to ring Carol and tell her about that conversation. Do you want to stay with me or go and have a drink at the bar with the others?"

"I'll go to the bar," Fenella decided. "Just in case anyone else wants to confide in me."

Daniel chuckled. "If they do, make them wait until I'm there. I don't want to miss anything good."

Fenella nodded and then gave him a quick kiss before walking to the bar. The group was sitting together at a table in the back corner of the room. She got herself a drink before she walked over to join them.

"Margaret is here," Melanie said. "Make room for Margaret."

They were sitting around a large table that had a U-shaped padded bench around it. There was just enough room for the six people, the three couples, who were sitting around it. Mrs. Dawson was sitting on a chair off to one side.

"Squish up," Melanie told Karl, who was next to her.

"I'm as squished as I get," he replied.

She laughed and slid her arm around him. "I could sit on your lap," she suggested.

"As much as I love that idea, I think the table is in the way," he replied.

"I'll get a chair," Fenella said, putting her drink down. It didn't take her long to drag over a chair for herself and one for Daniel.

"You could have our spot," Howard said as Fenella sat down. "Gloria and I are heading to bed. We haven't had a night in a hotel in ages and our room has a whirlpool tub. We're going to enjoy it tonight because we're expecting tomorrow night to be a very late night."

"I don't know about that," Linda said. "The reception only runs from five to nine."

"But then we'll move back in here," Melanie said. "And we'll drink and talk and laugh and have a wonderful time until the wee small hours of the morning."

Linda shrugged. "Jack and I may not stay until the wee small hours of the morning."

Melanie looked at her and raised an eyebrow. "Is he that good in bed?" she asked.

Mrs. Dawson drew a sharp breath. "What a highly inappropriate question," she said. "If that is the way this conversation is heading, I think I'll go to bed now."

"I think we could all do with an early night," Jack said firmly. "Tomorrow is going to be a very big day indeed, for some of us, anyway."

"Jack is right," Linda said. "Let's call it a night."

Fenella sat and sipped her drink as the others all finished theirs. Jack escorted his mother out while Linda followed. Howard and Gloria left together, holding hands. Melanie and Karl weren't far behind. He put his arm around her as they began to walk, pulling her close and holding her tightly as they stumbled to the door. A moment later, Daniel walked in. He looked surprised when he saw Fenella sitting on her own.

"They've all decided to have an early night," she told him when he reached her.

"Was Mrs. Dawson telling more stories about her wedding day?"

She laughed. "No, but Melanie asked Linda if Jack was good in bed and no one wanted to hear the answer to that."

Daniel laughed. "Then we should have an early night, too," he suggested.

"What did Carol say?" she asked when they were back in their room.

"That she's looking closely at both Melanie and Karl, but that she's also looking closely at a number of other people. She also thanked me for sharing the conversation with her. She's going to be at the wedding tomorrow, and the reception."

"Oh? Was she invited or is she simply turning up?" Fenella had to ask.

"She was invited, but I believe she may have asked Jack or Linda to invite her. It will be interesting to see how Karl and Melanie behave tomorrow with her watching, though."

"Howard and Gloria suddenly seem more devoted to one another, too."

"Yes, I noticed that. It was less striking than Melanie and Karl, but still noticeable. I mentioned that to Carol, too."

"Do you think one of them, either Melanie or Gloria, had an affair with George?"

"I'm wondering if they both did, actually," Daniel told her.

Fenella sighed. "Maybe Linda did kill him."

"It's a beautiful day," Fenella told Daniel as she opened the curtains in the hotel room the next morning.

"It's been nice every day that we've been here. I almost miss rain."

"I don't miss rain at all, but I am worried that it's going to be really hot today. I hope Jack was right about the ceremony not taking too long. I'm not used to being outside in the heat anymore."

"The wedding is hours away. What shall we do with our morning?" Daniel asked.

"Mini golf," Fenella suggested.

"Mini golf?" he repeated.

"The idea just popped into my head. There are several different places we can go. It might be fun."

"Sure, why not? It isn't meant to get too hot until later. Let's go and play mini golf."

Daniel won three straight rounds at the mini golf course. Their tickets had included a handful of tokens for the video games in the large building adjacent to the course, so they had some fun playing some of the games and amassing a small pile of reward tickets.

"What can we get with all of our tickets?" Fenella asked excitedly, feeling all of ten years old again.

"You have two hundred and six tickets," the man behind the counter told her. "This shelf has everything that costs two hundred tickets."

"Get the cuddly panda," Daniel suggested.

"Are you sure it's a panda?" she whispered. "It's a bit, well, deformed."

He laughed. "I think it's charming, if a bit odd."

"We'll have the green and yellow panda," Fenella told the man.

"Is that what it is?" he asked as he handed her the misshapen stuffed animal. "You have six tickets left. You can get a few pieces of candy."

Fenella selected a few gummy fish and then she and Daniel headed back to the hotel. "Do you want one?" she asked as she unwrapped a sugary treat.

"I earned at least one," he told her, tearing the wrapper off the candy she handed him.

"What do you think?"

"It tastes, um, red and sugary. You can have the last one."

Back at the hotel, they changed into their wedding finery, and then Fenella drove them to the campus. There wasn't a cloud in the sky, and Fenella could feel the sun beating down on her head as they walked from the parking lot to the lawn where the wedding was to be held.

"The arch is standing," Daniel said as they approached.

"It looks as if a strong wind will blow it down, though," she whispered back.

The grass was once again covered by a large white cloth rectangle. Rows of chairs had been arranged neatly in front of the arch, and there were already a few people in seats. Huge pillars on either side of the arch held large bouquets of red and white roses. Fenella waved to a few professors she knew from the university as she and Daniel took seats near the back.

Mrs. Dawson arrived a short while later. She looked around the lawn and then frowned and headed into the building. One minute before the ceremony was meant to start, she emerged, leaning heavily on Jack's arm. He walked her to the chairs nearest the arch and settled her into a seat. Fenella found herself blinking back a tear as Jack hugged her tightly and then turned and took his spot near the arch. Karl joined him a moment later. The dean had been sitting with his wife off to one side. Now he rushed up and joined the men at the archway.

"Sorry about that," he said. "I lost track of time."

Jack shrugged. "I'm rather eager to get this over with."

Karl and the dean both laughed and then the dean nodded at his wife. "Music," he said softly.

The music began and everyone turned to watch the door to the building. After a long minute, the door opened and Melanie walked out carrying a small bouquet of red roses. She smiled as she walked across the lawn to the arch. Linda stepped out a moment later. Everyone stood up and watched as Linda joined Jack under the arch.

"She looks beautiful," Daniel whispered.

Fenella nodded. Linda was stunning in a long white dress, carrying a bouquet of white roses. She looked very happy as she joined hands with Jack in front of the dean. The ceremony itself was very simple. The pair repeated their vows and exchanged rings as Fenella wiped away a few tears.

"I believe Linda has something she wanted to say," Dean Smith said after the rings had been exchanged.

Linda nodded. "Jack, when my marriage ended, I didn't think I'd ever find love again. I didn't think I'd ever trust anyone again. I didn't think I'd ever be happy again. I just want to thank you for teaching me to love, to trust, and to be happy again, in spite of everything that happened in the past."

Jack had tears in his eyes as he looked at Linda. "Linda, when I met you, I thought I needed someone to look after me, to cook and clean and help me cope with all of life's challenges. Now I know what I really needed was someone to love me and be with me, and that together, we can deal with whatever life throws at us. Thank you for completing me."

Fenella wiped away another tear as Daniel squeezed her hand.

"That was lovely," he whispered.

She nodded. "They deserve to live happily ever after."

"Ladies and gentlemen, I'm delighted to present to you: Mr. and Mrs. Jack and Linda Dawson, although technically, they're Dr. and Dr. Jack and Linda Dawson," the dean said. "You may kiss your bride," he told Jack.

Everyone clapped and Fenella noticed that even Mrs. Dawson looked a bit teary-eyed as the couple kissed.

"And now the fun begins," Melanie said happily. "Champagne for everyone."

After half an hour of photos, Fenella and Daniel followed the happy couple's limousine back to the hotel.

"That would have been a lot more romantic for them if Mrs. Dawson hadn't ridden with them," Daniel remarked as Fenella parked.

"It was only a short ride, anyway. At least she isn't going with them on their honeymoon."

"If they get to go."

Fenella frowned. "Is Carol going to keep them here?"

"I'm not sure."

They followed Jack and Linda into the hotel where the newlyweds were applauded by the staff.

"You need to wait out here," they were told as they headed toward the room where the guests were gathering for the reception. "You need to make an entrance along with your wedding party."

Linda laughed. "I don't think it really matters."

"I quite like the idea of making an entrance," Jack told her. "It's our first social event as a married couple."

She laughed again. "If it will make you happy, we can wait and make an entrance."

"We're here," Melanie shouted as she rushed into the lobby, dragging Karl behind her. "We got stuck behind a little old man who wanted to drive five miles an hour all the way here."

"It wasn't that bad," Karl laughed.

"Congratulations," Fenella told the happy couple as she and Daniel crossed the lobby.

"Thank you," Jack said, giving her a hug.

Linda hugged her as well. "Thank you so much for being a part of our special day," she said.

"Thank you for including us," Fenella countered.

"Not many people invite their exes to their weddings," Melanie said. "I don't think I've ever been invited to one of my exes' weddings — well, not when the bride knew that I'd been involved with her groom, at least."

The silence that followed the remark was awkward.

"We should go in," Daniel suggested.

"Melanie, I need to ask you something," Linda said in a low voice.

"What's on your mind, dear best friend?" Melanie replied.

"How did you know that Jason Jones was a terrible kisser?" Linda asked.

Melanie stared at her for a moment and then laughed. "I thought we covered this last night. You told me that he couldn't kiss. You must have done."

"Except I don't think I did," Linda replied.

"Maybe someone else told me, then. Middle school girls aren't shy about sharing their thoughts on such things," Melanie said.

"No one else in the school ever went out with Jason Jones, though. Everyone made fun of me for going out with him. No one else could have told you," Linda said steadily.

"Why does this matter?" Melanie asked. "I mean, it's your wedding day. Let's focus on that and go back over our childhood memories another time, okay?"

"No, it isn't okay," Linda replied. "You kissed Jason Jones, didn't you?"

Melanie sighed. "Maybe, probably even. What difference does it make?"

"The difference is that he was my boyfriend."

"Maybe I kissed him before you started dating him. Honestly, you can't expect me to remember the exact timeline of something that happened when I was thirteen or fourteen years old."

"Maybe not. Let's move things forward a bit, then, shall we?" Linda asked.

"Now what?" Melanie asked. "I mean, I know that it's your wedding day, so I'm trying to be understanding, but I really wasn't expecting an inquisition."

Jack put his hand on Linda's shoulder. "Are you okay?" he asked.

She took a deep breath and then looked at Melanie. "How did you know that George's pants didn't fit properly at our wedding?" she demanded.

Melanie blinked a few times and then shook her head. "Is that what this is about? Again, you must have told me or maybe George did. It was one of those funny wedding stories that we all have."

"Karl, did you know that George's pants were too big at our wedding?" Linda asked.

Karl opened his mouth and then shut it again. After a moment, he sighed. "I don't want to get in the middle of all of this."

"That's a no, then," Linda said. "The thing is, George and I agreed that we'd never tell anyone about the mix up with his rental tuxedo. I was furious with him about it, actually, because he was supposed to have gone and made sure that everything fit the week before the wedding, but he never went. When he turned up the night before the wedding to pick up his tux, he just grabbed it and left without even checking the sizes. When he dropped it off at my house, I made him try it all on and that was when we discovered the problem with the pants."

"I think all of the guests are here," someone interrupted.

Linda looked at him and shrugged. "In a minute," she said, turning back to Melanie. "George and I had a huge fight. I almost called off the wedding. In the end, we found a bunch of safety pins and pinned everything together as best we could. I told him that if he told anyone about it, I'd never forgive him."

"I probably noticed a pin or something. What is your problem?" Melanie snapped.

"My problem is that you and George both disappeared from our reception for about half an hour after the wedding," Linda said, tears streaming down her cheeks. "I told myself it wasn't anything, but

Dominic, he suggested that you and George were somewhere together. I insisted that you'd never do such a thing to me, but, well, if you kissed Jason Jones back in seventh grade, even though he was my boyfriend, then maybe you did have a fling with George."

Melanie shook her head. "You want to know what really happened at your reception? I got a headache from too much champagne. I went to try to find a quiet place to lie down for a few minutes and George followed me. He said something about his pants coming undone and asked me to help him fix them. When I started trying to help, he pulled his pants down and suggested that we could, um, have some fun together. I turned him down, of course, but I couldn't bring myself to tell you, not on your wedding day."

"We were best friends. You should have told me. You could have saved me years of heartache."

"I did what I thought was best. I'm sorry if I was wrong."

"You turned him down?" Linda checked.

"Of course I turned him down. He was your husband," Melanie laughed. "What sort of friend do you think I am?"

"And he never tried anything again?" Linda asked.

Melanie flushed. "I didn't say that."

"So he did try again? What secrets have you been keeping from me all these years?" Linda demanded.

"He used to drop hints all the time that we should get together, that's all. It was really just a joke," Melanie told her.

"It wasn't a joke," Linda said softly. "I think you should leave."

"Leave?" Melanie asked. "What did I do?"

"My husband made repeated advances toward you for close to thirty years and you never told me."

"It wasn't like that, not really," Melanie protested.

"You never told me, either," Karl said tightly.

She turned to him and sighed. "You know how men talk. They're always talking about sex. That's all it was. He didn't really mean it."

"I knew George," Karl told her. "He absolutely meant it. He wanted to take you to bed."

"Lots of men have wanted to take me to bed over the years," Melanie said.

"And most of them have succeeded," Linda added.

Melanie flushed. "I'm not going to apologize for being attractive to men or for enjoying sex."

"Are you willing to apologize for not being faithful to me?" Karl asked.

"I could ask you the same question," she shot back.

He sighed. "What were you really doing every Wednesday night from seven to nine for the first six years we were married?" he demanded.

"Taking classes in business management, remember?"

"Say that again," Linda said to Karl.

"Say what again?" he asked.

"She was out every Wednesday for two hours for years?" Linda asked.

"Yes, from before we got married, actually, until she finally finished her master's degree," he said.

"And there you have it. I finished my master's degree," Melanie said.

"George was out every Wednesday at the same time," Linda said in a low voice. "I never made the connection before. We never did group things on a Wednesday, but I just assumed that was because George had his weekly staff meeting on Wednesday nights. He didn't have a staff meeting, though, did he?" she asked, staring at Melanie.

Melanie sighed. "You're missing your wedding reception," she said.

"You had an affair with George for six years," Linda said. "And I never guessed."

"My dear girl, you were blind to George's faults. That isn't to say that I had an affair with him, but if he was going out every week at the same time, you really should have suspected something," Melanie replied.

"And so should I," Karl said. "Linda is right. You and George had an affair, didn't you?"

"I can't see what difference it makes, not now, not after all this time," Melanie snapped.

"You're my best friend," Linda sobbed. "I trusted you more than I trusted George."

"After she stopped going out every Wednesday, she started going out every Saturday morning for a few hours," Karl said. "She said she was going to the gym."

"I was going to the gym," Melanie shouted. "This is ridiculous. I'm going to the bar."

"George's staff meetings got changed to Saturday mornings," Linda said dully. "How many years did you cheat with him, then?" she asked Melanie through tears.

Melanie took a deep breath and then swallowed hard. "Too many," she replied. "We met just a few days before your wedding and we fell madly in love, but it was too late. He'd already asked you to marry him and he said he couldn't break your heart. I had to stand there and watch you marry the man I loved and it was the most awful day of my life."

Linda stared at Melanie. "You fell in love?" she said softly.

"I was the only one that George ever really loved," Melanie said angrily. "And we could only see each other for a stolen hour here and there. George was worried that you'd get suspicious, so I married Karl so that no one would guess."

"Gee, thanks," Karl said.

Melanie shrugged. "She wants to hear the whole story. George and I made love for the first time on your wedding day and we were together right up until he left you."

"He ended things with you when he left Buffalo?" Linda asked.

"When he left you, he had to get away. He couldn't stop to explain everything to me. He just went."

"And he broke your heart," Linda suggested.

"Of course not, because I knew our separation was only temporary. I knew he'd be back for me eventually. He just had to give you time to move on so that you wouldn't be upset when we got together."

"I'd still have been upset," Linda told her.

Melanie shrugged. "But you have Jack now."

"But you were supposed to be my best friend. And George was my husband."

"And what about me?" Karl demanded.

"I think we need to talk," Carol Gregory interrupted the conversation. "You didn't mention any of this when you gave me your statement after George's death."

"It wasn't relevant," Melanie told her.

"I think it's very relevant," Carol replied. "You said that you knew that George would come back for you, but from what I've been told, he came back to try to win Linda back."

"That was just for show," Melanie said. "A distraction from his real intentions."

"When did he tell you he was coming back to Buffalo?" Linda demanded.

"He didn't. He called me a few weeks ago. I told him about your wedding and the engagement party, but he didn't tell me he was planning on crashing the party."

"And then, at the party, you arranged to meet him later," Linda said. "That's why you went and talked to him."

"We had to talk. We had to plan what we were going to do next," Melanie explained.

"You killed him, didn't you?" Linda nearly shouted. "You met him here, and you got him to go outside with you and then you killed him."

Melanie shook her head. "It wasn't like that. I did meet him. We talked about what we were going to do next and then I left. Someone else must have been watching us talking in the parking lot and as soon as I drove away, he or she must have killed him."

"Let's go down to the station and talk," Carol said. "You seem to have a lot to add to your statement."

"I would never have killed him. I loved him. He loved me, too," Melanie insisted. "We were having some issues, but we would have sorted them out and then we would have run away together. We were meant to be together. He was the only man for me and now he's dead. I didn't mean to kill him. I just wanted him to understand how much he meant to me."

"Let's go," Carol said, taking her arm.

"You killed George," Linda said.

"I didn't mean to kill him. I was just so angry. He said he wanted you back and that he was going to try to make the marriage work this time. He actually said he didn't want to see me again. I had letters, though, letters he'd written to me over the years. Letters, notes, copies of texts, all sorts of evidence of our affair. I showed them to him and then I went over and threw them into the dumpster. I suggested that he should climb in and get them, otherwise I might get them back and give them to you."

"You got him to climb into the dumpster," Linda said.

"He climbed in and he grabbed the letters. As he started to stand up, I brought the lid down on his head as hard as I could. I thought it would hurt him, give him a headache, maybe. I didn't think it would kill him."

"We really need to go to the station," Carol said. A pair of uniformed policemen walked into the lobby. Carol waved and they crossed to her.

"We're taking Ms. Jensen down to the station," she told one of them.

He nodded and took Melanie's arm. "If you'll come with me, please."

"Wait," Linda said. She stepped forward and stared hard at Melanie. "You killed George," she said softly. "I'm not angry with you for that, though. It's sad but it didn't break my heart. Finding out that you and George had an affair for my entire marriage, though, that's heartbreaking. I thought you were my friend. I trusted you with my secrets and I loved you like a sister. I hope you spend the rest of your life in prison for what you did."

"I didn't mean to kill him."

"But you did mean to sleep with him, over and over and over again," Linda replied before she burst into tears.

Jack's arms went around her and she sobbed as the police escorted Melanie out of the room.

"I need a drink," Karl said bitterly.

"I'm going to need statements from all of you," Carol said. "I'll do it as quickly as I can, because I know you all have better things to do."

"Someone needs to tell the guests that things are going to be delayed," Jack said.

"We'll take care of it," the manager assured him.

An hour later, after having told a policewoman everything that had happened in the lobby after the wedding, Fenella was allowed to head to the reception.

Daniel was waiting for her right outside the door. "Linda and Jack went up to their room to regroup," he told her. "Karl has been drinking steadily since he finished talking to Carol. She's gone back to the station now to talk to Melanie."

"What a mess."

"Let's get drinks," Daniel suggested. "Dinner is on hold until Jack and Linda come down."

"What if they never come down?"

"Then we'll all just get drunk and hungry without them."

Fenella laughed and then let Daniel lead her to the bar in the large room that was being used for the reception. Jack and Linda arrived only a few minutes later. It was clear that Linda had been crying, but she held her head up high as the DJ introduced her and Jack to the crowd. Everyone clapped and then the party began in earnest.

"It's been quite the day," Jack said to Fenella more than an hour later, after dinner had finally been served and eaten.

"Indeed. Not the start to your marriage that you were expecting, I'm sure," she replied.

He shrugged. "At least we know what happened to George now. Linda's still in shock that Melanie did that to her for so many years, but she's tougher than she seems. We're both looking forward to getting away on Monday. Carol has agreed that we can go, at least."

"What about tomorrow?" Daniel asked. "Is the brunch still happening?"

Jack sighed. "We're probably going to cancel it. It seems wrong to spend another day celebrating in light of everything that's happened."

"Let's go to Niagara Falls tomorrow," Daniel suggested a while later. He was holding her close as they danced to an eighties classic.

"That's a great idea. I'm tired of all of these people," she sighed.

"Not me, I hope."

"Never you," she replied before they kissed.

15

"I was right all along," Mona said happily.

Fenella opened her eyes and looked at the clock. "It's the middle of the night," she whispered.

"I won't stay. It's really quite taxing, coming all the way to America. It was worth it this time, though, to find out that I was right about Melanie."

Fenella shrugged. That wasn't necessarily the way she remembered things, but it didn't really matter. "Congratulations," she muttered as she rolled over and went back to sleep.

"Good morning," Daniel whispered in her ear some hours later.

She opened one eye. "Good morning? What time is it?"

"It's half seven and it's pouring with rain."

Fenella frowned. "But we were going to go to Niagara Falls."

"I'm going to ring Carol and see what she has to say about that. I'll ring her from the corridor so you can go back to sleep if you want to."

Of course, as soon as the door shut behind Daniel, Fenella found herself wide-awake. Sighing, she threw back the covers and headed for the bathroom. The shower did its best to wake her up. She was combing her wet hair when Daniel came back into the room.

"What did Carol have to say, then?" she asked.

"Not a lot. She'd prefer it if we didn't cross the border into Canada just yet, though."

"We can still go to the Falls. I feel like we need to get away, at least that far."

He nodded. "In spite of the rain."

"We'll get soaked at the Falls if we do the caves or the boat."

"I want to do both," Daniel told her. "I want to do every touristy thing there is to do."

They were in the car, on their way, before Fenella brought the conversation back to George's murder.

"Did Carol tell you anything about the case?" she asked.

"She told me that Melanie has admitted to causing George's death, but she insisted that it was an accident. She said she just wanted to hurt him. She didn't think dropping the dumpster lid on his head would kill him."

"What happened to the letters that Melanie threw in the dumpster, then?"

"Apparently, Melanie climbed in and retrieved them after, well, after."

"She climbed in over his dead body?"

"She couldn't afford to leave the letters in the dumpster."

"I suppose not, but that's pretty horrible."

"Apparently, George had decided that he wanted Linda back, but he wasn't interested in resuming his affair with Melanie. She was already angry with him for leaving without saying anything to her. It appears that she was rather desperately in love with the man."

Fenella sighed. "What a mess. Poor Linda."

"I saw her and Jack this morning. They both looked very happy. I think she's going to be okay."

"I hope so. I'm surprised Carol told you as much as she did."

"Everything she told me is going to be in an official press release later today. They're eager to announce that the murder has been solved."

Fenella nodded and then focused on driving. It had been quite a while since she'd driven over the Grand Island bridges in the rain, and they seemed a good deal higher when she wasn't busy reassuring Jack that they weren't high at all. A short while later, she parked the car and looked at him. "We're here. Niagara Falls. Let's go."

It was still raining. They'd both worn raincoats, but Fenella still felt as if she was getting soaked as they walked toward the Visitor's Center.

"Do you really want to do it all?" she asked as they went.

"We don't have to, but I may never visit again. I think I'd like to see everything."

A few hours later, they found a small restaurant and ordered lunch.

"The caves were amazing," Daniel said. "I loved being right behind the Falls."

"And we were already soaked, so we couldn't get any wetter."

He laughed. "I was expecting there to be more people, really."

"The weather will be keeping them away, I suppose."

"What time is our boat ride?"

"Two o'clock. Maybe the rain will let up by then and we'll only get soaked by the Falls and not the rain."

They talked about their plans for the next week while they ate.

"All of this is assuming no one else gets murdered," Fenella muttered as they got up to leave the restaurant.

"No one else is going to get murdered," he said firmly. "We have a whole week to enjoy ourselves. Let's make the most of it."

Half an hour later, they were two of only a handful of passengers on a boat sailing straight toward Niagara Falls.

"How close do we get?" Daniel shouted over the roaring water.

"I'm not sure. It's been years since I did this," Fenella replied. "I think we'll have to turn around soon, though. We've definitely slowed down."

Daniel put his arm around her and pulled her close. "It's almost romantic," he said in a loud whisper.

"It's noisy, but it's beautiful."

"It's been a long week, but I'm glad I came with you. I would have hated knowing that you were dealing with all of this on your own."

Fenella smiled up at him. "I'm grateful you were here, and I'm really glad it's all over."

Daniel nodded and then whispered something.

"I didn't hear that," Fenella told him.

He laughed. "I love you," he shouted.

"I love you, too," she replied.

"The thing is, I've been thinking." He stopped and stared out at the waves.

"And?" she asked after a minute.

"Your money is always going to be an issue for me."

"You can't possibly be dumping me right now," Fenella blurted out.

Daniel looked confused and then shook his head. "No, not at all. Quite the opposite, really."

"The opposite?"

He sighed. "Your money is an issue, but what's more important than anything is that I love you. I've had a wonderful time with you this past week, even though we've spent it caught up in a murder investigation involving your ex-boyfriend, which isn't the most romantic way to spend time."

Fenella chuckled. "It's been a weird week."

"Weird, but also oddly wonderful. Just being with you all the time, that's been amazing. I wanted this to be romantic and special, but I also don't want to wait for weeks or months for the perfect moment, either," Daniel said, raising his voice louder with every word. "Fenella Margaret Woods, I love you more than I ever imagined that I could love another person. Will you marry me?" he shouted.

Fenella stared at him for a moment, unable to speak.

"Don't leave all of us in suspense," a woman standing nearby said.

"If you don't want him, I do," someone else said.

"Yes," Fenella said softly.

"That was a yes, wasn't it?" Daniel asked.

"Yes, yes, YES," Fenella replied, shouting out the last word.

He pulled her close and everything around them vanished for a moment. When Daniel lifted his head, the other passengers were all applauding.

Fenella blushed and laughed. "That would have been awful if I'd said no," she said.

Daniel nodded. "I was planning to ask in the privacy of our hotel room for that very reason, but there was just something about standing out here in the pouring rain and mist that made me realize that I didn't want to wait any longer."

"I'm glad you didn't wait."

"Me too," he said. "I, well, I have a ring for you," he said, reaching into his pocket. "If you don't like it, we can exchange it for something else. It's probably not nearly as fabulous as the things you've inherited from Mona, but when I went to look at rings, I found this one and I thought it was exactly right."

He opened the box and Fenella gasped. The large emerald cut diamond was surrounded by smaller sapphires. "It's stunning," she said. "But it must have cost a fortune."

"My house sold for more than I'd anticipated. I was going to use the extra money to pay back some of what I borrowed from you to buy the new flat, but I thought this mattered more. I wanted you to have something amazing."

"It's definitely amazing. I love it."

"Shelly said you would. She also told me your ring size. I hope she got it right."

"Shelly knew you were going to propose?"

"I promised her that I'd let her know how it went as soon as I'd done it," he told her. "I'd better text her."

Fenella laughed. "Send her a picture of the ring on my finger," she suggested.

"How about a picture of you two together with the Falls in the background?" a woman suggested. "I'd be more than happy to take it for you."

The pair posed for a few pictures with Fenella's left hand in every shot.

"Thank you," she said to the woman when she returned Fenella's phone to her.

"Happy to do it. Congratulations," she replied.

"I forgot to notice how close we got to the Falls," Daniel said as they disembarked.

Fenella laughed. "I feel as if I missed the entire thing. Maybe we should do it again."

"Or maybe we should go back to the hotel, change into dry clothes, and go and have a wonderful meal somewhere together," he suggested.

"That would be a better choice," Fenella laughed.

"Congratulations," a voice said behind her as she and Daniel began to walk away from the boat dock.

Fenella turned around, ready to thank whoever had spoken. She nearly fell over when she recognized Mona standing on the deck of the boat.

"I'm going to spend some time playing tourist," Mona told her. "I'll see you back on the island next week." She faded away before Fenella could reply.

SECRETS AND SUSPECTS

Release date: August 13, 2021

After finding a skeleton while visiting the properties that she'd inherited from her aunt, Mona Kelly, Fenella Woods is only a bit worried about what she might find when she visits the safe deposit boxes that Mona had in banks around the Isle of Man. Having said that, she's still shocked when she walks into one of the banks just as a body is found in one of the vaults.

Nigel Corlett was the bank's manager, but no one can explain how he'd ended up dead inside a time-locked vault. There is no shortage of suspects, as it becomes clear that Nigel was involved with many different women, some of whom seem to have been a bit obsessed with the handsome man.

Can Fenella help the police work out how Nigel got into the vault after hours? Can they work out exactly how many women he was actually seeing? And can Fenella persuade the owners of the Seaview in Ramsey to let her best friend, Shelly, have her wedding reception there when they're supposed to be closed for the season?

ALSO BY DIANA XARISSA

The Appleton Case

The Bennett Case

The Chalmers Case

The Donaldson Case

The Ellsworth Case

The Fenton Case

The Green Case

The Hampton Case

The Irwin Case

The Jackson Case

The Kingston Case

The Lawley Case

The Moody Case

The Norman Case

The Osborne Case

The Patrone Case

The Quinton Case

The Rhodes Case

The Somerset Case

The Tanner Case

The Underwood Case

The Vernon Case

The Walters Case

The Xanders Case

The Young Case

The Zachery Case

The Janet Markham Bennett Cozy Thrillers

The Armstrong Assignment

The Blake Assignment

The Isle of Man Romances

Island Escape

Island Inheritance

Island Heritage

Island Christmas

The Later in Life Love Stories

Second Chances

Second Act

Second Thoughts

Second Degree

Second Best

Second Nature

BOOKPLATES ARE NOW AVAILABLE

Would you like a signed bookplate for this book?

I now have bookplates (stickers) that I can personalize, sign, and send to you. It's the next best thing to getting a signed copy!

Send an email to diana@dianaxarissa.com with your mailing address (I promise not to use it for anything else, ever) and how you'd like your bookplate personalized and I'll sign one and send it to you.

There is no charge for a bookplate, but there is a limit of one per person.

ABOUT THE AUTHOR

Diana started self-publishing in 2013 and she is thrilled to have found readers for the stories that she creates. She spent her childhood and teens years wearing out her library card on a regular basis and has always enjoyed getting lost in fictional worlds.

She was born and raised in Erie, Pennsylvania, and studied history at Allegheny College in Meadville, Pennsylvania. After years working in college administration in both Erie and Washington, DC, Diana moved to the UK following her marriage.

While living on the Isle of Man, Diana had an opportunity to earn a master's degree in Manx Studies, focusing on the fascinating history of the island. Eventually, she and her husband and their two children relocated to the US, where they are now settled in the Buffalo, New York, area.

She also writes mystery/thrillers set in the not-too-distant future as Diana X. Dunn and Middle Grade and Young Adult fiction as D.X. Dunn.

Diana is always happy to hear from readers. You can write to her at:

Diana Xarissa Dunn
PO Box 72
Clarence, NY 14031.

Find Diana at: DianaXarissa.com
E-mail: Diana@dianaxarissa.com

Made in the USA
Middletown, DE
27 October 2023

41465800R00136